EXHALE

—————

AN MM SHIFTER ROMANCE

JOEL ABERNATHY

ONE

"IT'S time to face facts, Jack," the Sheriff began once the novelty of humoring a bereaved husband's conspiracy theories wore off. Being a murder scene was fun for a while, but sooner or later, everyone wanted to get back to the rosy picture of small-town life Clarksville was so good at projecting—as long as you didn't peel back the edges. "You're the only one with a glaring motive here, and your alibi's airtight. Now, unless your drinking buddies from down in the shaft have a change of heart and tell me you *weren't* with them at Tab's that Sunday night, I suggest you come to terms."

"You saw that letter I found," I gritted out. "Francesca was having an affair with some prick from Romania. You don't think you should be looking for *him?*"

"We did look, Jack," he said, rubbing his eyes like they were getting sore from seeing me so often. "Fact of the matter is, your wife came here when she was twenty and no one, including you, by your own admission, has a fucking clue as to who she was before then. Hell, for all you know, the guy who sent that letter is some old flame she left back in Romania who couldn't get her out of his head."

"The 'guy who sent that letter' killed her," I seethed. "And he knew about her life *here*, with me. That's something."

"If we were sitting in the NYPD offices, maybe it would be," he said, throwing his pen down on his desk. "Fact remains, we're in Clarksville. Now, not a damn soul has mentioned seeing a stranger in town for the last year and if anyone had, they would've fessed up by now."

"So start questioning them," I demanded. "You're the Sheriff, I shouldn't have to do all the legwork."

His eyes narrowed and he gave me that look he'd given me so often in high school. The look that said, "The only reason I'm not beating your ass right now is because I don't want you to tell anyone about the shit we got up to that night when we were both drunk behind the bleachers."

"Your 'legwork' already has you on thin ice, and my patience keeps getting thinner," he said, lowering his voice. Like the deputy gave a shit. The guy was always high and at the moment, he was picking dirt out of his fingernails while he listened to some wingnut on satellite radio. "Thank your lucky stars that you're home now and not sitting in state."

"I *would* find that a lucky break, Ben, *if* I'd killed my wife and *if* the man who actually did wasn't still out there," I shot back.

Ben pinched the skin on his forehead just over his eyes together, digging his fingers in deep. I'd envied those blue eyes of his once, and he'd called mine the greenest he'd ever seen in a rare moment of poetic inspiration. In a time we both wanted to forget, he'd tangled his hands in my shaggy brown hair and over the years, I'd kept more of it than he had even if I had a few grays I owed to the joys of parenthood. We were both thirty-four, but his chalk white skin had wrinkled more than my tawny beige. The guys in the mine liked to joke that I was the only fucker who could keep a "tan" in the mines, and usually I just laughed because I was on the edge of the generation that had been cautioned to sweep our Melungeon heritage under the rug and the one that saw it as an identity to wear proudly.

"I don't think you quite understand the situation, *Jack*," he said in a way that suggested he was taking on the -ass in his head. Had to be tough, transitioning from the school bully who could get away with everything to the one job in town where you actually had to pretend like you gave a shit, with the possible exception of the mayor. "All you have to go off of is that letter. A letter Franny kept for God only knows how long, with zero information about the guy who sent it other than a first name that could just as well have been a synonym."

"Pseudonym," I corrected under my breath.

His bushy eyebrows stuck together like two caterpillars having a war. "What?"

"Nothing. You could at least *pretend* like you give a shit about the fact that someone came here and killed a resident of *your* town."

"I do care. I've spent the last seven goddamn months doing little other than caring," he growled, slamming his palm down on the desk. "We got nothin'. Sooner or later, you're gonna have to accept the fact that Franny was mixed up in some fucked-up shit and you didn't know her as well as you thought you did."

His words cracked like a whip against my flayed ego, but he was right. Of course he was right.

I didn't know Franny at all. That's what I was grieving more than her death, and I didn't know if it was because I was still in denial like Ellie's therapist thought or because I was the kind of shitty husband who deserved to find that letter. I couldn't tell if I was numb because I was in shock or because I'd always been that way and it just took this to make me see it.

"You need to be honest with yourself, Jack," Ben said in a pitying tone that made me want to punch him even more than the sanctimony did. "This isn't about finding the guy who killed Franny."

"That so?"

"For God's sake, everyone in town could see your marriage was over before it started," he scoffed. "You think going all Tarantino over her death makes up for the fact that your entire relationship was a sham?"

My fists clenched up and I had to remind myself that killing the sheriff when I had a fifteen-year-old who still needed someone to pay for her braces and someone at home when she got back from school was not even a thought I should be entertaining.

"You can look at me like that all you want, but we both know it's the truth," he continued. "You're hardly the first gay guy to knock up a one-night stand in high school, and I'll give you credit for committing to the long con, but it's gotta give at some point. See this as your chance to start over. I don't make a habit of saying this to the primary suspect in a murder investigation, but get the company to transfer you, take Allen and get the hell out of this town before you both rot in it."

"Ellie," I gritted out for what I was sure was the ten-millionth time that week. Beverly "The Mattress" Holk could change her last name every other week to match her new husband's, but when the one openly trans person in the history of Clarksville swapped a few letters out, no one could get it right. "Her name is Ellie."

Ben gave me that other look. The tired, "I'm trying to be progressive, but you people just make it so damn hard," look every halfway decent person in town gave me whenever I stood up for my daughter. The thing fathers were *supposed* to do. The same look Francesca had always given me when I corrected *her* and it was just the two of us.

"All the more reason to start over somewhere new. Somewhere you can just be a mine supervisor and his teenage daughter. Hell, I hear Nashville's got a rainbow scene that stretches from one end to the other. You'll love it."

I narrowed my eyes and the words on the tip of my tongue were probably going to get us chased out of town with pitchforks, but I let them slip anyway. "That where you go on all those 'fishing trips' you take to get away from Kay?"

All the humor drained from his expression. "Watch yourself, Jack. I've been patient with you up to a point, and you're passing it faster the more you open your mouth."

I pushed away from his desk. "My bad. I don't know why I

thought anyone in this town would actually be interested in doing their job," I said, letting the door slam shut behind me.

Some words only had meaning because they were the last a certain person ever said to you, whether you realized it in the moment or not. When Francesca told me, "I'm going to the store, text me a list if you need anything," I assumed it was a lie because most of the words that came out of her mouth in the last year of our marriage were, but it didn't mean much at the time. Only later, when I was surrounded by police and glaring through flashing ambulance lights, trying to hold our teenage daughter together when my whole world was falling apart, did it occur to me that *that* was the last thing she was ever going to say to me. The last time the dwindling European flavor of her voice would caress my ears.

Our marriage had been hanging by a thread for years, and the fact that we should both outlive it seemed like a guarantee. Every day, I waited for the papers, the natural sequel to that letter I'd found in her sock drawer.

That was the thing about being a desperate person in a dying marriage. You did things you never thought you'd do, things you'd always judged other people for. Things like snooping through your spouse's things looking for proof you didn't want to find that they respected you as little as you feared. Things like keeping a lover's letter nestled in your hosiery and taking it out to read and fold back so many times it took on the texture of thin cotton rather than paper.

When the police had called that night and told me they'd found Franny's body in the lake by Greg Klipp's farm, the first thought on my mind should have been, *This can't be real. My wife's not dead. It's a trick.*

Instead, it was, *How the fuck am I supposed to tell Ellie?*

She had just turned fifteen when it happened. Old enough to understand why the police were combing our house for evidence and looking at me like I was the primary suspect, not old enough that I wanted her to have any knowledge of that letter. Handing it over to the police in private had felt like a betrayal. The guilt was worse than the shame of providing proof to the men whose brothers I supervised in the coal mine, whose children went to school with mine, that my wife had a lover.

The suspicion in the sheriff's eyes had been joined by pity that was now depleted the first time he'd read over those flowery words.

Dragostea Mea,

You cannot run forever. How long will you live like a commoner in this little mountain town with an uneducated man who cannot satisfy you?

You were mine from the beginning, but I will not claim you as is my right. Ours is eternity, and I am a patient man, if a possessive one. He may have you—until you grow weary of pretending to be what you are not.

But rest assured, my Francesca, I will have you beg on your knees before you return to me. You will bear my mark as you bear my soul. I wonder, has your country lover ever touched you so deeply?

Yours,

Nicolae

I knew what Ben was thinking. Either I was the one who'd slit Franny's throat and dumped her body in the lake in a jealous rage after finding out about her latest lover, or it was the bastard who'd been railing her in secret for no telling how long.

I knew handing over that letter would be motive the police needed to wrap up the only case of non-meth-related violent crime to darken the streets of Clarksville, Kentucky in the last thirty years. I also knew it would change the way everyone in town looked at me, but that was nothing new. Over the years, our little family had given the small minds plenty to talk about. At least this time the spotlight was on me and not Ellie. Poor kid had already been through enough shit.

Vengeance consumed me in those first few months, but as the investigation hit one dead end after another, the town gradually turned its focus to other gossip. Apparently even the sheriff wasn't interested anymore.

Some days, it felt like a whole lifetime had passed since the night Franny had told me she was pregnant. I'd always remember the look on her face when she came out of my mom's bathroom, clutching the white stick that spelled out the rest of our lives in two blue lines. Others, I realized that nothing had really changed. We'd all grown up on the outside, and swapped the clothes that had divided us so neatly into classes back in high school—the jocks, the preps, the losers—in exchange for uniforms that made the distinction even clearer, but we were all still the same.

I'd taken the job with Big Mountain Coal because it was the only entry-level career where a high school dropout with a baby on the way could expect to earn a decent starting salary. At the time, it hadn't mattered that I was selling my health when I signed that contract. Even if I had, it probably wouldn't have changed my decision. The job was a double-edged sword. It took the same toll on my body that it had taken on my family's land, the same toll the drugs had taken on my mother. Even now that we could easily afford a doctor, I found myself putting off those exams because I wasn't sure I wanted to know just how bad the cough that had nagged me for the last five years really was. Nonetheless, the job was the only reason Ellie had grown up in comfort rather than the constant strain of poverty that had been the backdrop of my childhood.

Maybe Franny and I had never had a fairy tale romance, and our little home was far from a castle. Hell, there was more fighting than there was anything else, especially once Ellie had come to us about taking the first step toward her transition. I'd just always thought what we *did* have, what we'd both fought so hard to build, was enough.

It was enough for me, anyway. Despite her cracks about me just being pissed I'd "gotten stuck with a woman" when we really got into it, I'd never once felt the need to be with anyone else, man or woman, while we were together. No matter how hard I'd tried to reassure her that she was enough for me, I could tell those doubts persisted. Now at least I knew it was projection. She was sure our marriage wasn't enough to hold my interest, but that was only because it wasn't enough for her.

Ben was right in his own bastard way. It *was* a chance to start over, and maybe I hated myself too much to take it on my own, but Ellie deserved better than always being a spectacle. Francesca had made me promise once, when we were first married, that no matter what happened, we would never leave Clarksville.

Well, *she* had promised to be faithful, and that was before our family had become the only subject anyone felt like talking about. I'd kept my promise to her for fifteen years, but maybe it was finally time to do something for myself and my daughter.

Maybe it was finally time to let go.

TWO

"WE'RE MOVING?" Ellie echoed, her golden-brown eyes so wide I could see all the way around her irises. "You're kidding, right?"

She had her mother's eyes. Her long, straight black hair, too. She had my complexion and my dorsal bump, much to her chagrin. Two years of hormone blockers and changing nearly every other aspect of her appearance had admittedly been a lot to swallow, but I hoped that was the one thing she'd never change.

I just wanted her to love herself and be happy with what she saw when she looked in the mirror, and deep down, I knew that was all Franny wanted, too. We just had different philosophies on how that was going to happen. She saw transition as the death of our son, while I saw that every year we begged her to "just wait and see," the closer we were to burying our daughter.

Given the choice between a dead kid and learning to accept the one we had, it was a no-brainer. Maybe my frustration with Francesca's inability to see that was what had pushed her toward Nicolae. Maybe it was my fault she was dead. In trying to save our daughter's life, I knew I had made my wife the enemy when I accused her of doing the very same thing.

There was so much I wished I could have done differently, so many words I wished I could have taken back and replaced with the ones I should have said, if I'd just waited a bit and spoken in love rather than in anger.

Either way, Francesca was gone now and if we didn't get out, I was going to lose myself to the constant reminders of my failure as a husband, as a father, as a man.

"It'll be good," I said, taping up the bottom of another box I'd taken from the grocery store. "We could use a change of pace. Somewhere that actually has more than one stoplight and some decent restaurants. I hear Nashville's got a great school system. You can join an actual art program instead of having to negotiate with your principal to get credit for sketching during study hall."

She was looking at me like I was absolutely insane, her arms folded over the Oxford sweatshirt Franny had ordered online the day she first started showing an interest in college. When Ellie had gotten too old for bedtime stories, they'd kept their nightly routine alive with Francesca's tales of all her world travels, and Oxford was part of that. They'd already planned out how Ellie would craft a brilliant essay that would get her into the MFA program.

Franny always clammed up when I asked her about her past, and she never gave Ellie details about the whos and whats, but she'd always get so animated when she started talking about the cathedrals in France and the mountain castles in her native Luxembourg.

Sometimes, I'd lean in the doorway just listening and Ellie would be so enraptured in her mother's dramatic tales of ancient curses and mysterious beasts that lurked in the woods that neither of them would notice me. It was only in those moments, where I was on the outside, that I felt like we were the family I had always hoped we would just fall into. Sort of like iron shavings grouping together because we were made of the same stuff, and it was easier that way than being apart.

"But I already have a school," she protested. "I'll be a junior this fall, and you have a job."

"The company already approved my transfer to Nashville. The pay's better, and so is the standard of living," I answered, taping up another box. We still hadn't sold the house, and the market in Clarksville wasn't exactly booming, but the pay difference would be enough to allow us to get a decent apartment in the city while we waited for it to sell. "As for your school, you really want to pass up the chance to go to Nashville for those 'small-minded assclowns'?"

She scowled at me for using her words against her. "So they're jerks, that still doesn't mean I want to pick up and leave the only home I've ever known because you're having a midlife crisis."

"Hey," I said, pointing at her. "I'm barely over thirty, this is a third-life crisis at best."

She rolled her eyes. How did teenagers keep the damn things in their heads when they were always doing intracranial gymnastics? "Beside the point, dad. This is crazy. You know that, right?"

"What's crazy," I said, stopping just long enough to look at her, "is staying in a town where we're treated like second-class citizens. Crazy is keeping you in a school my tax dollars pay to hire teachers who constantly misgender you and force you to use the bathroom in the goddamn teacher's lounge."

Her face went blank, but I knew my words were sinking in. For the last two years, Ellie had come home almost every night with tears in her eyes, and I knew the only reason she clammed up when I asked her why was because she knew it would start another fight. I felt like shit for not being able to protect her, for not being able to at least create a home that was a sanctuary for her when the outside world was so fucking needlessly cruel, but now we actually had a chance. I just had to make her understand that.

"This isn't about school," she said in a quiet, knowing tone. I was pretty sure every teenager in the history of humanity thought they were wiser than their parents, but when she got that look in her eyes, I actually found myself believing it. It was the same look Francesca had when she'd reach a point beyond stubbornness and bickering. A point where she seemed almost feral. There was something dangerous in that look, something inhuman that triggered a prey-like response in my mind that made zero sense, especially when it came to my own child. "It's about Mom."

My spine stiffened. "Ellie, don't," I warned.

"I know it is. I'm not a kid, I hear the things people say," she muttered.

"People in this town are always saying shit. Doesn't make any of it true," I said, shoving our throw pillows into the box. They just filled back up with air, so I grabbed the wrought iron statue that Franny had always been obsessed with—a woman reaching out to touch a wolf's head—and put it down on top of the pillows to weigh them down.

"So mom *wasn't* having an affair with some foreign creep?"

Her words knocked the wind out of me. It took me a second to stuff down my initial response, a trait I had perfected a little too late to save my marriage. "Excuse me?"

"That's what everyone is saying." She looked somewhat less confident when I turned to face her, but I could see that stubbornness shining in her eyes. This one wasn't going to be solved by telling her to go to her room. She swallowed hard. "Is it true?"

I could hear the plea laced into her question. The desperation. I could either lie to her, which was something I took a decent amount of pride in never having done, or tell her the truth and break her heart. The fact that I knew the revelation would hurt her far more than it had ever hurt me was just more proof that my marriage had died a long time before this "Nicolae" took part in it.

"Of course not."

"Don't lie to me!" Tears spilled down her cheeks, and that feral light shone in her eyes like the sun. "I'm not a child!"

"I'm telling the truth," I said, shrugging. No amount of bitterness or betrayal would ever push me to the point where I was willing to taint Ellie's memory of her mother, even if it was only with the truth. I'd tried to protect her from Franny's harsher tirades about her transition, but this was the thing that would break her spirit. "People also say I killed her. You believe that, too?"

She frowned. "Of course not."

"It's just a rumor, El," I said, handing her a fresh roll of packing tape. "Come Monday, we're out of here. Start packing."

She took the tape roller, staring down at it with what was probably the most malice anyone had ever shown a roll of clear store brand adhesive. "Why do all our boxes say L-Mart on them?" she grumbled.

"Because only schmucks actually pay for moving materials," I answered without missing a beat. "Double up along the bottoms, that tape's been sitting in the garage since before you were born."

She sighed heavily and trudged up the stairs, but her door didn't slam loud enough to shake the house, so I took it as a crisis averted. For the moment, anyway.

The fact that Ellie would learn the truth of her mother's betrayal if we stayed in this town for long enough was all the confirmation I needed to get the fuck out. I knew Ben was only trying to get us out of his hair, but he was right. I wasn't ready to give up on finding the bastard who'd killed Franny, but the answers sure as hell weren't in Clarksville. Nothing was.

Not for us.

THREE

"SO, WHAT DO YOU THINK?" I asked, holding open the door to the new apartment with my back as I carried in a box of what felt like bricks. Ellie had insisted on bringing it in the backseat because she didn't trust the movers, and I knew better than to ask too many questions where a teenager's belongings were concerned.

She looked around the third-floor apartment, and the perma-scowl she'd worn on the entire four-hour drive started to waver. The high ceilings and long windows let in plenty of light and ambient noise from the bustling little city below, and we had a great view of the town square. The brick accents were a little rustic, but it added to the charm. Hell, there was even a fireplace.

"It's big," she said, clearly surprised as she rolled in her suitcase.

I set the world's heaviest box by the door and left it propped since the AC hadn't been turned on yet and the movers were soon to follow. "What, you thought I'd move us into a shoebox?"

"We haven't even sold the house yet," she said, running her hand along the granite countertop that divided the kitchen from the living room. "How are we gonna afford this place?"

"Since when do you worry about our finances?" I demanded,

looking around until I found the thermostat. I breathed a sigh of relief when the air conditioning kicked in with a groan. Summer in northern Tennessee was not something you wanted to navigate without central air. "We're gonna be fine. You just worry about keeping yourself out of trouble until Fall and let me worry about the grownup shit."

She rolled her eyes, flopping down on the vintage couch that came with the place. I just hoped bedbugs weren't part of the package. "You're the one who needs to stay out of trouble."

She probably had a point. I'd never so much as gotten a call from the principal's office that didn't involve other people's kids being shitheads. "Go check out your room while I grab the rest of the stuff from the car. Once the movers get here, we'll go check out the neighborhood and find something for dinner."

When I turned around, Ellie was still sitting on the couch. I knew she'd be angsting about the move for a while, but once she started at her new school, she'd realize it was all for the best. We needed a fresh start. I'd lived in Clarksville all of my life, too, but the fact that I only felt like I could breathe when we passed the city line was just proof that we belonged somewhere else. I still wasn't ready to even entertain the idea of dating again, and I wasn't sure I ever would be, but it would be nice to live somewhere I didn't feel like I had to hide who I was.

By the time I carried in the last of our must-haves, Ellie was gone. I found her in the second bedroom checking out the closet space. She turned and looked up at me behind a curtain of hair. "I guess this place is decent."

I clutched my shirt over my heart like I was going into cardiac arrest and gasped, holding onto the doorframe for support. "Those words, they're...almost positive, but... *teenager*. Does not compute... dad brain shutting down."

Her neon lips curled back in a snarl of pure mortification, so I knew I was doing my job. "You are *so* weird," she said, stalking past me through the door.

"There we go," I said, making a miraculous recovery as I followed her back to the living room. She opened the world's heaviest box and I shouldn't have been surprised to find it loaded with sketchbooks and art supplies. The tin box full of paints certainly explained why a few discs in my back had migrated to where they didn't belong.

"Shouldn't the movers be here by now?" Ellie asked, peering through the curtains of the bow windows.

I checked my watch and realized it was half an hour past the time the guy on the phone had promised, the last time I'd called to check in. At least it wasn't like we had any gold bars for them to run off with. "I'll give 'em a call," I said, taking out my phone. It rang about a dozen times before I gave up. "Probably stopped somewhere for food."

I was sure I'd be charged for that little detour, too. They'd already tacked on at least thirty hidden fees once they had our shit on the truck. The next time we moved, at least it would be to a house nearby.

Despite the logistical hangups, I was already feeling the promise of the first major life decision I'd made that wasn't just a reaction to something else. This was going to be good for both of us. I could feel it.

Once the sun started to set and there was still no sign of the movers, I made the executive decision to call in an order at the Chinese restaurant a few blocks over. "You wanna come with me? Check out the hood?"

"Not really," Ellie said, curled up on the couch with her sketch-book, drawing out the lines of the fireplace.

I hesitated at the door, but decided now wasn't the time for another pep talk. I'd moved her out of the only state she'd ever lived in just seven months after her mother's murder, and we still weren't any closer to answers than we'd been after Franny died. It was finally starting to set in for her that we might never get those answers, and as that chapter in our lives came to an end, the future probably seemed as gray and vast and terrifying to her as it did to me.

Age didn't really do anything to change the fear. I just had enough years behind me to be even more afraid of getting stuck in the past. It was like quicksand, and the more you struggled, the deeper you sank in.

"Dad?" she called. I looked back to find her actually looking at me.

"What's up, kiddo?"

She bit her lip and I could tell she wasn't sure how to say whatever it was she wanted to tell me. Franny always did that. "It's nice," she said finally. "The apartment, I mean."

I smiled and it felt odd enough that I wondered when the last time had been. I'd been plagued with little other than guilt and doubt the entire trip, and those words made me feel like something other than the complete failure I'd felt like for the better part of a year. "Yeah. It's not forever, but I think it'll be a good place for us." I locked the door from the inside and said, "I'll be back in ten minutes, max. If the movers show up before then, don't open up. They can wait a few minutes since they're three hours late."

I pulled the door shut and walked down the front steps, pausing at the mailboxes in the lobby. I scanned the small glass boxes until I found the one for apartment seventeen and grabbed the pen hanging from a chain on the wall to scribble out the old tenants' name and replace it with Mullins. It felt good, that first little mark of ownership. It felt like I was finally taking control of my life.

I just didn't realize how quickly and entirely it was about to spiral out of my control.

FOUR

AFTER DEALING with a cashier who insisted I hadn't put an order in, I returned home with some combo platters and egg rolls, feeling very much like I imagined a victorious male lion might after letting the females in his pack do all the work and dragging home an antelope carcass for his young.

Downtown Nashville had its charms, and it also had its assholes. I'd gotten acquainted with both in the last thirty minutes or so, but at least the city had life. I'd watched Clarksville's gradual transformation from an idyllic little town in the mountains to a place where dreams came to die, unless of course your dream was to toil away in the mines until illness or painkillers got you. In that case, it was at the very top of the list of go-to destinations.

When I walked up around the apartment building and saw that the moving truck was still nowhere in sight, I was both relieved and annoyed. I'd paid three-hundred more than the estimate the first company had given me because their online reviews said they were reliable, and I didn't feel like putting my moving insurance to the test. I'd gone more than three decades without being one of those "I'm calling the manager" people, but as soon as I had some food in my stomach and a beer or two, corporate was getting a call.

The front door was propped open a little, which seemed weird until I saw the elderly lady on the floor below us at the mailboxes. She gave me a not-so-neighborly scowl and said, "You must be from apartment seventeen."

"Yeah," I said, offering my hand. So she was a little cranky. I was still going to make an effort to be on better terms with these neighbors than I'd been with the assholes who kept throwing beer cans into our yard. "I'm Jack Mullins."

She eyed my hand like she was assessing her risk of contracting a disease if she shook it before she finally decided it was worth the risk. "Bess Perkins," she said in a clipped tone, clutching the oversized rocks around her neck. Man, Ellie was gonna get a kick out of this woman. "I live right below you, and I don't mind saying, I hope you quiet down once you're settled in. This is a quiet neighborhood and all that racket won't do."

"Racket?" I arched an eyebrow. "Sorry if we disturbed you. The movers are late, but I'll try to tell them to keep it down when they come."

"It's not the moving that bothers me," she huffed. "It's all that screaming."

My world stopped. In one moment, it just stopped, but I was already moving, taking the stairs three at a time while Mrs. Perkins yelled at me from below. The front door was open and I blew through it, looking around the empty room. It felt like everything was happening in slow motion, like I was trying to run through water as I tore through the house, screaming for Ellie and somehow knowing she wasn't going to answer.

Her room was empty. Her sketchbook was open facedown on the floor in front of the couch, the pages bent. There was no other sign of struggle, but there was really nothing in the place to be amiss. I ran back to the stairs my elderly neighbor was only beginning to climb.

"How long ago did you hear the screams?" I demanded.

She stared at me, her wrinkled face frozen in shock. Evidently, this was the most eventful thing that had ever happened in the neighborhood. "Maybe ten minutes ago?"

"And you didn't think to call the cops?" I seethed, taking out my phone to dial 911. She made some indignant excuse, but I ignored her. The phone was ringing and the operator picked up, and as I rattled off our address and the few details I knew about Ellie's disappearance, I felt like I was outside of my body.

In that moment, all my fears that I was handling Francesca's loss the wrong way were confirmed, because all the terror and grief and frustration and bewilderment I should have felt then was hitting me now, and it was a fate that was so much worse than dying.

The police came and dragged me back home from searching the streets. I didn't know if my behavior was so erratic that they assumed I was a suspect or not, but at least they took it seriously when I told them what had happened. They somehow understood through the rambling and the panic, and unlike Ben, they listened. They asked questions, too, and I answered them to the best of my ability.

She was fifteen.

No, she would never run away.

No, she didn't do drugs. We'd been here all of four hours, she hadn't had time to "fall in with the wrong crowd."

No, the name on her student ID didn't match the name on her birth certificate yet.

Yes, we were "*those* Mullins" and this was the second world-ending tragedy that had hit us within a year.

Yes, I was the world's shittiest father.

That last one remained unspoken and unanswered, but we all knew. I told them about Nicolae. I showed them the letter, but they didn't seem to think there was a connection. More likely, it was a local gang that had seen an easy target. They told me to expect a ransom. Someone would be around all night, in case there was a call.

They would try to trace her phone, but that was all that could be done.

It wasn't enough, and I wanted to go out and look for her, but they told me it was necessary for me to be around in case the kidnappers tried to reach out. They usually did within twenty-four hours.

Hers didn't. I spent that night bombarded with every horrifying scenario my imagination and all the other news stories had to offer. I knew trans girls were a target for violence. The idea of anyone hurting my little girl was enough to drive me insane, and the only thing holding me together was the fact that she needed me here, ready in case that call came.

It never did. When my phone finally rang, my heart sank because I recognized the number. It was Pete, my second-in-command back in Clarksville. I almost didn't answer it, but the detective across the room nodded and I didn't have the energy to explain that there was no hope.

"Hello?"

"Jack? Man, you sound like shit."

I felt worse. "What is it?"

"There's some guy who came looking for you earlier today," he said, his voice slurred enough that I could tell he'd been down at Tab's with the boys.

"Yeah, okay?" I rubbed my eyes. The coffee the little intern with the cops kept plying me with wasn't doing much, but sleep wasn't even something that was on my mind. The exhaustion went deeper than any physical cause, such as being awake for the last twenty-four hours.

"He said he had a message for you, and it was urgent. Wanted to know why all your shit was gone and I told him you'd moved," he said casually. "Had a real funny voice, too."

My heart dropped. I looked up at the audio tech who'd checked out when she realized it wasn't the kidnappers, but she didn't notice. "What do you mean he had a funny voice?" I demanded.

"It was similar to your wife's. Uh, no offense. I just mean he was foreign, maybe French?"

"What did he look like? Be as detailed as you can."

"Yeah, sure, just don't get your rocks off," he taunted. I ignored him. "He was real tall, hair down to his ass. Kinda scruffy, but a pretty boy. Funny thing though, his eyes were like your wife's too. That weird sorta gold color."

"Did he say anything else?"

"Not really, just wanted to know where you went, so I told him you'd moved to Nashville. Oh, but he did give his name."

I covered my mouth, trembling with rage. I knew even before he spoke what name it was going to be.

"Nicolae."

Fucking Nicolae.

At least when I got off the phone, the cops seemed to take the Nicolae connection more seriously. The calls went out, updating the officers who'd been dispatched on the new information. The chief detective was starting to look at me like he pitied me more than he suspected me. Not that I could blame him either way.

I felt like I was coming out of my skin. Every moment that passed without another call was torture.

This fuck clearly wanted his comeuppance, and whether it was because Francesca had broken things off with him or simply because he hated me for taking her, I didn't know. All I knew was that Nicolae had become the most important name in my world, and my entire life was hanging on the moment he decided to call.

He had to fucking call. He had to want *something*. The fact that he'd taken Ellie rather than slitting her throat and leaving her for me to find was proof of that, I hoped.

Whatever it was, he could have it. What little I had in my savings account, my house, my life. If he wanted me to get down on my knees and beg for my daughter, I'd do it in a split second, and as soon as she was safe, I would spend every breath I had hunting him down like the dog he was and torturing him until he felt the pain I should have felt all along.

More hours passed. I lost track of them and lost interest in counting. Nothing happened. No call, no notes, no nothing. The man who had no trouble penning lurid words to my wife chose now to be silent.

The herd of cops and specialists and techs thinned out until there was only the audio tech and a single detective left. They were both new, both fresh-faced as they sent their colleagues home to rest.

The investigation wasn't over, they insisted, but when I finally got the guts to ask how long it had been, they told me we'd surpassed the forty-eight hour mark.

I knew what that meant. Everyone knew. The chances of finding Ellie alive were getting slimmer by the hour, and now, my hope was hanging by a thread.

The knock at the door all but snipped it. I wanted to believe that it was good news, but somehow, I knew the truth. That meant it could only be the kind of news that prolonged the agony or brought it all crashing down at once. I was expecting another uniformed officer when I opened that door, and instead, I found myself staring at a man who perfectly fit Pete's description. He wasn't kidding about the eyes, either.

The man was wearing a dark brown overcoat that just barely stopped before it hit the floor. His shoulders were broad and he was tall enough that I had to look up at him. His dark hair would have come close to softening his severe features, but the stubble and the hardness in his eyes made him look cold. Otherworldly. That look that so rarely came into Francesca's and Ellie's eyes seemed to live in his.

My voice went raspy, my throat clenched. "You're —"

"Detective Doyle," he said, holding up a badge that was complete and utter bullshit. Before I could call him out on it, his eyes narrowed and something about them held me in traction. I couldn't move or speak, even though all I wanted was to wrap my hands around his throat and choke out his last breath. "Relax. I'm with the FBI."

The officer who'd been stuck with my melancholic ass for the rest of the morning came over and gave me a strange look. "Detective Doyle?" he frowned, glancing at the badge. "Sorry, they didn't tell us you were coming."

"Standard procedure for this sort of thing, isn't it?" he asked, tucking the badge back into his coat before he stepped inside to look around. "Place is a bit sparse."

"The moving truck never made it," said Officer Barnes. "We called the company, and they say the drivers never reported in."

"I see," Nicolae murmured thoughtfully, as if he actually gave a shit. As if he wasn't the reason for all of this.

I stayed frozen, gripping the doorknob like it was attached to me. No matter how I tried, I couldn't make myself move or even warn them.

"Shut the door, Jack."

I wanted to tell him to go to fucking hell, to scream, "This is the guy! Are you all too dumb to see it?" Instead, I shut the door like he was the one in control of my actions.

Of course he knew my fucking name. The other officer didn't seem to think shit about it. They conversed for a few minutes and I just stood there by the door, watching them like some passive idiot, helpless to rail at him the way I wanted to.

"Why don't you two take an early lunch?" he finally offered. I wasn't sure if his voice had the same commanding effect on them that it did on me, but the audio tech and Barnes looked at each other and nodded. Once they left, Nicolae closed the door and waited until their footsteps faded down the stairs to notice me, like he was counting on the fact that I'd just be standing there like a good little bitch, waiting for his next command.

He stopped and looked me over, his golden eyes taking their time as they passed over me. My fists clenched and trembled at my sides, straining to break whatever hold he had me under. Every glance was an assessment, as if he was taunting me with his casual consideration.

"So," he said boredly, "you're the one she's been amusing herself with all this time."

The rage spilled over, allowing me to regain control over my body. I took that moment of freedom and swung at him, but he caught my fist and just the force of him pushing back made my wrist pop. "Enough," he scolded as burning pain throbbed in my joint. I didn't know if it was broken or just popped out of the socket, but his control wrapped back around me, making it impossible to cry out. It was like someone had thrown a blanket over my free will, keeping it bound and smothered.

That one word was all it took to render me powerless, and I hated him all the more for it. I hated myself, too. Nicolae took my hand and my forearm, and I saw what he was going to do in his eyes before he did it, but I was powerless to tell him to stop, too. He snapped my wrist back in place and the pain made me shudder, but this time, it wasn't enough to break his hold.

"I can tell you already know who I am. I'm sure your friend at the mines told you I was looking for you, but let me save you some time and energy. I'm not the one who killed Francesca, and I'm not the one who took Ellie," he said calmly, releasing me. My hand dropped to my side, but I still couldn't move on my own, only react to his movements. He must have seen the questions on my face, because he added, "The state you're in right now is a bit like sleep paralysis. Even though you're conscious, the vibrations of my voice are capable of placing your brain waves into a beta state, making you incredibly susceptible to verbal commands. In short, you're experiencing the effects of a trance."

I was trying to pay attention to what he was saying, even if it was complete bullshit, but I was distracted by the fact that every word out of his mouth brought the words on the page of that letter to life in a way I never wanted to experience. He was so fucking smug, so

European. I could hear him saying those words to Francesca, mocking me in the same breath as he tried to seduce her.

"Why the hell should I believe you?" I demanded. Speaking was a challenge, and I got the feeling that I was only able because he was letting me. Toying with me.

"Because you will never see your daughter again if you don't," he said in a voice that sounded like a shrug. "The people who have her are a hell of a lot worse than me, and trust me, finding them is far beyond the pay grade of those idiots downstairs."

"Prove it," I gritted out.

"I don't have to, but since you asked so nicely," he sneered, pulling something out of his pocket. He tossed it at me. "Catch."

My hands snatched the object in the air, proving that I was far more coordinated under his command than usual. I looked down to find myself holding a stack of photographs. Most of them were Polaroids, and the first was just a picture of Francesca looking exactly the way she had the day we'd met. She hadn't changed much over the years, just a few lines around her eyes from years of smiling despite me. The biggest difference that stood out to me was how much bigger that smile was in the photograph. How it actually seemed genuine.

The next photograph was similar, only it was Franny standing next to the man in front of me. He had his arms around her waist and her leg was kicked up behind her like an old-fashioned movie couple about to go in for that iconic kiss. They looked so fucking happy. So madly, deeply in love. It felt like I'd swallowed rocks, but something forced me to keep flipping through those old photographs, and it wasn't Nicolae's magic voice.

There were a dozen photos just like that one. Some were of Franny and Nicolae, others were her with a group of other happy, smiling, pretty people. None of them looked recent, but the quality made it hard to tell. When I'd finally had enough, I looked up at him. "What the hell is this supposed to prove?"

"Francesca was mine long before she was yours," he answered. "I know that you don't want to hear this, but I would have killed *myself* before I ever laid a finger on her. If you listen—and I mean truly listen, with the part of you that knows things you shouldn't know, and not your ego—you will know this to be true."

I did what he said, and to my chagrin, he was right. "How do I know it's not just you brainwashing me?"

"You don't, but if you don't have enough faith in your own instincts, there's nothing I can do about that," Nicolae said, shrugging. "At any rate, why would I be here if I already had what I wanted?"

It was a decent point that didn't make me hate him any less. "If you didn't take Ellie, then who did?"

"The same people who killed Francesca," he said, his eyes sharpening with a murderous glint that made me actually believe him, as little as I wanted to. "Her parents."

It took a second for that one to settle in. "Bullshit."

Granted, Francesca had never talked much about her family life, and I knew from the mood that came over her whenever the subject came up that it hadn't been rosy, but there was a difference between estrangement and murder.

"There are things you don't understand, and things I don't have time to explain to you here. Now, you can either come with me, or we can waste more time that could be spent finding your daughter."

"Why do you care what happens to her?" I demanded. "If you're the piece of shit who sent Franny that letter, why do you care about any of this?"

Those eyes were the only part of him that was expressive at all, and they took on a sadness that came as a shock. "Because Ellie is hers."

I waited for him to say more, but he didn't. Instead, he walked to the door. "I will wait outside for five minutes. Pack what you need or stay here and accept that you will never see Ellie again. The choice is yours."

With that, he left and I heard his footsteps echoing on the stairs. It took me a second to realize I was free to move and do what I wanted, and I reached for my phone to call Officer Barnes only to think better of it.

This was insanity. It was crazier still that I was even thinking of going with him, and yet...

Either Nicolae *was* responsible for Ellie's disappearance and he was lying, or he was right and he was the only one who had a chance at finding her. Either way, all roads pointed to him.

I grabbed the suitcase I hadn't even bothered to unpack along with my phone and walked out after him. His black car was waiting at the curb and he was leaning on it, a cigarette hanging from his mouth.

"And here I expected you'd spend the full five minutes on angst," he said, opening the door. He took the suitcase from me before I could stop him and tossed it in the back. "Get in."

I hesitated on principle before opening the door. "If you're shitting me —"

"You'll what?" he challenged, starting the car. "Kill me? You're more than welcome to try."

It was the challenge of a man who knew he didn't stand a chance at losing. I glared at him. "You owe me answers. Why would Francesca's parents want to kill her?"

"I owe you nothing," he scoffed without looking over at me. "Besides, you wouldn't believe me if I told you the truth."

"Try me."

"Fine." He flicked his ashes out the window and I breathed a sigh of relief since the smoke was making me cough. "They had a falling out many years ago, and discord in her family is not handled in a typical fashion."

"Apparently not if they slit your throat after sixteen years of not talking," I muttered.

"Our kind does not play by your rules. They will pay for what they've done, but it is hardly unconventional."

"Your kind?"

He looked at me again, like he was trying to decide something. "I am not human, Jack Mullins. Neither was your wife."

Now it was my turn to laugh. "Right. You know, for a second there, you actually had me going. I actually thought you might be something other than a nutjob."

"There are those who find it amusing to ease the odd human who stumbles upon our world into the truth of what we are," he remarked. "I am not one of them."

He veered off the country road and into the grass. I grabbed the handle over my head and gripped it for dear life. "Jesus H. Christ," I called out, "what the fuck are you—?"

The car came to a stop as soon as it had taken off the road and Nicolae got out, slamming the door shut after him. I watched through the windshield in bewilderment, ready to take the wheel and get the fuck out of there when I saw him disappear into the woods.

I was torn. Torn between going after him, between getting the hell out. In the end, even if I was probably following him to my death, I chose to follow him anyway. If there was even a chance he could help me get Ellie back, it didn't matter if he was completely insane. It didn't matter if he was the man my wife had loved enough to keep his letter for years. It only mattered that he was my only road to the one thing I had left in this world to hold onto.

I got out of the car and followed him through the grass, accumulating ticks as I went. If this fucker popped out at me, I was not responsible for what I did to him. I looked around, finding myself deeper in the forest than I wanted to be.

Had he brought me all this way just to ditch my ass in the forest? Was this some kind of joke to him?

A darker possibility occurred to me. That this was what he'd done to Francesca. Just as I was about to turn back, I heard it. The growling. The ground trembled with the vibrations of it and when I turned around, I found myself face to face with something that just should not have existed. A creature whose head reached the middle branch of the nearest tree in front of me, too perfectly sculpted and animated to be a man in a costume. Besides, there was no one that tall without wearing stilts. This thing was nine feet high at least. Its head was sharp and canine, with furry ears covered in the same dark brown coat that covered the rest of its muscular body. It looked like someone had stuck a wolf's head on a monster's body, slightly hunched over as it stood on its hind legs.

Werewolf. The word bobbed around on the surface of my thoughts for a while, but I couldn't bring myself to actually accept that I was seeing it. It would have been so much easier to accept that I was having a hallucination.

FIVE

BY THE TIME I thought to run, I could feel his breath on me, pure heat and enough of a shock to make me stumble backward. I stared at him in bewilderment. Those familiar golden eyes stared back, full of amusement rather than the hunger I would have assumed a thing that probably burned a million calories a minute would feel when looking at meat on two sticks.

All at once, he changed and the shock of it was enough to put me on my ass. I cried out as Nicolae was left standing in front of me. He was completely naked, his badly scarred flesh on full display. Every inch of him seemed to have been stabbed or clawed at one point or another. His hair wasn't quite down to his ass as Pete put it, but it covered his biceps until he reached out.

I flinched. "Stay the fuck away from me!"

He retracted his hand and stared at me, smirking like the prick he was. "I suppose it is a *bit* amusing."

"Fuck you. What the fuck was that?"

"So refined. I can see why she chose you over me," he said bitterly.

"What?" I was having a hard time keeping up. Now he was

talking about Franny again? "The hell are you talking about? She was cheating on me with you."

"Is that what you think?" He seemed genuinely perplexed.

"I found the letter."

Understanding crossed his face. "Ah." He paused, searching my face. "So she kept it, then?"

I didn't like the way he asked. Hopeful. I wasn't sure what the hell I was supposed to make of that. "When did you send that letter?"

"Answer my question."

"Answer mine."

He gave me a weary look as he reached into the grass for his pants and pulled them back on. So he'd prepared to scare the shit out of me. Nice.

"You just found out werewolves exist and you want to discuss my letter?"

"Did I stutter?" I finally stood once I was pretty sure he wasn't going to turn into that thing again and eat me.

And yeah, maybe he was right and my priorities were skewed, but I was still too shocked to accept the one thing, and the other... It never left my mind.

"About ten years ago," he answered.

Somehow, that answer cut as deep as if he'd come out and said he was fucking her the whole time. In a way, the fact that she'd kept that letter felt more intimate. Sex was sex, but holding onto something like that for close to the duration of your entire marriage... that was more. It felt like more.

"You wanna tell me how you managed that little magic trick?" I asked, brushing myself off. I'd decided almost as soon as I'd seen the thing that there was a logical explanation even though I was far from a logical guy. I couldn't accept that what I'd seen was real.

"It wasn't magic. I'm a werewolf."

"Yeah, okay."

"And yet here you are, talking to one. Either that makes me real or it makes you insane."

"Fair enough," I grunted. "Verdict's still out."

Nicolae rolled his eyes, buttoning his shirt back up. The muscle on his chest stretched it apart until he adjusted it down. The guy was enough of a threat in his human form.

"So you turn into a monster. And Franny knew about this," I said flatly, eyeing him for hints of how he did it, maybe the shimmer of a screen or hologram.

He squinted. "God, you really are an idiot, aren't you? Or she just kept you that much in the dark..."

"In the dark about what?" I snapped.

"Francesca *was* a werewolf, Jack. She was one of us, and so is your daughter."

"Bullshit!"

"Has anything I've told you this past hour turned out to be a lie?"

I walked back until I felt a tree to grab onto, because suddenly, my legs weren't feeling all that steady. "You... this is fucked up."

"Is any word that comes out of your mouth *not* profane? Just wondering."

I tried to swallow. No luck. "Franny was *not* one of you. Magicians or werewolves or whatever."

"She never disappeared on a full moon?" he asked knowingly.

I opened my mouth to deny it, but now that I was thinking about it, it was possible. She disappeared on a lot of nights. I'd never bothered to keep track which ones. I'd always just assumed she was fooling around with some guy after the last one I'd caught her with, but now that *the* guy was right in front of me claiming that their relationship had existed only from a distance, I wasn't sure.

"We have the same eyes. Surely you've noticed."

Sure I had. I'd done little but notice ever since he'd shown up, and I hated that one of the features I'd always loved most about her was part of him. More than that, I hated that I had known my wife, the woman I'd shared a bed and a life with for sixteen fucking years, so very little that this was even a possibility. I was beginning to accept it, too. The only reason I wasn't spiraling into insanity was because I was so damn stressed about Ellie that supernatural shit paled in comparison.

"Maybe you're telling the truth," I said, willing to concede that if only because she was dead and denial wasn't going to bring her killer to justice any faster. "Maybe Franny kept this from me for most of our lives. But there's nothing weird with Ellie. I know my kid."

He frowned and seemed troubled by something. I didn't even want to guess what that might be. "She is fifteen. Surely she has manifested some unusual traits by this point."

"No. Nothing. She's just a normal kid."

"Aside from being transgender."

My eyes narrowed. "You don't wanna go down that road, bud. Not with me. Not today."

"I wasn't making a remark," he scoffed. "Just a comment." He turned his head to the side. "You were ready to piss yourself a moment ago. Your heart's still racing, but your blood stinks of adrenaline. You're ready to fight me to defend your daughter's honor."

"Damn straight," I said without hesitation.

Nicolae watched me for a few seconds longer before chuckling.

"What's so funny, prick?"

"You are an odd soul. Idiotic, but brave in your own way."

I got the feeling he was trying to pay me a compliment. I just wasn't interested in accepting it. "Just keep your thoughts on Ellie to yourself. Better yet, don't think about my kid at all."

"And yet, you need my help to find her."

I fucking hated it when he was right.

"All I was trying to say is that werewolves shift for the first time during puberty. Perhaps her transition has delayed it."

"Well, you could have just said that," I growled.

"I tried." He cocked an eyebrow. "You wouldn't let me."

"Right," I muttered. "So you're saying Ellie can't turn into a giant fucking beast because she's *trans?*"

"We call it shifting, and yes. Assuming that she's on medication to delay the onset of puberty, that would delay the hormones that allow us to become 'monsters,' as you put it."

He seemed genuinely offended. I'd stuck my foot in my mouth often enough in my time, but I never thought I'd manage to hurt a werewolf's feelings. "And Francesca's parents, they're...?"

"Yes." His entire countenance shifted. "They are also were-wolves, and once they realize Ellie can't shift, they're not going to take it well."

"They'd kill her, too?" I asked, horrified.

"No. Fortunately, they need her."

I swallowed the bile in my throat. "Where are these fuckers?"

"Their pack is in Luxembourg, but the city itself is impossible for me to break into."

"What? Why?"

"It's an old war. Territory lines go back to medieval times, and there are forces at play that prevent a wolf from my line from crossing them."

"Forces?" I asked warily. "You mean like magic?"

He blinked at me. "I thought it would be better to limit your exposure to the supernatural one thing at a time."

"Bullshit. If my daughter's wrapped up in this, I need to know everything there is to know, no matter how fucked up it is." And no matter how much trouble I was having accepting all of it.

He watched me and I could tell he was trying to figure out if I could live up to that challenge. "Fine. We'll talk on the way," he said, walking back to the car.

I followed him and as soon as the car started again, I said, "Let's start where all of this did. Why would Franny's parents want her dead?"

"That's hardly where it began," Nicolae said, pulling on a pair of sunglasses to fight the mid-afternoon glare. "To put it simply, the Majerus wolves view Francesca as a traitor."

"Majerus? Franny's maiden name was Klein."

"Klein was her mother's maiden name, before she was mated into the pack. I'm sure she took it on to hide her identity."

"Do I even wanna know what 'mated in' means?"

He glanced over at me, his eyes invisible behind the black-blue lenses. "Our packs have been at war for the last two centuries, on and off. In the beginning, it was about territory even though we've all accumulated far more of it over the years than the little parcel that started it all. Francesca and I were part of an attempt at bridging the divide."

"You mean an arranged marriage?"

I could feel his rage, burning off him. "Things work differently in our world. You wouldn't understand."

"Not that different if she ran away." His jaw tightened and I decided to stop playing free and loose with my life. "So your packs are rivals. How many of there are you, a few dozen?"

"Several thousand in each," he answered. "Give or take."

"Several *thousand* werewolves?" I echoed.

"We make up roughly one half of one percent of the global population. You do the math."

"Yeah, but... how do people not know you exist?"

"The people who matter do. We keep them quiet about the same way you keep politicians and law enforcement and media quiet about anything," he said, shifting lanes to take the next exit onto another highway. "Bribery."

"Of course," I muttered.

"If that bothers you, werewolf life is going to be difficult for you to adjust to."

"Who said anything about adjusting to it at all?"

"Like it or not, you are part of the pack now," he said in a tone that made me think he didn't like it, either.

"How do you figure that? I'm human."

"Ellie isn't. I am the Alpha of the Ursache pack, and Francesca was my rightful mate. By proxy, that makes her child mine as well."

The thought of Franny "belonging" to this guy pissed me off

enough, but I was about to ream him out for thinking he had any claim to our daughter before I remembered that was probably the only reason he had any interest in getting her back safely.

"If you knew they were in danger, why didn't you do anything before?"

"I couldn't. Clarksville is protected territory."

"Whose?"

He looked over at me. "You wouldn't believe me."

"I just watched you shift into a horror buff's wet dream. I think we're a little far past skepticism."

"Fine. It belongs to the haints."

"*Haints?*" I echoed. "Is that some kind of crack at me for being a 'redneck'?"

"I told you you wouldn't believe me."

"Really. Haints. As in the ghosts my grandma painted the homestead blue to ward off?"

"A clever woman," he remarked.

"She was a superstitious nut."

"Most people in the know are deemed such by the small minded."

I frowned. "You seriously expect me to believe my hometown is owned by ghosts." Sure, the mayor was a bit pale and his parties were lifeless, but that was a stretch.

"Your hometown is the site of one of the bloodiest battles of the Civil War, not to mention the final resting place of countless men who met their deaths in the mines. Plenty of spirits reside there."

I swallowed hard at the reminder of the perils of my own profession. Not that it mattered. All I had to do was survive long enough to make sure Ellie was safe and get her the hell away from these werewolf freaks. The rest was just icing on the cake. "So if wolves are afraid to cross haint territory, how did Franny get away with it all these years? And how did you get into my old office?"

"The office is just outside of the territory. A lone she-wolf and her fledgling pup aren't much of a threat, but my guess is that she had a token."

"A token?"

"A sacred object, usually something made of iron or crystallized salt. It's more or less a visa for the spirit world, and it must be given and blessed by a conjurer who acts as an intermediary between the wolf and the spirits in a specific region, granting permission for them to reside in occupied territory."

"Iron?" I muttered, trying to think through the inventory of our belongings. I was pretty sure I'd remember Franny keeping a salt lick around as decor.

"It's usually something portable. Jewelry, perhaps a picture frame or a—"

"A statue?"

"Yes, it's quite possible."

"Franny had a wolf statue she insisted on keeping on the coffee table. Gaudy-ass thing."

His expression soured. "I gave that to her as an engagement present."

I pursed my lips. Well, this was awkward. "Guess she liked it."

He snorted. "Enough to have it blessed by a conjurer, at any rate."

"By conjurer, I assume you mean witches are real, too?"

"Of course they're real. But a conjurer is different. Appalachian folk magic is unique in its —"

"I know about Appalachian folk magic," I snapped. "I'm Melungeon, for God's sakes. I grew up throwing salt over my left shoulder and rubbing warts off on paper like everyone else. I just never thought it was more than..."

"Superstition?"

"Yeah." I stared out the window, watching the exit signs pass. "Guess I'm not much of a believer in anything."

"Well, you might want to start if you want to get Ellie back."

"Of course I want her back." I fell silent, thinking about all the bombs he'd just dropped on me. "If Clarksville is protected, how did Franny's parents get to her?"

"Her body was found in the lake, just outside the original town line," he answered, gripping the wheel a little tighter. "I imagine they hired a proxy to check up on her as I have in the past, and they lured her out somehow."

I could relate to the anger in his voice. In Clarksville, I'd been convinced that I was the only person who even still remembered Franny's death, and it was clear that everyone else resented me for being a reminder. When he spoke, I got the feeling that it was still just as fresh for him, and as much reason as I had to hate this man, I pitied him.

Sure, I hated him too, but he still loved her. It was evident in the way he said her name, the way his jaw tightened whenever he spoke of her death. If anything, he was still grieving her the way I should have been and I hated him all the more for it, but out of the two of us, I couldn't help but wonder who was the bigger chump. Me, the guy she'd been lying to for the last sixteen years, or him, the one she'd run out on.

Maybe it was a draw. All I knew was that if she *had* been cheating on me, despite what Nicolae claimed, at least now it made sense. This was no small-town hick I could compete with on even terms. The guy was her past and her future, and it wasn't just the monster he turned into that made him formidable. Judging by the looks of his clothes, that antique ring on his right hand, and the car we were driving, he had the means to give her everything she deserved, too. The only mystery was why she'd stayed with me.

That question was what kept me from trusting Nicolae's intentions when it came to rescuing Ellie. If Francesca had run from him, what did he have in store for our daughter?

He went quiet for the rest of the drive to the airport and I decided to save the rest of my questions for later. Neither of us was in a talking mood.

SIX

IT TURNED out that in addition to a rental that hadn't even hit the American market yet, Nicolae also had access to a private jet.

Fucker.

I sat as far from him as the plane would allow, even though I probably should have used the opportunity to get answers. His energy made it clear he wasn't in the mood to give them, and the truth was, I didn't want to know.

A few hours wasn't enough time to process all the bullshit he'd dropped on me. Hell, a few years wasn't enough, but sixteen? That might have started to make a dent in my disbelief, and yet Franny hadn't uttered so much as a word about what she was. Not even, "Hey, honey, my car's due for an oil change, and while you're at it, let's talk about how I turn into a giant furry nightmare on full moons."

It would've been *something*.

A shadow fell over me, a bit too all-encompassing to be the petite stewardess. I looked up to find Nicolae watching me with an unreadable expression on his annoyingly chiseled face. He sat down, leaving a single seat between us, but his long legs stretched out and made it feel like less space. "There are some things you need to understand before we land."

"Okay," I said warily. He hadn't talked to me for the first five hours of the flight, not even to tell me where we were going. When I'd asked, he'd simply grunted and opened up his smartphone to do whatever the fuck werewolves did online. Probably stalking vampires on Tinder, because why the hell wouldn't those be real, too? Of course, he'd taken *my* phone before we even got into the air.

"I am the Alpha of the Ursache pack. It's a title that comes with many responsibilities, and a reputation to uphold."

So here it was. We were finally going to have the "other man" talk. I just wasn't sure which one of us the label applied to. "Alpha. What is that, like the wolf king or something?"

He snorted another laugh. I wondered if he was capable of actually producing a chuckle. "It's more like the president of a large company."

I looked around the luxury jet. "Yeah, that figures."

"There are rules of behavior that all members of the pack are expected to follow. Being a human, the expectations for you are of course lower, but I need you to at least try to conform."

I narrowed my eyes. "You turn into a crotch-munching hell monster and you're worried *I'm* gonna embarrass you?"

"That kind of talk is exactly what I'm referring to," he said in a tone of disapproval. "You are the consort of an Alpha she-wolf and the father of the heir to the Majerus pack. I can't have you talking like a drunken sailor."

"Consort?" I echoed, holding up the hand that wore my wedding band. "I was her fucking husband."

"Human law means nothing in our society," he scoffed. "You are a *consort*."

"And that somehow embarrasses you less?" I asked in disbelief.

"Our society is matrilineal. It's not uncommon for Alphas of either sex to take consorts." His eyes flitted over me disapprovingly.

"Less common to take a human as one, but I suppose it can't be helped."

I sat up straight and pulled down my shirt, because I didn't like the feeling I got that he was looking at me like I was a slob. "And does the consort schtick come with a title?"

"I suppose you could go by Sir Mullins at formal events, if you like, but we're all on a first name basis."

I'd been kidding about the title part, but I decided not to tell him. "And when we land, what are the chances I'm gonna be ripped apart by your wolf buddies?"

"If you weren't under my protection? One-hundred percent," he said, leaning back against the padded seat.

I gulped. "Seriously?"

"We're not normal wolves, Jack. The ones who aren't Alphas may look normal, but we have all the predatory instincts of human beings in a package capable of doing damage to the furthest extent. Our hierarchies are rigid because they have to be. Without law and order, we would not be able to exist in secrecy."

He didn't need to expound more for me to know that was because they'd leave a path of destruction that was more than noticeable enough to end up on the nightly news. "So you... eat people?"

"We don't have to, but we often do. It's common for us to get worked up on the hunt, the younger wolves especially, if they're not kept in line."

"What keeps them in line?"

"Me," he answered.

"Message received. '*Fuck with me and you're dinner.*'"

The amusement in his eyes pissed me off, but I was newly afraid of getting on his bad side. "I will not allow harm to come to you, but it is in your best interest to make my job as easy as possible."

"Why *wouldn't* you allow it? And don't pretend like you don't hate me, 'cause I sure fucking hate you."

He stared boredly at his nails. They were a normal length again, but I'd never forget the blades they grew into in his wolf form. "You see me as a threat. Competition. I see you as the collateral damage of Francesca's tragic decisions. Is that clear enough?"

"Perfectly," I muttered. "And Ellie? How do you see her?"

His gaze softened in a way I didn't want to acknowledge. "She is all I have left of Francesca, and I will do whatever it takes to protect her. You can count on that, if nothing else."

I didn't want to. I didn't want to count on anything from this prick, the guy who'd held onto a big enough piece of my wife's heart that she'd held onto his letter to the very last. It was infuriating to know that he was my only shot at saving our daughter, but I couldn't deny the sincerity in his words or the way they resonated with me deeper than anyone's words ever had. Even deeper than Francesca's halfhearted professions of love.

Whatever Nicolae's reasoning was, I was finally starting to believe that we shared a common goal. Keeping Ellie safe. Bringing her home, wherever the hell that happened to be these days. As long as he kept his word, I'd follow his rules and try not to tarnish his precious reputation. My daughter's life was worth far more than my pride.

"Then we won't have any problems."

Nicolae nodded and stood to go back to his original seat. I took out the magazine in the pouch in front of me and tried to look like I was reading, even though ergonomic luggage was the furthest thing from my mind. It was another two hours before we landed, give or take, and by the time I stood up, my legs felt like jelly. I grabbed the bag that now held my every possession that wasn't holed up in a missing moving truck somewhere and slung it over my shoulder.

When I followed Nicolae off the plane, I was surprised to find a car already waiting for us just off the runway. Everything else about the werewolf lifestyle was still a mystery to me, but I could probably get used to the expedited travel.

The man waiting in front of the car nodded in deference to Nicolae, but it was hard to tell if he was another werewolf or just observing the formalities of whatever the hell country we'd landed in.

I knew we'd passed over the Atlantic, so we had to be in Europe somewhere. "Where are we?" I finally asked.

"Romania."

Of course.

"Get in," Nicolae ordered, opening the backseat door. I hesitated, even though it felt more like he was bossing me around than getting the door for me. Reluctantly, I slipped in and pulled the door shut, reminding myself that I was playing nice for Ellie's sake. Even if it meant letting Nicolae treat me like his bitch.

God, this was gonna be hell.

Nicolae talked to the driver for a few minutes, looking down at his phone every so often like he was confirming plans. He finally got in next to me and I caught a glimpse of the driver's eerily blue eyes in the mirror before he took off.

The odds that he was a wolf were looking better by the minute. Nicolae stayed silent, working on his phone for the entire ride, and something told me he wasn't trying to upgrade his farm. I watched the city pass by through the tinted windows. I knew next to nothing about Romania, but whatever city we were in was sure active at night. Part of me was afraid to ask if vampires were real, too. I wasn't sure I really wanted to know.

I'd never been more than a couple of hours outside of Clarksville until our recent move, and a high school trip to Nashville hardly counted as being well traveled. I couldn't help but wonder how many times Francesca had taken this route. If the glimmering neon lights set like eyes in the mountain range were the home she'd been dreaming of whenever she'd get that nostalgic smile on her face as she gazed out the window on a rainy day. The city was beautiful and cosmopolitan, just slightly ethereal in a way that made me question if I was dreaming. Just like her.

The car finally came to a stop in front of one of the highest buildings in what had to be the downtown district. I'd expected us to keep driving out into the mountains. After all, didn't wolves like forests?

"This is it?" I asked doubtfully.

"What were you expecting?"

"I don't know...not a luxury condo," I said, looking up at the numerous floors.

Nicolae snorted and got out of the car. "We only have to shift on full moons, and living in the city keeps our instincts in check."

"In other words, you live among food because it's a good test of will."

His head was turned just enough for me to see his smirk before he walked into the building. The driver stayed behind, so I followed Nicolae into the lobby. The woman at the front desk immediately leaped to her feet and bowed her head.

"Sir," she said in a tone of reverence.

I stood frozen, unsure of what I was supposed to do. Nicolae ignored me and nodded to her on his way past. "At ease, Marie. Call Mason and let him know that we've arrived."

"Yes, sir. Welcome home."

Nicolae walked over to a glass elevator and I stepped in, my stomach tangling into knots as the elevator car climbed the floors. "You guys not a fan of metal or something?"

"We're not a fan of being trapped in enclosed spaces and not knowing who's waiting on the other side," he answered.

"Fair enough." I followed him out onto the top floor, which seemed to be a single apartment. Just a huge one. "You live here?"

"These are my personal quarters where I sleep and do most of my work, yes."

"Fancy," I said, looking around. Everything was stainless steel and glass and every room other than the bedrooms could be seen from the entryway. It was the exact opposite of the modern home Franny and I had shared for sixteen years, and yet again, I found myself wondering what the hell she'd been thinking when she made the decision to come slum it with me.

It was one thing when our life had been this thing we'd both built together. Our house was cramped and kind of crummy when you got right down to it, considering all the leaks and paint that seemed to peel in a new room as soon as we'd painted the last, but it was *our* house. Knowing *this* was what she had given up made me feel all the more inadequate in retrospect. I'd hoped that maybe I would find the ghost of her here in this place she'd run from, because I had stopped feeling her in Clarksville from the moment she died, but the only echoes I felt were of a woman I didn't know. A stranger who belonged to a strange world I had no hope of understanding and wouldn't have ever wanted to, if it hadn't been for Ellie.

"This will be your room," Nicolae announced, opening a door at the end of the hall.

I peered in to find a surprisingly normal room equipped with a bed, a desk and a TV. It was posh, like the rest of the place, but there was no sign that a wolf pack called this condo home. Maybe they saved the weird shit for the bottom floors.

"I'm staying here? With you?"

"I need to keep an eye on you," he said, as if that should be obvious. "I'm going to let you have the run of the place, so don't make me regret it. There's an ensuite bathroom in your room, and food in the refrigerator. If a door is closed, assume it's closed for a reason."

"Got it. Now, when are we going to go after the Majerus bastards?"

He gave me a severe look. "Ellie was taken by a pack of werewolves, not a group of amateur kidnappers. Getting her back is not going to happen overnight."

"Fuck that! If I wanted to wait and see, I would have stuck with the FBI."

"Fine. You want to go charging onto Majerus territory and get yourself killed, be my guest," he said, folding his arms. "All you're going to accomplish is ensuring that when I *do* rescue Ellie, I have to tell her that she's an orphan now."

I clenched my jaw, furious at his nonchalance when it came to my kid's life, but I knew he was right. If *Nicolae* wasn't charging in, I sure as hell didn't stand a chance. "When?" I gritted out.

"I'm making arrangements now. This is a matter of strategy, not brute force," he said sternly. "If you want to help your daughter, try not to get in *my* way."

"And if they hurt her while you're twiddling your thumbs?"

"Do you know why Francesca's parents killed her, Jack?" His tone made it clear he thought he was speaking to a child. Someone so far beneath him I didn't deserve respect. He must have realized I wasn't dumb enough to give an answer I obviously didn't have, because he continued berating me. "Because when Ellie was born, Francesca became expendable. She humiliated the family by running away, and in the interim, relations between our packs broke down. Ellie is their chance to start over."

I frowned. "And that means...?"

"They need her to continue the Majerus line. She's invaluable, and for that reason alone, no harm will come to her in their care."

"Surely they had more kids," I protested.

"Claire was deemed infertile by every doctor in her pack," said Nicolae. "Damon took consorts and had other children, but only an heir from Claire's line could be considered for the role of pack Alpha. Francesca was their miracle," he murmured. "Ellie is her only hope of continuing the Majerus line and maintaining control. If she doesn't produce an heir, the role of Alpha will go to one of Damon's other children and the pack will splinter."

That didn't sound good. "So you're saying they want to marry Ellie off the same way they did with Franny?"

His eyes clouded with anger. "Yes."

"She's trans. When they realize that —"

"They won't hurt her, but she will be expected to take a female mate when she comes of age and produce an heir, the same as any other Alpha."

"Well, that's fucked," I snarled.

"Mating is a political act for werewolves, and producing an heir is considered a duty, not an option," said Nicolae. "She will be permitted to take a male consort, if she chooses, but neither love nor attraction is a requirement when it comes to these things."

"My kid is not gonna be 'permitted' anything," I said firmly. "Not by you or those freaks who killed Franny."

Nicolae was giving me that look again. The look that said, *I can't believe I'm wasting time explaining this to an inferior life form.* "It's rather a moot point now, isn't it? It's not something that will be an issue for quite a few years to come."

It wasn't going to be an issue at all. As soon as I got Ellie, we were both out of there, so I decided it wasn't worth it wasting what little energy I had arguing with this nut about his ass-backwards society. And he looked down on *me* for being a redneck.

"If you'll excuse me, there is much I still have to do." With that, Nicolae left and the implication that he expected me to stay in my room for the remainder of the evening was clear. Not that I was eager to spend any more time with him, either.

It took me all of five minutes to unpack my belongings and I finally decided to take a shower since I realized I hadn't bothered to since Ellie had gone missing. Probably good to get in the habit of showering regularly again if I was gonna be surrounded by dogs. The less I smelled and looked like an item on the menu, the better.

By the time I got out of the shower, I could hear another deep voice conversing with Nicolae's out in the living room. The one good thing about an apartment with few walls was that sound carried. I cracked the door to hear a little better and the fact that they were actually discussing security in the Majerus pack gave me hope that Nicolae meant what he'd said about getting Ellie out.

"And the human?" the other man asked after a lull.

"He's human. Exactly what you'd expect." I heard the sound of ice dropping into a glass as Nicolae spoke. Evidently, mention of me drove him to drink.

It's mutual, buddy.

"I'm doing what I can to minimize talk of him in the pack, but they all know he's here." The man's tone was troubled.

"Don't bother," said Nicolae. "He's here and he isn't going anywhere."

"I still don't understand why." His companion sounded even more vexed about my presence than Nicolae was. "We need the girl, not him."

"He's necessary to ensure that her transition into the pack goes smoothly," Nicolae answered. "Besides, I feel there's more to him than meets the eye."

Well, he was dead wrong about that.

"He's a country miner. What more is there?" his companion scoffed. I decided he was to be known henceforth as the Prick.

"Surely something if Francesca saw fit to whittle away sixteen years with him."

Ah, there it was at last. The bitterness. Funny how that was what put me at ease far more than any of Nicolae's reassurances about his good intentions. At least it made sense that he was keeping me around because he was curious as to just what Francesca had seen in me.

That made two of us.

I closed the door softly and turned the TV on since the white noise was the only way I stood a chance at falling asleep. It still took me a few hours, according to the clock on the dresser. Every time I closed my eyes, the image of Ellie being dragged out of that apartment, her screams echoing through the halls as she cried out for me, kept me awake. When I finally did sleep, there was no escaping the fear, or the guilt.

SEVEN

SOMEWHERE AROUND DAWN, while the sky was still blue, I woke to the feeling that someone was watching me. It had always been a common occurrence to wake up and find Franny watching me the way she was now, at the foot of a stranger's bed. She looked the way she had right before she'd died, her beautiful features hardened with disappointment as she stared down at me.

Usually, when I'd find her watching me, I'd ask what she was doing and the answer was always the same. "Just wondering what it's like when you dream."

I'd always just chalked it up to her being kind of a weirdo and figured that normalcy was the one thing I had going for me. The one thing she could possibly be drawn to. She was so wonderful and strange, from her constantly shifting moods to the melancholy that sometimes overtook her for months at a time. She'd told me once that I was boring and simple and that was why she loved me. There were no surprises, good or bad.

I hadn't taken it too personally, because she was a goddess and I was a mere mortal graced with her presence. Everyone knew it, from her to the men she entertained while I was at work.

I knew this wasn't like the other times she'd woken me with her watching. This time, she wasn't real. Even though I doubted I was fully awake yet, I was conscious enough to know that she couldn't really be here. I sat up and let the sheets fall, and she kept watching me with that serene, knowing expression that reminded me of how much more she knew about... everything.

I'd just never imagined there was quite *that* much more to know.

"Hello, Jack," she said warmly.

"You're not here."

Her lips curved as she looked around the room. "Can't get anything past you," she said casually, standing. The hem of her pink cotton dress pooled around her ankles as she walked to the other side of the room. "How are you liking Romania?"

"It's not exactly a pleasure trip," I said, climbing out of bed. The part of me that wanted to go over to her and take her into my arms, even if she wasn't real, was tempered by the part of me that knew she'd disappear if she didn't simply push me away. "Ellie—"

"I know what happened," she snapped, turning on me with a look of pure spite in her gaze. It was the look I was used to seeing in her eyes, so it didn't come as any surprise. The way it filled me with longing did. Longing just to see her look at me that way one last time in reality. "You failed, Jack. I trusted you with our child, and you failed us both."

"I know." My throat tightened and I took another step toward her, walking softly in case I alerted the real me somewhere up in the waking world. "But I'm going to fix it. I know I didn't protect you, but I'm gonna bring her back."

"You or Nicolae?" she spat. "I gave up everything to get away from him and you've delivered our son right into his hands."

I flinched. Even in my goddamn dreams, we had to have this argument. "We don't have a son, Franny. For God's sake, do you still not get that?"

"You're the one who doesn't understand! You know nothing of this world. The world I gave my life to keep him out of," she seethed, her hands trembling as she made fists of them at her side. "I made you promise not to leave Clarksville. One thing. I asked *one* thing of you, but you couldn't even do that, could you?"

I swallowed hard. "I did what I had to do, for both of us. You left us. You left *me* without a fucking clue about what was going on, about how to help her through this. After sixteen years, did you really not think I deserved the truth?"

She opened her mouth to speak, but her eyes narrowed as they locked on the door. I turned to see what it was that had drawn her attention away from me, but by the time I looked back, she was gone.

I felt an intense pressure on my chest that brought me back to reality, and to my body. When I opened my eyes, I cried out in alarm at the sight of two bugged-out eyes as blue as the sky staring back at me through a mess of reddish-brown curls. The little imp barely weighed more than a sack of potatoes, but all of it was concentrated on my chest as he crouched on top of it with his bony little feet. When I screamed, so did he and the alarm made him use my chest as a springboard as he leaped onto the floor, landing crouched like a wild animal.

I was sure it was another dream as I flipped the light switch on the wall. The little goblin shrieked like the light was about to turn him to ash and shielded his eyes. He was a scrap of a thing, barely five if that, wearing footy pajamas covered in Batman logos that might as well have been fur for the way he was snarling at me. "What the hell?" I muttered, stumbling my way out of bed.

The goblin-child grabbed the door and threw it open before scampering out into the hall. I pursued him to the kitchen where Nicolae was standing over a fresh pot of coffee. The kid climbed his leg and clung to his back, staring at me over Nicolae's shoulder with the wide-eyed fixation of a baby bear who knows it's safe behind its behemoth parent.

Nicolae scowled over his shoulder at his cling-on, but his lack of alarm made it clear this was far from an unusual occurrence. He looked back at me, his frown deepening. "What did you do?"

"What did *I* do?" I cried. "I just woke up to find that little creep sitting on my chest gawking at me!"

Nicolae sighed, peeling the boy off his back and holding him at arm's length as he kicked against the cloth confining his feet and made fierce snarling sounds in protest of being removed from his safe perch. "Andrei, what did I tell you about sneaking into other people's rooms?" he scolded.

The boy ignored him, kicking and grunting. Nicolae set him down and he dove for the elevator, reaching up to jab the buttons as many times as he could until the doors slid open. He dove into the car and glared at me as he crouched behind the elevator panel, like *he* was afraid of me. I stared in confusion until the doors slid closed before turning to Nicolae and asking, "What the hell was that about?"

"That was Andrei," he answered, sitting at the counter. He poured a cup of coffee and slid it over to me. "That's what we call him, at least. He's a pup my men rescued on a recent mission."

"Rescued? From where, a zoo?" I asked, sitting across from him.

"From the woods. He's only recently been able to shift into his human form, and as you can see, he's having some trouble adjusting."

I blinked. "So he really is feral?"

"In a manner of speaking."

"I thought you said werewolves can't shift until puberty. He can't be more than what, five?"

"We assume. We haven't been able to track down his parents yet, and I imagine when we do, we'll find that they're dead," he said, growing somber. "As for him being able to shift, that's true except in cases of extreme trauma. It's not uncommon for young wolves to revert to their beastly forms to cope."

"Oh." Well, now I felt like shit. "So you adopted him?"

"Regular wolves care for those who cannot care for them-selves," Nicolae said, pouring a dash of creamer into his own coffee. It was a surprisingly human thing to do. I wasn't sure why I couldn't picture the guy eating or drinking like normal, even though he was at least as much man as he was beast. "We're not so different."

"I see. You still could've warned me. I would have at least locked my door."

Nicolae smirked. "But then I wouldn't have been able to see that look on your face."

I flipped him off and took a sip of coffee. He might have been a weirdo, but he made a decent cup of Joe.

"I was going to come check on you anyway. You were making quite a racket in your sleep."

"Rough night," I muttered, running a hand through my hair. "Who was that guy I heard here last night?"

"That was Mason, my chief lieutenant," he answered.

"What, like a military?"

"More like a police force, but yes. Sometimes that, too."

"So you really are at war with the Majerus pack?"

"Among others," he answered. "Our race is ancient. We're always at war."

"Sounds like a real hoot."

"You will be accompanying me to an event tonight," he announced, ignoring my comment.

"An event?"

"Several members of the pack have returned from an extended stay in friendly territory, and it's my responsibility to welcome them. It will be a good opportunity to introduce you."

"I'm not crazy about the idea of partying while my daughter's missing."

Nicolae gave me a look, leaning over the counter. "Let's get something straight. Your daughter is not *missing*. I know exactly where she is, right down to the coordinates. She is not a hostage. Right now, according to pack law, she is with blood relatives who have as much right to her as I do."

"But they murdered Francesca!" I cried.

"And proving that will be incredibly difficult if not impossible."

"You said it yourself, Francesca was your mate and that means Ellie belongs to you." I couldn't believe those words had actually left my mouth, but the only way to argue this insanity was on its own terms. What little I knew of them, at any rate. The look on Nicolae's face when my words sank in was so much more troubling than anything he had said this far.

"Francesca was my rightful mate," he said slowly. "But the ratification of our mating is on tenuous legal ground."

"What the fuck is that supposed to mean?"

"It means that Francesca ran on the night we were to be mated. We consummated the arrangement, but she left before she was marked as mine."

"*Marked?*"

"When two werewolves are mated, we bite to leave a permanent mark that announces belonging," he explained.

"Right. Kind of like wedding bands, only for freaks."

Nicolae smirked. "I told you, this world would not be easy for you to understand. There is a reason we seldom allow humans into it."

"Then how do you make more werewolves?"

"We are born, not turned. No human has ever survived a werewolf's bite without going insane and having to be put down." He hesitated. "Not in recorded history, at least."

I shuddered. I wasn't sure which would be the worse side of that coin. "So you and Franny were never actually mated," I said. A day ago, that would have come as a sweet relief, but now...

"No," Nicolae replied bitterly. "She ran before it was official, but you are now one of four living people who knows that. Claire and Damon could try to claim Ellie on that basis if they knew, but..."

"They would have to admit they were the last people who saw her alive," I muttered.

"So you see the dilemma. In either case, Francesca's disappearance is enough to call my claim into question. It's their word against mine."

My head was throbbing, burdened by all the questions I was

afraid to ask. There was one that stood out among the others, and I had to know. "When you say you and Franny consummated the mating before she left, you mean...?"

"The same as it means to humans." He took a sip of his coffee, watching for my reaction. Like he was trying to see if I was keeping up enough to arrive at the same question that had obviously occurred to him. The question that would answer so many others.

"Ellie could be yours," I gritted out. Now, it made sense. The whirlwind of lust that had led to Ellie's conception, and Francesca's desire to rush into marriage. I'd always wondered, but knew it didn't change anything, even now that the possible sperm donor was right in front of me.

"It is a distinct possibility," he answered. "In fact, given the rarity of human-wolf hybrids, I would say it's far more likely."

I could tell what he was thinking. For once, that smug expression was far from a mystery.

"I'm sorry you had to find out this way." He sounded almost sincere about it, too.

I laughed, staring into the black liquid in my cup. "Guess it makes more sense than the alternative. Why the hot new girl in town was in such a hurry to shack up with the most average guy in all of Kentucky."

Nicolae's expression shifted a little. He seemed surprised by my self-awareness. "You're taking this better than I expected."

"You expected what, a temper tantrum?" I asked. "Maybe that I'd throw a punch?"

"Humans males are at least as volatile as we are. You're just not capable of doing as much damage."

I grabbed a bottle of what I hoped was vodka off the counter that had been left out from the night before and dumped it into my coffee mug. "It doesn't change anything."

"Are you sure about that?"

I looked up at him, swallowing my anger. "It doesn't," I said through my teeth. "If it turns out that Ellie really is mine, are you still going to want her back?"

"Of course." He seemed offended by the same insinuation he'd made of me seconds earlier.

"One thing I don't get," I admitted, hoping the alcohol would make my hands stop shaking. It wasn't withdrawal. I hadn't touched the stuff much since Ellie was born, but I couldn't blame all my nervous energy on the wakeup call from hell I'd gotten, courtesy of Andrei. Franny's ghost was still with me, her words all the more biting in the context I now had. "If you think Ellie is yours, why not just stake your claim that way? Surely that's a more convincing argument than I could make as Franny's... consort."

"To explain it to you would require an understanding of pack law that you simply don't have."

"Try."

He sighed. "*If* Ellie is my biological child and *if* I make a claim to her on those grounds, the status of my mating to Francesca will still be an obstacle. Pack law always favors the she-wolf in matters of custody. The Majerus pack will use the fact that she ran away as proof that Francesca did not want our child raised by me, and the Court will almost certainly decide the matter in their favor." The hurt in his voice took me off guard. "On the other hand, your status as Francesca's consort is indisputable. As I said, we are matrilineal. If *you* are assumed the biological parent, as Francesca's consort, you are Ellie's rightful custodial parent. Are you following me?"

My head felt like it was going to split open, but I answered, "Yeah. Mostly. According to your laws, Franny belonged to you, I belonged to her, Ellie belongs to me and that means we both belong to you, by proxy."

He stared at me for a second, and I found his surprise over the fact that I understood more insulting than his snarky remarks. "Yes. That's about the long and short of it."

"Maybe you wolves just aren't as complicated as you like to think," I said, taking another sip of my drink.

Nicolae didn't smile, but his eyes did somehow. "Perhaps not."

I reached for a muffin in the basket on the counter. I hadn't had much of an appetite over the last few days, but now that I knew Ellie was at least safe from physical harm for the time being and we had a plan for getting her back, however bizarre it seemed, I was famished. "So all that's gonna hold up in your Court?"

"That is my hope. Our packs being at war complicates things and will require an impartial arbitrator," he explained, folding his hands as he watched me. I realized he was probably judging the way I buttered my muffin, so I ate it dry. Fucking snob. "There are still some logistics I need to work out before I file an official claim, but the first step is introducing you to the pack."

"Why?" I asked, realizing I should have waited until my mouth wasn't full.

He arched an eyebrow. "Just... try to keep yourself out of trouble until the designer comes."

"Designer? Why, and where are you going?"

"She's going to need to fit you for some formal wear for tonight. I'm going to work."

"There's gotta be something more useful I can do than sitting on my ass getting fitted for party clothes," I protested. I'd never been away from work for this long, and on top of worrying about Ellie, it was driving me insane.

"I'm afraid we don't have any ores to mine at the moment."

"One, fuck you. Two, I mine *coal*. It's a fossil fuel, not an ore."

"I've been meaning to ask, how did you get into that, anyway?"

I stared at him. "Uh. Pretty much the same way any southern schmuck does. I was eighteen with a wife and a kid on the way, and I needed a job that paid well."

"Right." He finished his coffee and stood, draping a coat over his arm. "Well, try to behave yourself while I'm gone."

"Worry about that rabid puppy running around your building, not me," I called after him.

Just like that, I was alone in the kind of place I'd once been certain only existed in magazines. The condo was rich in every sense of the word, but I wouldn't have traded it for the happy little shack we'd owned any day. Even if those happy memories had become fewer and further between toward the end.

EIGHT

TURNED OUT, I was pretty fucking bad at not snooping. I tried every door that was shut while Nicolae was gone, but they were all either disappointing or locked. By the time those elevator doors finally opened, I would have been glad to see him.

Instead, a petite woman with cloudy golden-brown ringlets and skin a rich brown ochre came bounding out, carrying a designer satchel on her left arm. She paused to peer down at me over her thick blue frames and pursed her berry blue lips. "Oh, boy. Nicky said I'd have my work cut out for me, but he didn't say it was this bad," she said in a thick European accent that wasn't quite as eastern as Nicolae's. French, maybe.

I stood from the couch and wiped the chip dust off on my jeans, well aware that I was probably making the very first impression he'd prepared her for. "You must be the designer. I'm —"

"Jack, I know," she said, her lip curling slightly as she looked down at my hand. She finally took it and smiled pityingly. "Charmed. The name is Leonie, but you can call me Lee. Everyone does."

"Nice to meet you, Lee. So you're the uh, pack designer?"

She laughed, setting her bag down on the coffee table. "I'm a designer who's part of the pack, but even Nicolae doesn't pay enough for me to exclusively cut cloth for this feral lot."

"Well, sorry you're having to work on such short notice."

She waved me off, pulling a measuring tape from her bag. "Don't be silly, I'm not creating anything from scratch. Just getting a look at you so I can make the proper alterations. Strip, please."

I blinked. "I —"

"Nothing I haven't seen before, cookie. Now, your clothes. Take 'em off." Reluctantly, I started unbuttoning my shirt and she sighed. "It's not a bloody strip show, love, off with it. You're not the only appointment I have today."

"Right. Sorry," I muttered, peeling off my shirt, followed by my jeans. Leonie paused, looking me over. "Well, you've got a nice body under that baggy flannel, haven't you?"

"I thought you said it *wasn't* a strip show."

She smiled innocently, standing in front of me. "Arms out."

I complied, trying not to feel like a mannequin on display as she took my measurements. She noticed the black tattoo on my bicep and arched an eyebrow.

It wasn't the first time I'd been self-conscious about the design. It wasn't exactly my cup of tea. Hell, neither was getting inked in the first place. Francesca had insisted it would be fun to get matching tattoos, even though the little crescent moon and stars she'd gotten on her ankle was a hell of a lot easier to hide than the weirdly detailed crest she'd printed out for me. But hell, I was young and eager to impress my girlfriend, so I'd stuck out the torture session at the hands of a tattoo artist who was more drunk than I was.

"So, you uh, turn into a wolf, too?" I asked, eager to distract her from asking about the tattoo.

"Every full moon since I was fourteen," she answered, pausing. "What's the accent, Texas?"

"Tennessee," I answered.

"Quaint. And a human," she mused. "Haven't had one of those around in *ages*."

"Did the last one survive?"

She laughed like I'd just told a hilarious joke and gave my arm a teasing swat before stowing her gear back in her bag. "Don't worry, love, I'll have something fixed up for you by tonight's run."

"Run? I thought it was a party."

She paused at the elevator, turning back around to face me as she pushed her glasses back up on her nose. "Oh, dear. Nicky really didn't tell you much, did he? I suppose he's still a bit miffed about the...Francesca thing," she mouthed.

"You knew Francesca?" I asked hopefully.

"We all did. World-class bitch, that one," she huffed. "May she rest in peace, of course."

"Uh..."

"Oh, I know humans are so attached to their mates," she said with a sympathetic sigh, propping her cheek in her dainty hand. "But you must understand, darling, nothing's all that personal here. We all have our place within the pack, and we stick to it. That includes Nicolae."

"And Francesca?"

Leonie's gaze softened. "She didn't know her place," she said in a way that sounded more like sorrow than smugness. "If she had, she'd still be alive. If you want my advice, you'll learn from her mistake and help your daughter take her proper place when the time comes."

The doors opened and Nicolae stepped out. His appearance didn't seem to come as a surprise to her like it did to me. "Leonie," Nicolae said, nodding to her.

"All set, love," she said, giving his arm a squeeze as she traded places with him and got onto the elevator. With a mischievous smile, she added, "It was nice meeting you, Jack. I'm honored to have gotten a sneak preview before everyone else."

The elevator doors closed, leaving me to look to Nicolae for answers. "What was that about?"

"That was Leonie being Leonie," he answered, going into the kitchen to pour himself a glass of liquor. I'd grown up in a town where booze passed for medication, but I'd never seen anyone drink quite as much as Nicolae did. Then again, he was huge, so it would probably take a bathtub full of vodka to make a dent in his sobriety.

"She said something about there being a run tonight. I thought you said it was a party."

"No, I said I was going to introduce you to the pack. The Majerus pack does parties, but that's not really our style."

"So, what's a run?"

Nicolae paused like my questions were irritating him and he needed to regenerate his patience. "Wolves are simple creatures, even if our society is not. When we celebrate, when we mourn. When we need to rally together, we hunt."

My throat started to tighten up again, the same way it had when Nicolae had first showed himself to me as a wolf on the side of the road. "You hunt what?"

His blank stare was all the answer I needed.

"Christ! What the fuck is wrong with you?"

"We are men and we are beasts, Jack," he said calmly. "You asked how we could live here, among prey, and this is the answer."

"So it makes it more civilized if you do it in an organized fashion?" I demanded.

"I never claimed it was civilized, nor that we have any interest in being civilized. Not according to your standards." He took another drink. Straight vodka. "Would it help if I told you the evening's prey happens to be a serial rapist?"

It did, and he knew it. "Still. We have laws for a reason."

"The law failed to convict him three times. I'm sure the law is doing nothing to help his victims sleep easier at night. One was Ellie's age."

My stomach churned. He knew how to erode my moral defenses, I'd say that much. "It's not about the scumbag. I can think he deserves to die and still think it's fucked up that you use people in a canned hunt."

"It's hardly that. He'll be given a loaded weapon and released into the forest. You won't be required to watch, only to accompany me and meet the rest of the pack."

"Right. Because everyone needs a fancy suit to attend a blood sport."

"I know this is going to be difficult for you, but try to keep in mind that the quicker you adapt to the way things are, the more you will be able to help Ellie. You do want that, don't you?"

I want her as far away from you psychos as possible. "Yes," I gritted out.

"Good boy," he taunted, setting aside his glass as he walked past me. "Try to relax until tonight. There's no point in stressing yourself out."

I waited until he disappeared into his room to flip him off.

LEONIE'S ASSISTANT came to drop off my suit a few hours later, and I still didn't feel like I'd adequately prepared myself to go have appetizers and small talk with werewolves right before they set off to rip someone apart for sport. Not that I had an issue with their chosen target, but still. There was something about it that was so... inhuman.

No shit.

By the time I was dressed and waiting for Nicolae to take me wherever the hell we were going, I had come to the realization that it wasn't the violence that bothered me. It was the fact that Francesca had been a part of it. I consoled myself with the knowledge that she had run away to keep Ellie out of this world, even if that also meant that I had failed them both by unknowingly dragging her back into it.

Nicolae came out of the room and I stood up, ready to get the evening over with. The sight of him stopped me short, proving that he could take my breath away in more ways than one. I hated myself for reacting that way, but the man was a fucking god come down to grace the mortals with his presence. His long, dark hair was down, gliding over his broad shoulders where it became camouflaged in his black suit. It was the same cut and fabric as mine, but standing side by side, we would have looked like the basic and deluxe versions of the same package.

He looked me over like he was trying to decide whether or not my appearance was acceptable. When he reached out to brush some lint off my shoulder, I flinched instinctively, and the smug look in his eyes made me wonder if he'd done it on purpose. "And here I was worried Leonie would dress you in flannel just to spite me."

"It's a practical fabric," I grumbled, following him downstairs.

He ignored me, of course, and continued to do so until we reached the parking lot. "No driver this time?" I asked as he stopped at an even more obnoxious car.

"I needed my hands free to make sure you weren't going to make a run for it last time," he replied, getting behind the wheel.

"And what makes you so sure I'm not?"

"You are, for all your lack of complexity, a devoted father. I know you wouldn't do anything foolish to jeopardize Ellie's safety or her standing within this pack."

"Is that a threat?" I asked, buckling in. I didn't trust this guy's driving and he was probably perfectly capable of surviving a crash and walking away without a scratch.

Nicolae looked over at me. "It's whatever it needs to be to help you understand the gravity of your situation."

I decided to take my turn ignoring him as we pulled onto the road. "You still have my phone, right?"

"Mason has it. He's monitoring it for all incoming calls, of course."

"Don't you think I should at least be around in case Ellie calls?"

"Trust me, they won't let Ellie call you. If anyone calls, it will be Damon, and I'm not taking the risk of letting you talk to him."

He had a point. I probably wasn't going to say anything overly productive to the bastard who'd killed my wife and kidnapped my daughter.

"I'm going to be a broken record until this truth sinks through," said Nicolae. "The best thing—the *only* thing—you can do to help Ellie is —"

"Play by your rules, adapt to your world," I muttered. "I get it."

"As long as we're clear." He took a road that sure as hell didn't lead anywhere good and about fifteen minutes later, we were in the fabled middle of nowhere without another car in sight.

"Where is everyone?"

"They came on foot," he answered, parking well off the road. "I would have, if I didn't have a human to transport."

"Right," I muttered. I caught sight of headlights through the trees and realized that could only be another wolf with a human to transport. I didn't pity tonight's prey, not by a long shot. As far as I was concerned, getting hunted down and ripped open by a pack of angry werewolves was a fate far better than any child rapist deserved, but it was a reminder that these people were anything but human. They were predators, and I didn't want Ellie having any part of them.

All I could do was hope that the Majerus wolves were slightly more civilized, but given what they'd done to their own daughter, that seemed absurd.

"Come," Nicolae ordered, falling back into his habit of ordering me around like I was one of his dogs.

I stopped and it took him a full ten seconds to realize I wasn't right behind him. The moonlight showcased the impatience on his pale face. "What is it now?"

"I'm playing by your rules. I'm doing this fucked up thing, I'm trying to come to terms with everything you just dropped on me last night," I said, taking a step toward him. "But you've gotta cut me some fucking slack and stop treating me like I'm your goddamn pet. I get that in your eyes, I'm lower than dirt because I'm human and because I work a 'shit job,' but as far as Francesca goes? You and me are in the same boat, pal, so how about you stop pretending like you're so much better?"

Nicolae listened in absolute silence, and his sudden movement was so swift I was completely unprepared. He had me up against a tree, his hand so tightly wrapped around my throat I could barely breathe, before I'd even had the chance to blink. "Pretending I'm better?" he taunted. "You're human. You're so weak that Francesca didn't even trust you with the truth of what she was, and if it hadn't been for you, she would still be alive. If you hadn't trapped her in that dead end town, she would have realized her mistake and swallowed her pride, but instead, she settled for you and now she's dead because of it."

He grabbed my wrist with his other hand and dug his nails in deep. I let out a muffled grunt but managed not to cry out, since I was sure that would just be the highlight of his day. His nails cut through my flesh with such ease that I was sure he had the ability to partially shift them, even though he still looked human everywhere but his eyes. They shone with malice as they drew my blood to the surface and wiped it across my palm before holding my hand up to make sure I could see. "Her blood is on your hands, and if you fuck things up, Ellie's will be too."

"Fuck you," I spat, looking him dead in the eye even though it burned. There was hatred in that gaze that hurt physically. Maybe that was what made him an Alpha.

He held me there, crushing the breath out of me, and I could tell he was thinking about just snapping my neck right then. I could feel the power in his grasp and knew he could, without even trying. Instead, he let me go and I fell to my knees, gasping.

"Clean yourself up," he said, straightening his tie. "You look pathetic."

I coughed, wiping my palm off on the wet grass. I used the tree to help me stand and took a moment to catch my breath. By the time I did, he was already gone, but I could see the lights of the torches through the trees. I rubbed my neck and waited until I was sure I'd composed myself to follow him.

The sight of the dozens upon dozens of wolves waiting in the woods took me off guard far more than the outburst from Nicolae that I'd expected all along. They all fell silent and stared at me, but only the faces of a few toward the front of the pack were illuminated in the glow of the torches. I caught sight of Leonie toward the front. She had traded her designer dress for all black, and she stood out even from the other females by her small stature. Whether the men outnumbered the women or the ones gathered were a poor representation of the total population, I couldn't be sure, but I knew this was only a fraction of the whole pack.

Nicolae stood in silence, beholding me with the same somber expression on the faces of the rest of his pack. His demeanor made me fear for a moment that *I* was the night's prey and everything else had just been a ruse to get me out here.

Not that it was a necessary one. Nicolae had already proven he could easily overpower me. If I was the one they had decided to hunt after all, there was no reason to hide it. Just when I was thinking about whether running counted as suicide, Nicolae turned to them all. "Now, brothers and sisters. Come take your form before the moon and greet your new brother."

He said the words with such bitterness that he had to be mocking me. I stopped caring when the pack got down on their knees, one after the other, and the shift happened before my eyes. It had been bizarre enough to see Nicolae changing back, but to see their human faces lengthening and growing monstrous was too much to handle.

If I hadn't been frozen in place in horror, I would've run. At least most of them were actual wolves, albeit huge ones, rather than the bipedal beast Nicolae turned into. There were a few of those around the crowd, but even they were smaller and less intimidating than he had been with his godlike stature.

All at once, the pack rushed me and I cried out, ready to run when Nicolae's booming voice silenced me. *"Hold still."*

I did. Not because I wanted to, but because his voice left me no choice. It held me in its paralysis as it had that day when he'd come into the apartment. I shuddered as the teeming herd of wolves pressed in around me, their cold noses against my hands, my legs, under my sleeves. Their tails wagged like dogs, but there was something in the way they were investigating me that seemed anything but friendly. There was a little one with fur the same golden-brown shade as Leonie's hair who pressed her nose into my hand in an almost affectionate gesture before she turned away and darted into the woods with the others who'd grown bored of me.

Only when the last of the wolves had left did I collapse as if Nicolae's spell had finally broken. I could feel him watching me as I panted on my hands and knees, coming back from the certainty that I was about to meet my death. "What the hell was that?" My voice was strained, and there was glee in his gaze when I finally looked up at him.

So much for thinking he was over Francesca choosing me over him. And I'd thought I was the one who was bitter.

"That was your welcome into the pack," he answered, his arms folded. "They needed to know your scent."

"Why?"

"So they'll be able to find you in case you try to run." He turned, pulling off his tie as he walked to join them. "Stay here. It shouldn't take more than an hour, and I don't recommend trying to find your way back to the car on your own. They've all been instructed not to touch you, but you know how wolves are when they get worked up and smell prey. Things happen."

No chance of me moving an inch. I waited to breathe until he was out of sight and heaved my lunch into the grass. By the time the human prey's anguished screams filled the air, I was just coughing up bile and blood.

Nicolae was right about one thing. This night had been an introduction to the pack I would never forget, and now I knew everything I'd ever wanted to know about werewolves. Or him.

NINE

I'D LEARNED my lesson about locking my door at night on my second day at Nicolae's, so when I woke to the sound of someone knocking, I had no idea what was in store for me. I was relieved to find Leonie standing in the hall, peeking coyly through her fingers. She was by far the least intimidating werewolf I'd encountered. Not that that was saying much.

"You decent?"

"More or less," I said, pulling on my robe. I wasn't crazy about wearing another man's clothes, and less so about the fact that Nicolae had ordered them specifically for me, but I'd only brought a few changes of clothes and none of them were pajamas.

"Nicolae wants me to babysit you."

At least she was honest. "Sorry."

"It's fine," she said, wandering into the kitchen to pull a wine cooler out of the refrigerator. I wasn't even aware we had any. "Not like it's runway season. Besides, you're the talk of the town."

"You mean the pack?"

She grinned. "There's not really that much of a difference."

"Right. There are thousands of you, aren't there?"

"Four thousand, give or take," she answered, sitting at the counter across from me. "We're one of the larger packs in Europe. So, I'm supposed to give you a crash course in werewolf law and etiquette. Think you're up for it, lumberjack?"

"I can try. You're sure the prettiest teacher I've ever had."

Her cheeks turned ruby red and she gave my hands a playful shove. "There's that country boy charm, but it doesn't fool me. I've seen the way you look at Nicolae," she said with a glimmer in her dark eyes.

"What, you mean the disgust and jealousy or the way I fear for my life whenever he's threatening me?"

She sighed. "He's gotten a bit rough around the edges ever since Franny left, but it's all bluster." She hesitated. "Well, mostly. He would never hurt you, you know. In a way, you're the only link he has to her."

I wasn't sure that was a comfort. If anything, it made him even creepier. "What was she like when she lived here?"

Leonie gave me that pitying look she so often wore. "I'm supposed to be teaching you about the rules, but I suppose it can't hurt. Francesca was a typical Alpha female," she said with a shrug. "She knew what she wanted and what she didn't, and nothing mattered outside of that."

"Nicolae said something about her being an Alpha... that's just because of her family line, right?"

"It's a bit more complicated than that," she answered, taking another sip of her sugary drink. "Wolves are hierarchal. In the wild, those roles are less rigid and some packs don't follow them at all. Alphas are so different, they're practically a different subspecies, as you saw last night."

"Subspecies?"

"Think of it like this. The vast majority of us are betas. Worker bees. We fight, we breed, we go about our daily lives in service of the pack. We're just... normal. The Alphas are the elite. The one percent."

"So they're douches who feed off everyone else's hard work. Got it."

She laughed. "Not exactly, but I do love the cynicism. It's very *en tendance*. Alphas are natural leaders and that comes with responsibility. An Alpha is expected to live and die for the rest of us. Their free will doesn't matter. From the moment they're born, they're expected to train and care for the pack, to put our needs above their own, and taking a mate is no exception."

"So they marry for duty instead of love."

"That's the idea." She sighed. "Francesca broke the rules, and as an Alpha, what she did is considered unforgivable. She put her wants ahead of both her pack and ours. Ahead of peace."

"So that justified her parents in killing her?"

"No," she said carefully. "Not according to pack law, but there are the official codes and then there is the moral code. Even if it did get out that they were the ones who killed her, there would be those who supported Claire and Damon's decision."

"That's sick."

"That's life, darling. The sooner you get used to it, the better."

"Right. Because Ellie is also an Alpha," I muttered.

Leonie looked shocked. "Well...yes. Nicolae told you?"

"No, but it's not hard to put it together. You said an Alpha is known from birth, which means it's hereditary."

"That's true."

"So, who's Nicolae planning on marrying my daughter off to for his own gain?" I asked dryly.

"Jack, try to understand, it's just politics," Leonie said, taking my hand. "All she has to do is have an heir by the time she's thirty. She and her mate don't even have to live together, and the tradeoff is so much greater. She'll have opportunities she never would have had back home."

I didn't doubt that. It was just a matter of what was going to be taken away from her to pay for those "opportunities" that mattered. "If you had a child and you'd watched her fight so hard and so long just to be the person she wanted to be, would you see this as a gift or a threat to everything you'd worked for?"

"I... I don't know. I've never been human. I don't know what it's like."

"Well, points for honesty," I said, forcing a smile. "Anyway, you were trying to tell me about Alphas before I derailed you?"

"There's not too much more to tell. Of course, I'm sure you know about the voice by now."

"Yeah. Nicolae's used it on me a few times," I muttered.

She smiled. "You can see why success comes easily to Alphas, then. It makes business negotiations easier."

"Negotiations?" I scoffed. "More like all he has to do is say, 'open up the vault and give me all your money.'"

Leonie tilted her head. "It's not quite *that* extreme. Not unless you're an omega."

"An omega? What, like the bitch wolves who always get the shit beaten out of them because they're at the bottom of the pack?"

"No!" she huffed. "And don't let anyone hear you speaking like that, or you'll end up with a black eye yourself."

"Sorry, didn't mean to offend. Are you...?"

"Me? An omega?" She pressed a hand to her collar and gave a breathy laugh. "Oh, hardly. I'm just your run of the mill beta, albeit a fabulously dressed one," she mused, gliding her fingertips along the curve of her jaw. "Omegas are even rarer than Alphas. They're...special."

"Special how?" I asked warily.

"Special as in they're made to bring packs together. There's just something about the presence of one that's very..." She paused, her eyes darting up toward the ceiling as she searched for the word. "Calming."

"So they're the wolf equivalent of aromatherapy?"

She gave my hand another swat. "You. It may not sound important, but trust me, when you've got a pack of hundreds of werewolves who're all just a single 'your mom' joke away from tearing into each other's throats, it matters."

"So, where's the omega of this pack?"

"We don't have one. Like I said, they're rare and when one shows up, the packs tend to fight over them."

"That's ironic."

"That's just how we are," she said, dipping her finger into her empty bottle. "All of the omegas in other packs are mated to Alphas, and it's quite a status symbol to have one."

"That sounds a bit objectifying."

Leonie shrugged and said, "I've never heard one complain. They live pampered lives. Fragile things, you know."

"I can imagine." At least Ellie wasn't one of them. Being an Alpha seemed to come with enough bullshit without being the kind of wolf that only existed as a status symbol for the others. "If Alphas are different in their wolf forms, are omegas different, too?"

"Not really. They look like betas, but their scent is different. The most noticeable difference happens around the full moon."

"Do I want to know?"

She smirked. "They go into heat, and that's about what you'd imagine."

I grimaced. "That's awkward."

"It's the reason they're protected as carefully as they are. When a full moon comes, an omega's calming presence has the opposite effect on any Alpha who happens to be in the area."

"Glad I'm not one of them, then." The only thing I could imagine as being worse than having men like Nicolae hunger for my blood was having them hunger for my body."

"It's not likely you'll come across one anytime soon, but if you do happen to be introduced to a mated omega at an event, you should never address him or her directly. You address the Alpha."

"That's too weird for me," I muttered. "I'm not gonna treat another person like someone else's property, werewolf or not."

"That's *etiquette*," she corrected. "It's for the omega's protection. Or at least, that's where the rule comes from."

"Somehow, I doubt I'm a threat to any werewolf. Even an omega."

She gave me a patient smile. "Our rules aren't made to accommodate humans. We're not used to having your kind among us."

"Except when you hunt us down in cold blood."

Leonie sighed. "I told Nicolae it wasn't a good idea to bring you last night. I don't know what he was thinking."

"I do. He's pissed at me for 'stealing' Francesca from him and he wanted to put me in my place."

She pursed her lips and I could tell she was torn between wanting to defend her Alpha and acknowledging the truth. "Perhaps he did. But it's important that you learn it, Jack. That's the only way you're going to survive in our world. You have to understand that we all exist in relation to one another, and now, like it or not, you exist in relation to Nicolae and to your daughter. You can make her life easier or harder, and trust me, there are enough people within the pack who are going to be doing that already."

I frowned. "What do you mean?"

"Francesca made a lot of enemies, and not just because she ran. She was a very... *difficult* woman at times," she said, obviously wary of my reaction. "She could be cruel when the mood struck her. There are those who will hold Ellie responsible for her actions."

I listened thoughtfully. Maybe I should have come to Francesca's defense, but Leonie wasn't saying anything I didn't already know. Francesca's moods changed like the wind. She could be smiling and doting one moment, and the next, screaming and throwing shit because someone had loaded the dishwasher wrong. She was as mercurial as she was loving, as cruel as she was kind.

"So she's in as much danger here as she is there."

"No. Not at all. She's not in physical danger so much as political," Leonie explained. "The power an Alpha wields is a double-edged sword. Even Nicolae has enemies, but he will protect her."

I recalled his words about the likelihood that he was her biological father and part of me hoped he was right. He could protect her more than I could, and as much as I hated admitting it, I wasn't going to let my pride get in the way of her wellbeing. If I did, I didn't deserve to call myself her father, whether my blood was in her veins or not.

"Thank you, Leonie. You've given me a lot to think about."

"You're going to do well here, Jack. I can feel it," she said gently, standing to pull on her scarf and jacket. "I'll be back tomorrow. There's still much we have to cover, but I think that's enough for today."

I nodded, walking her to the elevator. I knew exactly why Nicolae had sent her. She presented his truths in a far more palatable form, but it didn't matter. I still enjoyed her companionship. It passed the endless hours while Nicolae was away and kept my mind off the Majerus pack.

Unfortunately, her words had led me to the troubling realization that if Ellie was an Alpha, there was nowhere I could take her that was far enough to free her from her role in life. It was in her blood.

TEN

IT HAD BEEN four days since the "run" in the woods, and I was no closer to getting those screams out of my head. Nicolae was seldom around the condo, at least, which proved to be a blessing. I didn't know what to say in those moments he was around, so I avoided him and for the most part, he let me.

He seemed oblivious to the effect of those words he'd spoken in the forest. The few times we had talked, he'd been almost pleasant, just like before. I knew he wanted me to fear him, so I wasn't sure why he was acting so surprised now that I acted like I did.

The wolf I now recognized as Mason came in and out most days to discuss various happenings within the pack with Nicolae. It wasn't until he'd slipped up once and called Nicolae "father" that I realized the truth of their relationship.

It might have been obvious, if it wasn't for the chilled, professional nature of every word that passed between them. After all, Mason had Nicolae's handsome features right down to the uncomfortably blue eyes and diamond jawline. His hair was just as dark, even if it was cut short. Maybe it was just that Nicolae didn't look old enough to have a son Mason's age, but I knew from Leonie's lessons that wolves aged slower than humans did. She came over nearly every day to have coffee with me and fill me in on all the knowledge Nicolae didn't have time for. I still felt like I knew next to nothing about wolves, and the more I learned, the more that feeling grew—but I was studying harder than I ever had in my life with the knowledge that the more I learned, the more I could help Ellie.

The more I learned about them, the easier it would be to escape from them, too. But I had already come to terms with the fact that it wasn't going to be a simple matter of running as soon as Ellie was back. Nicolae's influence was vast, and with two prominent packs who wanted Ellie, hiding would not be easy. We had only gone undetected as long as we had because Clarksville was protected.

All my life, I'd dreamed of escaping that town, and now it seemed like the only sanctuary left for us. The only place we could be free of Nicolae and the Majerus pack.

That night, Nicolae came home in good spirits, which immediately put me on edge. Before I could disappear into my room, he called, "Wait."

"What is it?" I asked warily. Please, God, not another run.

"We're going out," he announced. "I have news from the Court, so get dressed. The clothes Leonie brought you, not yours," he added, already pouring himself a drink.

My heart had sank the moment he walked in the door, but now it was in my throat. Was this it? The news we'd been waiting for? Nicolae had kept me on a need to know basis ever since the run, and what he thought I needed to know about the claim he was filing with the Court to petition for Ellie's return was next to nothing.

I dressed quickly and found him waiting at the door. "You look nice," he remarked.

I stared at him. For all I'd learned to pretend, I still couldn't pretend like a kind word was natural coming from his lips. "Come on," he said when he got tired of waiting.

I followed him onto the elevator and decided he was in a good enough mood that I could venture to ask, "Where are we going?"

"There's a restaurant the pack owns downtown," he replied. "I figured you've been cooped up so long these last few days that you'd like the chance to get out."

I wasn't quite sure that cooped up was the right word for it. I could come and go as I pleased, and the condo itself was like a city, full of shops and restaurants. Most days, I just didn't feel like exploring. All I did was wait. Feel useless. Sleep without resting. It was an endless cycle and every day that passed, I felt more trapped by my own inability to do anything that mattered.

I didn't want to believe that Nicolae's words were part of it, but deep down, I knew they were. They haunted my dreams and stung more than Francesca's jabs ever had. Maybe it was because Nicolae so easily articulated everything she'd always wanted to say and hadn't had the courage to. Or perhaps, everything she'd always pitied me too much to say.

You trapped her...

She settled for you...

If it hadn't been for you, she'd still be alive.

And was he wrong about any of it? Of course not. It was nothing I didn't already know, but hearing it in his voice... the same voice that could command me and override my will with its powerful frequency. It made it impossible to keep living in denial, even for the odd moments I'd allowed myself before.

The restaurant wasn't far. The wolves owned most of the block, as I'd come to realize. "Money talks, and no one's louder than Nicolae Ursache. Not in this country, darling," Leonie had remarked at our last meeting.

Why Nicolae had decided to take me out was another matter. Something told me it wasn't because he was just in the mood for a chat. I was pretty sure I fell somewhere between a fake plant and a wall when it came to people he would want to talk with.

I followed him inside, and the dim lights made my eyes ache. The restaurant was full of the drone of meaningless conversation and the lighting was giving me that "none of this is real" feeling I usually only had after a few too many drinks. The hostess greeted Nicolae by name with a flirty little smile before taking us to a private table by the window.

The city was beautiful at night, and it occurred to me that I still didn't know where we were. The menu was engraved with "Avenue, Fine Dining in Bucharest." At least now I didn't have to ask Nicolae. He'd probably just mock me for being geographically illiterate.

"Is there a reason you brought me here?" I asked once he had a little wine in him. I was pretty sure even he wasn't going to come at me in the middle of a crowded restaurant, but he needed me alive, but after his freakout in the woods, I was more reticent to trust him than ever.

Trust was a funny word. It didn't mean what I once thought it did. I'd once trusted Francesca, and look where that ended up.

"As I said, there are things we need to discuss," he said, leaning back from the table. The fancy-ass chair was hardly built to accommodate a man as big and broad as he was, but I doubted he'd fit in a booth any better. As it was, his legs were already stretched out under my side of the table. "I've spoken with the Court and filed my petition for Ellie's return."

That made me perk up. I could tell from the look on his face that my reaction amused him, but I didn't care. That was one step closer to bringing Ellie home, or at least back to me. "That's great news. That means we can go get her, right?"

"Not yet. There still has to be an investigation." He took a sip of his wine, leaving his rare steak untouched. "The Court will want proof of paternity, which means they'll want access to you."

I frowned. "I thought you said—"

"It doesn't matter. It's unavoidable that they'll want to know who she belongs to biologically, but as long as they think she's yours for the time being, that's all that matters."

It took a moment to swallow the implication, but I reminded myself, and not for the first time that day, that it didn't matter. "So what's the next step?"

"That is what I wanted to talk to you about." The way he was watching me made it all but certain that I wasn't going to like his plan. It was just a matter of wondering whether I'd survive it. "As I mentioned, due to Francesca's impetuousness, my claim to *her* is tenuous. However, her claim to you is not."

"I thought you said human marriage meant nothing to wolves."

"It doesn't, but surely Francesca marked you as hers by wolven tradition."

"Marked me?" I frowned. "What are you talking about?"

"You'll have her family crest somewhere. She wouldn't have let you go sixteen years without it. Maybe she scratched it into your ass while you were passed out drunk and you've never even seen it."

"Crest?" I murmured, touching the spot on my arm where that bad ink job sat. "My tattoo?"

Nicolae reached over and started unbuttoning my shirt. I pushed his hands away, but he tugged my shirt down over my left shoulder enough to reveal the top half of the tattoo. "Hey!"

"That's it," he announced.

I looked around to make sure we weren't being watched, but the table was secluded enough. Suddenly, I wasn't sure that was a good thing. "The fuck are you saying, Francesca tricked me into getting a tattoo I hate so she could show she owned me?"

"It was for your protection, if that makes you feel any better. So other wolves, among other things, wouldn't touch you."

"It really doesn't," I muttered. This whole thing had been an exercise in emasculation. My buddies had always joked that Franny wore my balls around her neck on a gold chain, but those days, I at least felt the need to check just to make sure.

"In any case, I have an offer to make. One that would guarantee my claim to Ellie as my daughter without question."

God, those words stung. "Whatever it is, if it's to protect Ellie, I'll do it. You know that."

"You might want to wait and let me tell you what it'll require of you first."

"So say it, then," I muttered, chugging wine.

"I would have to take you as my mate."

I started coughing and the wine got up my nose. When I finally collected myself, Nicolae was looking at me like I was some savage again, even though he'd timed that fucking bombshell. "Excuse me?"

"I'm afraid I'm not joking," he said, all smug and more prickish than usual. It didn't help that he looked the way he did. If I didn't hate his fucking guts, I'd have been attracted to him.

Who was I kidding? My dick didn't have those kinds of standards.

"I'm *human*." That was by far the least troubling aspect of the equation, but it was as good of a place to start as any.

"It doesn't matter. Just because we don't take humans as mates doesn't mean that we can't. It's just frowned upon, because there's the risk of a bite turning one feral, but it's not forbidden."

"I still don't get how this is supposed to help Ellie."

"My claim to Francesca is in question, but her claim to you is valid by law. If I take you as my mate and mark you as she did, there will be no doubt. You and all that belongs to you, including Ellie, will be mine," he answered. "It's ironclad."

I listened even though part of me was still convinced he was fucking with me. "And being your mate, that would involve...?"

"Mating?" He raised his eyebrows. "Yes, that's generally how it works. Forgive me, I didn't imagine that would be an issue, considering that you are homosexual."

"*Homosexual?*" I wasn't sure whether to address his terminology circa the nineteenth century or his assumption about my sexuality.

"We've been sharing close quarters for a week now, Jack," he answered casually. "Your pheromones don't lie. Even the day we met, when I stood before you naked and human, I could sense your desire even through the fear and hatred."

His accusation seemed to erode what little dignity I'd managed to keep with every word. Of course, I knew the wolves probably had a heightened sense of smell, but pheromones? That shit was fucking humiliating.

Worst of all, it was probably true. I hadn't been consciously checking him out that day. My thoughts were definitely on other things, but I *was* attracted to him in spite of myself, and the realization that I hadn't kept it under wraps was more than a bit flustering.

"If this is your idea of a joke—"

"It isn't. Of course, the choice is yours, but I would advise you to think quickly. The sooner you're marked, the sooner Ellie will be returned."

My head was aching already, and not just from the wine. I'd already made up my mind. Still, I knew my perceived indecision was the only leverage I had to get answers. "What would being your mate entail?"

"You are a human, so the rules are different from one Alpha mated to another. You would be treated as my property, but with that lowered status comes protection."

"How generous of you."

He smirked. "You've already been part of one sham marriage. What's another?"

My blood was boiling and I wanted to run my steak knife through his hand, but instead, I sat there and behaved because taking shit from him meant sparing Ellie. "I'll do it. But you know that, don't you? You just like to taunt me, because it makes you feel better about the fact that even if she stopped loving me toward the end, at least Francesca did love me at one point. That I made her feel something you never could."

Nicolae's hand moved so fast I didn't see it until it was wrapped around my wrist, crushing my bones. I refused to flinch, but holding his gaze was harder than bearing the pain. He yanked me out of my chair and over to his side, his other arm wrapping around my back as he pulled me onto his lap like I weighed nothing. To anyone who happened to be at just the right angle to peek into the private section, it might have looked like a lover's embrace rather than the power play it was.

"I will not kill you because I am honor bound," he said in a whisper that felt like knives gliding along my neck. It made me shudder, and not entirely for the reasons it should have. "But I don't have to touch you physically to ruin you." His hand closed around the back of my neck and something about that touch, as uncharacteristically gentle as it was, made me fall apart. My fingers bit into his shoulders and my heart thundered so loudly he must have heard it. My eyes fell shut and I tried and failed to swallow as his lips grazed my neck, pure temptation and torture. "And I will take great pleasure in doing so, Jack Mullins. Francesca's human *pet*," he spat before dumping me onto the floor.

By the time I'd caught my breath and pulled myself up, Nicolae was already reaching into his pocket. He lit up a cigarette and tossed a credit card on the table before standing and smoothing out his jacket. "Keep the card. Most of our kept mates find shopping to be a diversion. I trust you can find your way back home."

"I trust you can find your way back to hell," I muttered, getting back to my feet. Not exactly my best comeback, but my head was still spinning for all the wrong reasons.

The rough handling didn't bother me. It was Nicolae's uncanny ability to rip away my defenses and reveal the very hidden desire he stirred that made me feel vulnerable. To know that he was not only aware of it but planning on using it against me to exact a revenge far subtler than bloodshed.

I dusted myself off and finished the bottle of wine to steady my nerves and come to terms with what I'd just agreed to. To willingly subjugate myself to the man I hated, the man who'd laid claim to my wife's heart before we'd ever even met and held onto it long after.

For her, I reminded myself as I waited for the check to come. *Anything for her.*

Even if it meant belonging to a monster.

ELEVEN

THE DOORS to the top-floor elevators didn't open often. When they did, it was always Nicolae or Leonie. The one was guaranteed to ruin my day while the other was the highlight of it. Leonie's lessons were getting shorter and I knew it was only a matter of time before she declared me as educated about their customs as I was going to be. I was pretty sure she saw through my feigned ignorance over the subject matter, but if she did, she was generous enough not to call me on it.

By the end of my first three weeks in the Ursache pack, I knew the pack ways as well as the streets of Bucharest. It was safe to travel anywhere on foot as long as I stayed within the city limits. All of Romania was Nicolae's territory, but the city itself was so heavily saturated with pack members that no enemies would dare cross that line.

Some days, I walked from dawn until dusk both because the fresh air and exercise helped my cough and because it was an excuse to stay out of the house. I knew Nicolae could easily find me if he wanted to. He probably had people following me, but I preferred not to know for sure. He had barely talked to me since that night at the restaurant, when he'd announced his plan to claim me as he'd never gotten the chance to claim Francesca.

I knew what this was, beyond the utility of saving Ellie. It was Nicolae's vengeance. He couldn't shed my blood, so instead, he was killing my dignity. I could see it in the way the other werewolves looked at me. I'd gone from being a strange newcomer to them all treating me like the family pet. Always underfoot, something to be coddled and tolerated. I preferred being an outsider.

If Nicolae wanted to make me feel like less of a man, he'd certainly accomplished that. What he didn't understand was that it didn't matter. Whatever he had planned for me that night, the eve of the full moon, it was nothing compared to the shame I'd feel if I didn't go through with it.

The idea of bearing his mark bothered me more than sleeping with him, admittedly. He spoke of it like a chore that had to be done in the interest of formality, and I knew he wasn't looking forward to it. If anything, I was. Not because I wanted to act on my attraction to him but because I hoped that the physical act would purge it from my system.

The sooner it was over, the better. The sooner we were bound, the sooner he would realize he'd already won and lose interest in tormenting me and the sooner he could stop being the center of my world.

That night, I expected Nicolae to show up and announce that it was time for us to hate fuck our way into a marriage of convenience. Instead, Mason showed up and he made Nicolae look friendly by comparison. Nicolae's second-in-command was immediately recognizable as an Alpha thanks to his superhuman physique and his nasty attitude. According to Leonie, he was as displeased by my presence as the fact that the wolf who was next in line for Nicolae's power had been raised as a human.

"Where is Nicolae?" I asked, wary of being alone with a guy who could break me like a shortbread cookie. Not that his boss was much better.

"He's coming," Mason answered. A dark-haired man stepped off the elevator with a plastic black carrying case, but he looked far more like the tatted up cliche I would have expected upon hearing about a gang of werewolves. His eyes were decidedly wolflike as they looked over me. I got the sense of familiarity that I'd seen him in the crowd that night.

Mason didn't bother to introduce the man. He hadn't ever officially introduced himself either, just showed up to glare at me and mutter the odd order while he spoke with Nicolae every now and then.

"What's going on?" I wasn't sure what this night would entail, but I certainly hadn't expected two spectators. Wolves were freaks, sure, but this was a bit much.

"You'll find out when Nicolae gets here," Mason said impatiently, turning away from me. A few minutes later, Nicolae showed up looking somber as ever. He certainly hadn't dressed up any more than usual. Then again, he was always wearing a suit, unless he was home for the night. The sight of him sitting on the sofa, nursing a beer while he pored over papers in a thin white tank top that showcased every muscle stuck in my head a bit too easily.

I hated the guy, but there was no denying he was sex on legs. The worst part about him was that he knew it.

"Good. You're all here. Let's get started," Nicolae said, pulling over a chair from the kitchen. He looked at me and without a second's hesitation ordered, "Take off your shirt."

I looked from Nicolae to the other two men in the room in disbelief. "What the fuck? No, not in front of them."

Nicolae rolled his eyes. "We're not *mating*. I'm marking you."

"I just spent the last three weeks in werewolf college, I know what that entails."

"If you were a werewolf, yes. I can't place a mating bite on you. It would start the transformation and you would surely turn feral and die," he said slowly, as if speaking to a child. "Instead, I'm going to place my crest on you with ink as Francesca did. Understand?"

I swallowed my embarrassment and peeled off my shirt. Sometimes I thought he intentionally kept me just out of the loop enough to make a fool out of myself. The look of satisfaction on his face as my shirt hit the floor confirmed it.

I'd always been pretty fit, thanks to my job, but standing half-naked in a room full of manbeasts who could and probably would have eaten me for breakfast if it wasn't for Nicolae's "protection" made me feel like I did when I was a shrimp getting judged in the locker room. I thought I'd prepared for every awkward scenario this night could bring, but I was so fucking wrong.

"Sit down, facing the chair," Nicolae ordered. Warily watching as the nameless tattoo guy set up his gear, I took my seat, resting my arms over the back of the railing.

"Think I could get a skull and crossbones while you're at it?" I asked in hopes of lightening the mood.

The tattoo artist just stared humorlessly at me, making it clear that Mason was far from the only member of the pack who disapproved of my presence.

I swallowed the remark on the tip of my tongue, because the guy was going to be drawing tiny needles down my skin and I didn't want to give him more reason to make it hurt. I watched as he mixed the ink in little cups and filled three with solid black. It all seemed routine enough, until Nicolae rolled up his sleeve and the other werewolf pulled a switchblade out of his pocket. I flinched as he drew a cut sideways across Nicolae's forearm and collected the blood in another cup before mixing it with the ink.

Nicolae's face showed no sign of pain as he was cut, but he did smirk when he saw me gawking. "When we bite another wolf, we bite ourselves first to inject our blood into them. Since my saliva contains the pathogen that would turn you into a rabid monster, this is the only safe way to do it."

"In other words, you're the flu."

He ignored me. The remark was just my attempt at getting at him in some small way and he knew it. As usual, it failed.

The artist stood and brought his tray of ink over to the chair next to me. When he reached for his tattoo gun, I decided to be grateful they weren't insisting on the old stick-and-poke.

"I'll take it from here, Owen," Nicolae announced, holding out his hand.

Owen and Mason both stared at him in confusion. "Sir?" asked the former.

"He is my mate. I'm not going to let another mark him. Just place the stencil and I'll take care of it."

Mason set his jaw, and while his eyes were on his Alpha, I could feel all his hatred directed at me. If looks could kill...

"Yes, sir," Owen said, handing off the gun. He pulled what looked like a white sheet of paper with a clear film on one side out of his bag and peeled it apart. "Where do you want it?"

I started to answer, but Nicolae beat me to it, reaffirming that the question was not for me. "On the base of his neck, between the shoulder blades."

For a moment, neither Mason nor Owen said a word. The look they exchanged confirmed my fears that Nicolae had chosen the most degrading possible spot to place his crest.

I gritted my teeth and leaned forward as Owen pressed the stencil to my flesh. He ran a wet washcloth over it until the design was in place and peeled off the film.

Nicolae pulled up another chair and the moment his hand rested on my left shoulder blade, a chill went through me even though the spot he touched became so hot that I gasped. It was an automatic reaction, and more audible than I'd feared given the way Owen and Mason were looking at me. I could feel Nicolae staring, too, and knew I'd fucked up somehow.

Was this another one of his Alpha tricks? Was he testing me to see if I'd react? The heat faded with his touch, but I still felt it, like he'd started up a chain reaction under my skin. Deciding that pretending like nothing was wrong was my only option, I clenched my jaw and gripped the back of the chair, determined to bear through it.

After a few moments of hesitation, Nicolae finally pressed the needle to my skin. The back of my neck was a far more sensitive spot than the bicep had been, and the burning from the blood-laced ink and needle was almost intolerable for the first few minutes, but I stuck it out and breathed as little as possible. As Nicolae followed the outline Owen had drawn, etching his mark on my skin forever, the heat of his touch became harder to bear than the pain of the needle. I was sure he could sense my distress and knew he'd just take it as yet another sign that I was a weak human.

Sweat beaded on my forehead, dripping down my temples as I struggled to keep my breathing even. When I finally looked up, Owen and Mason were still watching us. The former seemed as uncomfortable with the whole thing as I was, while the latter seemed enraged. I was in no mood to humor his baseless aggression, so I glared right back at him and he actually seemed surprised enough to look away.

"Are you almost done?" I gritted out, figuring that I could get away with being impatient without it being taken for weakness. I'd gone numb to the pain after the first ten minutes or so, but sitting still was driving me crazy. Not nearly as much as his touch, though. Everywhere it rested, it made my skin crawl and not in the way it usually did. I bit back a moan as he flattened his palm against my shoulder blade to brace himself for the last bit of shading.

"Stop whining. This ink may well be the only thing standing between you and death someday."

In that moment, I wasn't entirely sure I would have preferred this to death. It wasn't the pain or even the strange restlessness his touch caused. It was the fact that I was horny as hell, and I was pretty damn sure that I was going to pay the price for not hiding it better. If Nicolae could read my pheromones, so could the others.

At long last, the needle left my skin and Nicolae wiped his work clean of blood. I tried not to think about how mine was mingled with his now. Why the wolves kept such an unsanitary tradition was beyond me. It was just a mark. A weird, tacky version of an engagement ring. Why did it matter if his blood was inside me?

"Bear witness," Nicolae said, standing.

Owen nodded in response and Mason did so only with great reluctance. "We affirm the mark," they said in unison.

"Leave us." Nicolae's voice was rough, but I didn't detect anger in it like I'd expected. By the time I finally rose, my body was stiff and my skin burned, but I could still feel his hands on me like they'd never left. I watched him pouring himself a drink from across the room. Because evidently, werewolves and functional alcoholism went together like peanut butter and jelly.

Owen and Mason disappeared into the elevator and I finally let myself breathe. I reached behind me to rub my tense shoulder in hopes of getting some relief and wondered why the hell the heat had to be up so high. It was the middle of summer.

I didn't hear Nicolae move at all, which made the sensation of his fingers running down the spine all the more alarming. I spun around to find him looking at me through those glaring blue eyes, his face as stern and handsome as ever. He reached out before I could speak and ask him what the fuck he thought he was doing, pressing his hand to my cheek. He grazed the stubble there before running his fingers down to brush the side of my neck.

This time, the shudder that ran through me was violent. So much so that I felt myself on the verge of collapse, like he'd short circuited my brain. He caught me against his strong chest and for a moment, I thought he was going to chastise me. Instead, the gaze that met mine was full of curiosity. "Interesting," he murmured, looking at me like I was his new prey.

Maybe I was. Maybe that was all I'd been this whole time. I wished I was capable of seeing him as what he was, a predator and that alone. I wished I could force my heart to race with fear and dread every time he came out that door rather than anticipation.

"What is?" I asked hoarsely.

"Your response," he answered, running his hand down my bare chest. I had suffered through an hour-long tattoo without making a sound, but a moan of agony—that's what I convinced myself it was, at any rate—escaped me as his hand rested over my heart. He took my hand again and bared my wrist as he'd done that night in the forest, only rather than biting into my flesh with his claws, he blew lightly on the inside of my wrist.

My knees gave out with a rush of breath. "You son of a bitch," I exclaimed.

A wicked smile touched his eyes, but his lips remained firm and always slightly scowling. I couldn't take my eyes off them and my tongue darted out to wet mine instinctively as he pulled me closer.

That made him smile.

TWELVE

"I DON'T BELIEVE IT," Nicolae murmured.

I tried to pull away, but he wouldn't let me move. His grip tightened around my wrist, but this time, he wasn't trying to cause me pain. There was something else he wanted, I just couldn't tell—

"You respond to my touch like an omega would," he finally said in answer to my confusion. "Every erogenous zone makes you squirm. And your scent..."

I swallowed, humiliation crawling over me like insects. "I don't know what you're talking about."

"Don't you?" His knuckles brushed my side and I caved into him, my head falling to the crook of his neck.

"You're hypnotizing me," I accused, gripping his shoulders because I no longer knew how to stand up.

"I wonder," he whispered in my ear, entirely supporting me with the arm that was wrapped around my back while his other hand cradled my head with gentleness that was so unnatural to him. "Did you respond to her touch this way?"

I gave him a hard shove and stumbled back. More offensive than the question was the answer. I had, in the beginning. I'd never experienced any desire for women, but the way I felt when Francesca touched me was bewildering. It was addictive and terrifying and confusing. I'd latched onto it, to her, in the desperate hope that every relative who'd told me I just hadn't met the "right woman" was right. And for a while, that spark had been enough to bridge the gap between who we were and what we both needed.

It was still so much different from what Nicolae was doing to me. It was fainter, subtler, quieter. This was... God, it was exhilarating and at the same time, it made me want to dive out that window and hope for the best, because falling twenty stories seemed safer than staying here to let him keep playing with my head this way. To say nothing of the games he was obviously capable of playing with my body—

"Have you changed your mind?" he asked wryly.

"No," I gritted out. "I'm just not in the mood for your hypnotic bullshit."

"I'm not hypnotizing you," he said with bite in his tone that made it clear he didn't appreciate the implication. "Why would I do that when I want you to bask in the knowledge that you begged for everything I'm going to do to you tonight and loved every minute of it?"

His words made me shiver again, without touching me. How could malice sound so sweet? How could I want *him* this much?"

"Fuck you," I seethed.

He pushed me up against the wall, pinning my hands as he glared down at me, his eyes full of lust. I felt some force pulling me toward him, daring my lips to brush his, but I knew that I'd regret it. Not because I had any shame or decency, no. Because it would confirm what he already knew, if not from my scent, then from my erection grinding against his. At least he had the excuse of being pissed off. Of being an Alpha who, according to Leonie, were always ready for action.

"Do you want to rephrase that?" he asked in a harsh whisper as his hands tightened around my wrists.

My lips parted and so did my legs, making room for his thigh as he ground up against me. I didn't want to say the words, but I was so desperate, so in need of this thing that was too repulsive to even speak out loud, that the words escaped me. "Fuck me..."

"See?" he taunted, his eyes lit with satisfaction as they wandered over me and he gripped my chin in his hand to force my head up. "Begging already."

Before I could respond, his lips took mine with the violence of a hurricane and I let the destruction wash over me. I'd never kissed anyone like that. Not any of my experimental lovers, not my wife. It was foreign, but familiar, especially the taste of him when his tongue delved into my mouth, demanding and claiming and searching all at once. I swallowed the smoke and liquor on his breath and he swallowed my moan as his tongue went deeper and his hands gripped my waist.

I realized he was trying to unfasten my jeans and tried to help him, because if I was going to abandon my dignity and sell out everything I stood for, I figured I might as well go all in. Instead, he pushed my hands away with a punitive snarl and his nails nicked my skin as he tore my jeans and boxers down in one go.

Until this moment, I'd been convinced that the only pleasure Nicolae was going to get out of this encounter would be my subjugation, but one look in his eyes told me otherwise. I knew the lust in them because it mirrored the darkness in my own soul, and as he took his fill of my naked body, I knew he wanted me as badly as I wanted him.

Maybe only in this moment. Maybe not for the same reason. But he wanted me and I wanted him, and the reasoning behind it all didn't really seem to matter. Not now.

He took me by the hand, or maybe the forearm. My bones turned to jelly at his touch, so I was lost on the finer distinctions between my body parts until he threw me down on his bed. I scarcely had time to realize this was the first I'd seen of his room, exactly as cold and featureless as I'd imagined, before he was on top of me.

This time, when I reached to unbutton his shirt, he let me. I was surprised he didn't insist on fucking me while partially clothed just to drive in the stark difference in our stations, but when he disrobed, all I could think of was another proportional distance between us.

I'd never had dick envy. No, I wasn't porn star thick or anything, but I'd never had any complaints. Knowing my primary partner for the last sixteen years had also been with the man standing in front of me, that came as a surprise. Nicolae wasn't just thick, he had the girth of a fucking soda can. I didn't even bother to hide my shock and he didn't bother to pretend like he wasn't amused by it.

"Like what you see?" he asked dryly.

"I'll let you know when I've seen all of it," I muttered under my breath.

He laughed. He actually fucking laughed. As he lowered himself onto the bed again, his fully erect cock bobbed with the movement and grazed the inside of my thigh as he planted his hands on either side to observe me. "You look like you've never seen another man's junk before."

"I have," I said, swallowing hard. Not as much as he probably thought. "Just not...in this context."

"Context?" He raised an eyebrow.

"I haven't... you know. Bottomed." I'd just assumed that was what he meant by mating, but the pensive look on his face had me second guessing myself. Maybe that wasn't the plan and I'd made an even bigger fool out of myself. If he didn't already think I was the repressed closet case I probably was, he did now.

"That's a surprise. You seem like a man who takes it up the ass on a regular basis."

"The hell is that supposed to mean?"

He smirked. "You are easy to rile, you know that?"

His thigh went between my legs again and I grunted as he trapped my shaft between our stomachs. "You have me in an easily riled state," I wheezed as his weight came down on top of me.

"That I do," he mused, stroking my hair with unexpected tenderness. "I suppose I have somewhat of an obligation to make your first time go smoothly, hm?"

Anything he said in that accent sounded wrong in all the right ways, but fuck, how was I supposed to respond to that? I guess he didn't want me to, because he reached into his nightstand drawer and pulled out a bottle of lubricant. I watched, torn between humiliation and fascination as he squirted some out in his hand and marveled at how he could make even the act of lubing someone up seem sexy.

"Open your legs."

It was another command, but this one lacked the strange psychic resonance of his first. He wasn't compelling me, but my desire to obey was even more troubling knowing that I couldn't blame it on anything else. I felt the sting of humiliation as I parted my knees and his fingers slipped into my crack. I tensed up instinctively, but his fingers dove in, undeterred by my virgin ass's resistance.

"Fuck," I groaned as the ache gave way to pleasure. My cock throbbed as he started fucking me with his fingers, spreading the lube that was starting to tingle like it had some heated pleasure gimmick to live up to. Then again, maybe it was just that his touch had that effect on me.

"Relax," he ordered, pushing my knees up with his free hand to get a better angle. He crooked his fingers and I let out a cry. He'd barely even started touching me.

"God, you're fucking tight," he growled. "What're you trying to do, break my fingers off?"

"You know what you're doing," I panted. I just hoped he wouldn't stop. I didn't even care that I hated this man, or that he was just fucking me because he wanted to own me. Hell, he could leash me to the post outside in the parking lot and call me Fido as long as he kept...

"Good boy," he breathed, his breath hot on my dick. I hadn't realized how much lower he'd sunk, and when had he gotten that third finger into me? He was holding my left knee away because my hips were bucking too hard for him to keep hitting that spot I *needed* him to —

His mouth wrapped around the head of my shaft and I thought I was going to cum right there. Fuck, I came close, but his fingers had me stretched enough that the pain kept me off. I stared down in pure disbelief that Nicolae fucking Ursache was actually lowering himself to sucking me off.

And he wasn't doing it halfheartedly, either. He took to giving head with the same authoritarian intensity he had with everything else, and the sensation of his stubble grating against my inner thighs as his head bobbed up and down between them was too goddamn much.

My hands dug into his hair without my permission, but his growl didn't seem entirely foreboding. His fingers surged into me, three at a time, and he deep-throated my cock to keep my hips pinned as they fought to rise. If I was supposed to wait for permission to cum, it was beyond my current ability to do so. He seemed to sense it and sucked the life out of me those last few seconds as my ass tightened around his fingers until I filled his throat and he filled my head with splashes of light and bursts of color.

"Oh, fuck..."

"Are you even capable of articulate speech anymore?" he taunted once he finished drinking my cum.

"Dunno... ask me when I'm not still high off you sucking my cock."

He pulled his fingers out fast, and pretended like it wasn't to punish me. Not that I particularly cared. Of all the punishments I'd imagined Nicolae would have to dish out, this was by far the most generous.

"We're not done," he said, gripping my hair as he brought our bodies close once more. He kissed me hard, forcing me to taste myself, but the way he tasted was so much more... *everything*.

What had begun as a ritual and turned into a hate fuck had become something I didn't even understand myself. I didn't want to. Somehow, I knew that dissecting it would ruin it and while I was sure the guilt and shame would be my punishment come morning, I just wanted to drown in ignorant bliss right now. In him.

"Turn over," Nicolae demanded. I decided I liked the way he told more than the way anyone else asked. I got on my knees, not even caring that I was acting like a dog in heat in my haste to make myself accessible to him.

When had I become so desperate?

He was in the drawer again, and I assumed he was looking for more lube. I'd been hesitant to take him, especially when I saw the size of his dick, but now I just wished he'd get on with it and fuck me. When I felt the soft brush of fabric against my side, I looked over my shoulder in confusion.

"I need to restrain you," he said in a husky voice that made it sound like the best damn idea anyone had ever had, even if I didn't understand. I shouldn't have been surprised that a man like Nicolae had some kinks, but he was so domineering that it hardly seemed necessary.

"Why?"

"Because I'm a werewolf and you're human," he said harshly. It was hard to take it personally when the thought that he was just as desperate and impatient as I was turned me on so. "I could hurt you if you start acting like prey, and given the way you squirmed while I had your dick in my mouth, that seems likely."

I swallowed hard. *Prey...* that's really what I was to him. The realization shouldn't have come as a shock, but it *should* have been enough for me to get out of that bed, pull on my boxers and call the whole thing off. It *shouldn't* have made me hard all over again, but it did.

This man, this monstrous thing who seemed intent on chasing away every last remnant of humanity within himself, reminded me of my own mortality at every turn, if only because my heart felt like it was going to explode whenever he touched me. He was cruel and cold and I hated him, but he knew my body and parts of my soul in a way no one else ever had.

As he bound my willing arms behind my back and my face dropped into the blankets that still smelled so heavily of his musk, I felt myself slipping into a trance, and not the kind he'd put me under before. This was all organic, all born of the fact that I couldn't believe this was real. I couldn't believe I was on my knees for Nicolae Ursache, begging him to fuck me and ready to fall apart if he didn't.

His hands traveled down the length of my sides once more and like before, I shivered on cue. "Good boy," he coaxed again, his voice deceptively kind. I felt his thick shaft pressed against my left buttock as he repositioned to guide himself in.

I held still and bit down on my bottom lip, hoping the pain would keep me from squirming for him. When I felt his crown at my entrance, all bets were off. He'd thoroughly, aggressively fucked me with his fingers for so long I'd started to feel like he was part of me, but it still wasn't enough to fully prepare my body to make room for his girth. The tension was almost worse than the pain, and I craved both, shuddering when he finally worked it in. His shaft was heavily lubed, which was the only thing that made it possible for him to get in as deep as he was, and I couldn't tell if he'd used more or if he was just that slick from what he'd done to me.

The thought made me moan, but he seemed to misunderstand. "Just relax," he coached, spreading my cheeks open wider as he pushed himself further in.

"Hell," I groaned, arching back into him despite myself. It hurt like fuck, but my body wanted more when I should have been taking it slow. Nicolae grabbed my hips to keep me in place and stopped his steady descent into me.

"This is what I'm talking about," he said in a tone of scolding accusation, like I was a disobedient fool who needed to be chastised.

"I'll tear you if I don't go slow, and bleeding around a sexed-up were-wolf is not a brilliant idea, even for you."

His taunting was all the foreplay I needed, but somehow, the warning got through the fog of lust in my brain. "Since when do you care about hurting me?" I didn't recognize my own voice. It was the voice of a man who hadn't touched water in days, and I was thirsty, but it wasn't for that. Suddenly, I regretted not taking the opportunity to taste him. Oh, well. Another time...

And then I remembered that there wouldn't *be* another time. That this was a moment, a one-time necessity that wouldn't bear replication. Not when the lust faded and we were left with only ourselves. Him and me. Two men on opposite ends of everything. All we'd have was the hatred, and I'd cherish it because it was here, even now when he was bringing me pleasure I'd never experienced. The lust would taint that hatred and I decided I could stay high on the lingering essence of it.

Nicolae was silent. I knew he wasn't going to answer when I felt him pushing into me again, this time pulling out before he'd reached the halfway mark. He drove into me again and I cried out as his girth tortured my tight hole, stretching me to the brink of comfort only to push me past my previous limits. And still, despite the pain or maybe even because of it, the only thing keeping me from grinding against him like the desperate whore a single touch from him turned me into, was the fact that he was holding me still. I'd never really had a kink for being tied up, but the association with the cloth binding my arms behind my back and Nicolae's cock sliding in and out of my aching ass was creating a new fetish. My fists balled up and I bit the comforter to keep from screaming when he hit my spot. Maybe it was on accident, maybe he knew exactly what he was doing, but fuck, I'd never known something that felt that good could hurt so bad. I'd never known I needed pain to feel the reality of another person. To really *feel* him. His body. His weight pushing up against me. His heat, his pulse pounding against the membrane of my most sensitive place.

The vibrations of the growl building in his chest as his thrusts became faster, matching my need. Every thrust sent him deeper into my spot, and he filled me to the point of absurdity. I writhed, proving he was right to tie me up, as if him slamming into me over and over again simply wasn't enough. I begged for more, just like he said I would, and I didn't even care that I was proving him right. The tradeoff was worth it. More of him inside of me. Harder, faster, *more*.

"Nicolae." I breathed his name like a prayer. And it was. He was my god of sex and rage, and I was his sacred whore, offering myself up fully to his mercy.

And he had so little of it to give. He pulled out all at once and for the first time, I cried out in pain, not because it hurt but because his absence did. Before I could question his betrayal, he flipped me over and brought his weight down on me. His eyes were blazing, absolutely livid, and I wondered what I'd done to earn his wrath. Whatever it was, I'd get down on my knees and beg forgiveness if that was what it took to get him back inside of me. To finish what he'd started. If he didn't, I felt like the flames were going to engulf me.

My arms were crushed behind my back at an awkward angle as his weight pressed me to the bed, but I still parted my legs to accommodate him between them. "Nicolae..." It was a plea, a question, begging him to tell me what I'd done so I could fix it.

His hooded eyes softened with something like pity for a moment as they swept over me. I felt him at my entrance once again, pushing gently when I needed him to force and claim and thrust. "I want to see your face," he said in a harsh whisper that felt like sandpaper on my skin, chafing my already sensitive flesh and making my need all the more pronounced. It was cruel what he was doing to me. Or rather, what he wasn't. The cruelest he'd been yet. Couldn't he see I was dying? That every moment he kept himself from me, he was prolonging my torture?

Having his cock buried hilt-deep inside of me had taught me the unexpected lesson that my body existed only to be claimed by his, and I'd accepted it all too readily. I just needed *him* to do the same.

His forehead grazed mine, both slick with perspiration, and his dark hair fell over me like a burial shroud, which was going to be necessary if he didn't get back to fucking me. Did he *want* me to spontaneously combust? His hand swept my face and gripped it with gentle roughness. "I want to see your face when I come inside you." Somehow, those vulgar words sounded like poetry on his lips.

I nodded, eager to prove that I understood. My fingers dug into the mattress beneath me and I flexed them to keep my arms from going to sleep entirely. I just didn't care enough to ask him to make any adjustments. Wasted time. He drew his hand up the outside of my thigh and pushed my legs up and apart before he entered me once more. This time, my body put up only minimal resistance and he delved back into me all at once. It had only been a few moments, but my tight hole had already forgotten what it was like to have him sheathed within and I moaned into the crook of his neck as he reminded me. His hand slipped behind my head, but I wasn't sure if he was comforting me or just getting a better grip. Either way, I felt the heat spread up the back of my scalp, his touch washing over me like spring rain.

He started thrusting again, right back to where we'd left off, and when he hit my spot, all was forgiven. I unwound in his arms and the pain in my own was forgotten. He draped my calf over his back and forced my thigh to stretch, but the place he was able to reach with that new angle was so worth it. His body ground against mine and I threw my head back because it was all too much. Too much and not enough. His lips found my neck as his balls-deep cock throbbed inside me and he sucked hard enough that my head spun. When his teeth grazed my skin, something snapped within me. I should have been afraid that he would bite me, and I was, but I *craved* it still. I wanted it so much I froze when I'd been rocking and writhing with him a second earlier, desperate to reach climax. Whose, I wasn't sure. His, mine, it all seemed like the same thing in the moment.

Nicolae's breath was hot on my neck and I realized I'd turned my head into the pillow to offer my throat to him. It was unintentional, instinctual, yet I would have known what it meant even if I hadn't been told. In my lessons, I'd learned that for shifters, baring the neck was the ultimate sign of submission—the equivalent of rolling over on your back.

Well, I'd done both for him tonight. It would humiliate me come morning, of that I had no doubt, but it seemed right in this moment. It was what I needed, even if him taking me up on the offer would mean certain death.

Nicolae claimed that wolves were instinct-driven creatures who knew no reason when their desire, whether for flesh or blood, became great enough. Maybe humans weren't all that different.

Maybe I was just weak. For him. For the one person I needed to hate in order to maintain my own identity. If I didn't hate him, who the fuck was I?

Nicolae froze just as I did, gazing down at me. He'd promised to take great satisfaction in the look on my face when he had me at this point, so close to climax and so utterly dependent on him to allow it, but instead, he looked bewildered. His eyes darkened and traveled back down to my neck, his throat constricting visibly as if he was considering taking me up on the unspoken offer and his mouth was watering at the thought of it.

Knowing he wanted my flesh in that way, too, made me squirm and I felt the heat of his rock-hard balls grinding into my ass. Our bodies were trying to press even closer when there was no space left between us, like there were two black holes, one inside each of us, just sucking in everything until they became one.

His eyes widened and the next second, I knew why. He was already buried inside of me as deep as he could possibly go. Hell, if he got any deeper, he was gonna be fucking my heart. Nonetheless, I felt him grow inside of me, a thickening at the base of his shaft, stretching me beyond what seemed possible.

"What the fuck is that?" I asked breathlessly. It hurt like hell, and I felt like I was going to be split in two if he moved at all, but it also felt...

Good seemed both too generous and inadequate. The pain kept it from being pleasurable exactly, but the extreme pressure up against my prostate was making me squirm.

"Hold still," he growled, pressing his right hand to my chest. "You'll hurt yourself."

"What *is* that, Nicolae?" I demanded, my teeth clenched tight. I knew he was right. I could already feel that he'd torn me, but fuck, it was hard to hold still.

"It's my knot," he grunted.

"Your *what*?"

"I'm an Alpha wolf. You do the math."

"Fuck! You could've warned me—"

"I didn't know this would happen," he snapped. "It's not supposed to."

"This can't be the first time."

"It's not. Just the first time it's happened with someone other than an omega. I knew you had the other traits, I just wasn't expecting my body to respond this way."

It took me a second to replay all Leonie's lessons, wondering if she'd mentioned this part or just conveniently left it out. She got blushy whenever it came to more than the basics of were biology, so I wasn't surprised. It wasn't like I *needed* to know the mechanics of how the rare class of werewolves fucked. From the way Nicolae was acting, it wasn't something he'd imagined would come up, either. Unlike his fucking knot.

"It hurts," I muttered. "Can't you pull it out?"

"If I wanted to kill you, sure."

"So we're just stuck like this forever?" I cried, both horrified and strangely pleased.

"Just until it goes down."

"When will that be?"

"It depends on how long it takes after I cum. Usually twenty minutes, sometimes longer."

"Fuck!"

He gripped my hair and stared down at me with a stern expression on his face that made me forget about his knot—or at least the pain it was causing me—and realize my own climax wasn't all that far off.

"I need you to relax," he said in a gentle tone that made me doubt my theory that the strange effect he had on me was all about my latent repression of some masochistic sub fetish. Gentle, rough, it didn't matter. It all made me tremble like a leaf ready to break off the vine. The common denominator was him. "I'm sorry, this is going to hurt you no matter what I do, but I'll try to make it as easy as possible."

I nodded, because when he looked at me like that, I couldn't remember how to speak. He was *sorry* for hurting me? And here I'd become convinced that he lived for nothing else.

"Good boy," he murmured, bending his head to kiss my neck on the spot that still tingled from the caress of his fangs. It was usually a degrading term meant to keep me in my place, but somehow, it felt different this time. Like a term of endearment from a man who held nothing dear at all.

"Please," I whispered. I wasn't even sure what I was asking him for. His knot was already doing things to my spot that no sex toy ever had and all I had to do was think of moving to send waves of pleasure rolling through me. It had to be about the tingling in my neck that had become a burn.

Somehow, he seemed to understand. "I can't," he said into my neck, his tone almost apologetic. His tongue swept out over the same spot we'd both fixated on for some reason, him with his mouth and me because it was there. "It would destroy you."

I let out a moan that was dangerously close to a whimper and felt myself tighten up around him out of instinct. He grunted and surged forward before catching himself, as if the extra pressure around his knot had taken him off guard. "What the devil are you doing to me?" he breathed, searching my face for the answer. It was an accusation, but one that seemed to come from wonder more than anger.

"I want..." The words rushed out with my breath and I swallowed the rest because I knew they'd just come out in a senseless jumble. I didn't *know* what I wanted, I just knew I wanted it so badly it hurt. The agony of desire made me shudder and he nuzzled into me.

"Shh, shh," he soothed, stroking my hair as he started rocking his hips ever so slightly. Not thrusting, just moving enough to stimulate me anew each time. My dick was pressed so tight between his coarse abs and mine, ready to erupt any moment. I needed it so bad I was dizzy, but I didn't want it just yet. I needed something else, something I couldn't put into words, but he knew.

"I know what you need," he whispered. And he did. The gentle suction at my neck, the subtle movements of him inside of me, proved that my body was an instrument under his maestro's touch. He strummed every chord to perfection and without him even having to demand it, I fulfilled his prediction.

I begged.

"Please, God," I sobbed, not sure if I was calling out to Nicolae or not. "Please, fuck, please... Nicolae, please..."

Well, that settled that. Not like his ego needed the boost.

"Jack," he growled with such force I thought he was scolding me again. And then, he came. His seed exploded within me, pulsing and streaming violently until there was no room left in me to fill. I cried his name and a slew of other nonsensical things, most of them profane, as my orgasm bled into his. My cock shot a full load between our chests, but he didn't seem to care. He captured my lips and his nails dug into my scalp as he tugged my hair in his grasp and his hips gyrated into mine, bone and flesh knocking violently together. His balls slapped my ass as he thrust into me, even though his knot left no room to pull out. Every time he tried, it was agony, but it was also the most earth shattering experience of my life. When the last of his seed was in me and the last of mine was spilled between us, all I had left to my name was his. Nicolae, on my lips, in my veins, carved on my skin in indelible ink, forever.

He collapsed on top of me, panting and growling and it was the hottest sound I'd ever heard. My body convulsed with the after-shocks, but his knot showed no sign of going down. I was still too breathless, too shocked by my own reaction, to ask.

"Son of a bitch," Nicolae muttered into my neck, his arms wrapped tight around me. I tried to move a little, because my arms felt like they were going to fall off, and he growled.

I froze. "Can you at least untie me?"

He looked up and I could tell the growl hadn't been intentional, just an automatic reaction to keep me where he wanted me. He nodded, obviously still recovering himself. He unbound the cloth around my wrists, but the pins and needles made me groan.

"Sorry," he muttered. It was the second time that night he'd apol-ogized to me and I'd been certain that he wasn't capable of it. He started rubbing my arms and I cursed, but it was helping to bring the feeling back into my abused limbs. They were worse off than my stretched hole.

His hands found their way to mine and somehow, that light brush of his fingertips against my palms as he pressed my hands to the bed felt more private than anything else we'd done. I stared at him and he looked back at me, his face unreadable again. "*You*," he murmured, shaking his head like it was some great mystery.

I waited for him to finish his thought, to elaborate the 'you,' but he didn't. Instead, he gathered me into his arms and rolled onto his side. I winced at the change in position, but it was more comfortable once I adjusted. I draped my leg over his and came to terms with the fact that this was how we were going to stay for the foreseeable future.

Come morning, I would hate myself for enjoying this and espe-cially for hoping it lasted a little bit longer. Come morning, he would judge me for all of it, even though he'd been a willing participant. The instigator, if anything. But for tonight, he held me and I let myself be held. I let myself feel paradoxically safe in the arms of the man I had reason to fear more than any other. I let myself pretend I was someone else, because pretending that *he* was someone else would have defeated the whole purpose. And then I would have had to admit to myself that Nicolae, for all the ways he was wrong and unobtainable and dangerous, was exactly who I wanted him to be.

THIRTEEN

I WOKE up coughing to the pungent odor of a pricey cigar and found Nicolae across the room, half-dressed as he studied a paper in his hand. He looked like the wolf he was, even in repose. His long hair had been freshly washed and brushed out, and his muscular torso still glistened with water. Meanwhile, I probably looked like I'd been ridden hard and put up wet. There was truth to that.

I winced as I sat up and gathered the sheets around my waist. A shower was definitely in order. Just had to figure out how to put one foot in front of the other without making any humiliating sounds. I was not twenty-five anymore, and the way my body was punishing me for one night of debauchery made that clear.

God, I'd done so many humiliating things. The things I'd *said* were even worse. Did he remember all of them? Of course he did. He wasn't looking at me, but I knew he'd seen me awake.

"You should take it easy," he announced once I was in the doorway to the bathroom, ready to clean up for the walk of shame down the hall and back to my room.

"All I do is wait these days," I reminded him before closing the bathroom door. I looked myself in the mirror and I saw no sign of the clingy, horny creature I'd become the night before. What the hell had come over me? My first actual romp in the hay with another man and I came unhinged. Maybe what they said about repression was true.

The most unsettling part was that even now, in the light of day, it didn't feel like it had been about sex alone. At least, not for me. I had offered him my body, but it felt like I'd given something more without really being conscious of it. I wondered if he knew. I wondered if he cared at all, or if he'd just throw it away, whatever it was, like everything else that existed outside the parameters of his power game.

Nicolae cared for his pack, that I believed. I just wasn't part of it, and the sooner I made the brain-heart connection and accepted that absolutely nothing was going to come of the night before, the easier it would be.

The shower was both painful and comforting. The hot water soothed the muscles that had been contorted into positions they never had before, but it made me keenly aware of just how badly I'd torn the night before. I'd assumed Nicolae was exaggerating when he'd warned that he might hurt me if we weren't careful, but neither of us had been expecting his knot to make an appearance.

I still wasn't sure what to make of it. It was one thing to accept that Alpha anatomy was a bit different from the rest of us. Hell, Nicolae himself was so huge in every way that I could fully comprehend him being some superhuman species, and in a way, it made me feel less inadequate. I just wasn't sure what to make of the fact that his body responded to mine as something I wasn't.

Omegas weren't human, and I sure as hell wasn't interested in being one. No matter what the others said, it was a degrading life. Fine if you were born into it, not so much if you were the kind of person who'd been raised to stand on your own two feet and take no shit. It was yet another reason to stay away from Nicolae as much as I could now that our official duties had been resolved.

The door opened and Nicolae walked in, taking off his pants like he'd planned to come in and join me all along. "What are you doing?" I asked once I picked my jaw up off the floor.

"You're hurt," he answered, stepping into the shower with me. "I don't want you limping around."

"Well, sorry," I muttered, watching him quizzically as he sank to his knees. He grabbed my hips and turned me away from him. I caught myself with my hands against the stone shower wall. "What the hell are you doing?"

He ignored me, running his hands over my ass a bit too languidly for whatever excuse he was making to touch me. Not that he needed one. My dick was already at half-mast from the sight of his, and I bit my lip in preparation for his fingers, assuming he had plans for round two.

"That's a bit egotistical, don't you think? Your dick's not the panacea." My, how quickly I abandoned my plans to move on and cut ties.

He ignored me. Instead of probing me with his fingers, Nicolae spread me open and ran his tongue along my aching hole. "What the fuck?" I gasped.

"My saliva has a healing agent," he explained. "Just relax."

My face heated up to the point where the shower water felt frigid. This was fucking humiliating, but it felt... Oh, God, his tongue was inside of me. If he heard my strangled choking sound, he paid no mind and kept eating me out in the interest of "healing" me. When the pain started to ease, I realized he wasn't lying, after all.

Of course this was just some medical bullshit. The one time he chose to be considerate, it had to be this. If only I could send an SOS to my dick that this was the wrong time to get hard. Who knew the god of wolves ate ass like a professional?

When he finally stopped, the only thing that still hurt was my pride. That shit was mortally wounded.

"Thanks, but I think I would have survived without your were-wolf spit," I muttered, tempted to blast icy water just to tame my cock. Not that it would've done me any good.

"It reflects poorly on me if I don't care for you," he said, forcing me to face him. His gaze lowered and went right to the one place I didn't want him looking. "Speaking of which..."

Of course that's the reason. "You just tongued my ass, I'm not supposed to get hard from that?" I asked bitterly.

I expected him to offer some smug retort, but instead, I saw the same look in his eyes he'd had the night before and my breath hitched in my throat. Maybe his intentions weren't so clinical after all. Was he just healing me so he could fuck me again?

Just as I was deluding myself into thinking I wasn't sure if I'd let him, he touched my face and with that minimal contact came the reminder of how freely I'd given myself to him the night before.

No. You could only give someone what didn't already belong to them. As soon as Nicolae touched me, I felt like I'd come home. Like I'd never belonged to anyone else, including myself, and he was just finally reclaiming what had been his all along. It made the truth that he would never actually want me that much sharper.

"I want you to do something for me," he said in a low, enticing voice.

I should've told him I'd do whatever he wanted as soon as he went to hell, but instead I asked, "Yes?"

He leaned in, his lips so close to mine I could taste them. "Touch yourself," he whispered.

"Wh—what?"

His eyes hardened. Water to stone. "I don't make a habit of repeating myself."

My hand wrapped around my cock, and I was already wound so tight by the way he was looking at me that it twitched on contact. Every stroke was torture, like my body was punishing me for being turned on when I'd cum twice the night before, and harder than I ever had.

Nicolae's expression was still somber, but I could see the approval in his gaze. He folded his arms and leaned against the stone to watch me. The whole thing was far more objectifying than being on my knees for him had been, but it was hot as hell and I didn't need any imagination fodder as I stroked myself. Just the sight of him. Just seeing how hard he was from watching me.

I knew it wouldn't help his lowly opinion of me to ask, but I saw my opportunity and I took it. "Let me suck you off..."

His eyes widened slightly in surprise, and he seemed to consider it for a second before he gave a bored nod. I sank to my knees and grabbed the base of his shaft with my left hand before swirling my tongue around the head. His cock jerked in response, but he didn't say a word. I drew him into my mouth and he felt even bigger than he looked. I was going to break my damn jaw if I planned to take all of him.

When I dared to glance up, his expression was that of the least enthusiastic man to ever receive a blowjob. At that point, I was convinced he just took every opportunity to make me feel inadequate. If only he knew that all he had to do was exist.

"It's not an ice cream bar, it's not going to fall off if you suck too hard," he remarked, confirming that my efforts were every bit as lackluster as I'd feared. To be fair, the only practice I'd had was with other closet cases like me.

I glared at him and hoped it didn't look as ridiculous as it felt with my lips wrapped around the head of his cock. He grunted, so I knew I was doing something right. When his hand burrowed into my hair and his hips surged forward demandingly, I felt like I'd just won the gold star.

I started stroking myself faster, relieved that his criticism had slowed my libido a bit. It was hard to breathe with the water running down my face and his cock in my throat, but he tasted too good to want to stop.

"Finish yourself off," he growled, as if he knew I was about to. The taste of him and the occasional growl that escaped him when I did something he liked was making it hard to hold off. "I want your hands free."

He may have stopped compelling me, but my dick hadn't gotten the memo. My orgasm exploded, spraying the floor before the steamy water washed the evidence down the drain. It was quick and dirty, but the fun wasn't over.

I rested my hand on the pillar of his thigh as I caught my breath and he kept his hand in my hair to keep me there. "I'm going to teach you how to give a proper blowjob, since you're such a needy little bitch," he taunted.

Before I could flip him off, he took my hand and guided it down to his scrotum. "Roll them," he ordered.

I'd never imagined I would be taking a 101 class on how to give a blowjob, but the teacher was hot, so I followed along to the best of my ability. Nicolae's balls tightened up in my grasp as I kept sucking him, and he didn't have any more snide remarks, so I knew I was getting a passable grade. His other hand found my hair and I knew he was close. I let the length of his dick slide out of my mouth and the snarl of indignation that erupted from his throat gave me great pleasure. I gripped his shaft with my left hand and squeezed his balls tight with my right, torturing the slit of his dick with my tongue.

"You fucking —" He broke off with a throaty gasp, fully resting against the wall now. He shuddered as I took him back into my mouth and for once, I took delight in knowing that he was under my control. His precum was salty and smooth on my tongue and I kept teasing his slit with the tip of it while my lips suctioned off his crown. He gave another pleasured growl as his hips jutted forward so fast that his cock hit the back of my throat hard enough to bruise me. I drank down the hot burst of pleasure that filled my throat and laved the drops off his cock until I finally felt him soften in my mouth.

"I'll make you regret that," he warned halfheartedly, still catching his breath.

"What?" I asked, trying my best to sound innocent. He offered no hand to help me to my feet. "Were you close before or something?"

Nicolae grabbed my arm and pulled me up against him, delivering a crushing kiss that bordered on punishment and only felt like it when it came to an end. "This doesn't change anything. I need you to understand that."

My heart sank back into its proper place. "Of course it doesn't."

Nicolae released me and turned off the water. He grabbed a towel to dry off his hair and wrap around his waist, leaving me to finish up. It was a good thing, because I needed a moment to catch my breath and remember that I'd had dignity once, and I could probably get it back again if I stopped wanting what I couldn't have.

When I had started wanting him at all was another matter. He was still the man my late wife belonged to, in spirit and by law if that letter was any indication. He never let me forget it, either.

By the time I came out of the bathroom and started looking for my clothes, Nicolae was gone. My clothes were also ripped apart, thanks to the wolfman, so I stalked out into the apartment with a towel around my waist and seriously regretted it when I found myself in front of Nicolae and Mason, both staring.

"I see you've taken things a bit far beyond the mating night," Mason muttered, giving me a look that could shatter glass.

To my surprise, Nicolae turned on him, not me. "What I do with my mate is none of your concern."

"It is when I'm the one who has to explain your erratic behavior to the guard," Mason snarled.

Well, shit. Being stuck in the middle of a werewolf fight was just about the last way I'd planned to spend the day. Especially since I was the reason they were fighting.

"I should... go," I said awkwardly, inching toward the door.

"Stay where you are," Nicolae ordered. "This concerns you."

Mason said, "He's not pack."

"He's my mate. That makes him higher ranking than you, especially if you don't stop with the attitude," Nicolae warned. I'd never seen him as angry as he was now, especially since he'd been at the heights of pleasure only a few minutes earlier. Whatever Mason had done to piss him off, I didn't envy him. "If I hear one more word of questioning my decisions, you will be demoted to the rank you started at. Do I make myself clear?"

The Alpha's words seemed to hit him hard, and I almost felt bad for him. Until he cast me one last filthy glance before muttering, "Yes, father."

Nicolae must have caught me staring, because he scowled at me. "What?"

"Nothing, I just... nothing." Definitely not gonna touch that family feud with a ten-foot pole. We obviously had drastically different parenting methods, and I wasn't going to pretend like I knew what it took to run a wolf pack.

Seemingly satisfied, Nicolae took a seat and poured himself another drink. Maybe it was a good thing I was his mate and not his lover. I'd been through the twelve-step meetings and withdrawal with Francesca when she'd turned to alcohol after Ellie announced her transition, and I wasn't interested in getting another alcoholic were-wolf through recovery. Especially one who was as open about his spite as Nicolae was.

"Our mating has been announced," said Nicolae, as if he was just picking up where we'd all left off. "It won't be officially recognized until we've held a ceremony of recognition, of course, but as long as it's done sometime within the next month, the Court will have no choice but to recognize it and it shouldn't affect our petition of custody in any way."

Our petition. It sounded intimate, almost like we were family even though that was far from the truth.

"That means Ellie can come home?" I asked, afraid to sound as hopeful as I was in front of Mason. Nicolae already knew my weakness.

"Yes," Nicolae said, nodding. "The Majerus pack will have no choice but to return her for the duration of the trial, but it is contingent upon the ceremony going as planned."

Something in his tone had me on edge. There had to be a catch. There always was with him. "What is the ceremony?"

The last wolf family event I'd been to had been nothing short of horrifying, so I didn't have high hopes that their wedding customs would be cozy, either.

"*You* are," Mason sneered, taking great satisfaction in the chance to answer. "We hunt you."

I looked at Nicolae, hoping he'd tell me his son was bluffing. Instead, he glared all the more murderously at him, which was not a good sign. "Leave us. Now."

Mason left and let the door slam behind him.

"Please tell me he's kidding," I said.

"Take a drink and sit down," Nicolae replied, offering me a glass.

I stayed where I was. "Nicolae?"

"Take a *drink*, Jack," he said, meeting my eyes to let me know just how he felt about asking twice. Well, telling twice. I was pretty sure Nicolae Ursache had never asked for a damn thing in his life. He probably came out of the womb, cut his own umbilical cord and said, "Milk, bitch."

I chugged what was in the glass just to spite him and slammed it down on the coffee table. I regretted it by the time I sat down and almost missed the couch. "What the hell does Mason mean? You're going to hunt me? And why didn't you tell me he was your son?"

"Which question do you want me to answer?"

"All of them," I snapped.

"You say that like I was hiding it. He's my son, so what?"

"So, you act like you're barely even on a first-name basis!"

"Technically, we aren't. He usually calls me dad."

"You know what I meant."

Nicolae rolled his eyes. "We're wolves, Jack. We don't make a habit of coddling our young."

"Apparently not," I muttered, thinking of Francesca's parents. I decided Mason was probably lucky to be alive.

"As for the hunt, he's making it sound worse than it is."

"So he was telling the truth?"

Nicolae hesitated. "It's an age-old tradition. When a pack Alpha takes a mate, the mate is introduced to the core pack as prey. It's both to make certain that the pack has your scent—in case you ever try to run—and to test me."

I thought back to that night in the woods and realized that was why Nicolae had let them all crowd around me like that. The event seemed even more sinister in its proper context. "Test you? How?"

"My seven most trusted advisors will be pursuing you, and so will I," he answered casually, like he wasn't discussing the inevitability of me getting hunted down by his blood. "If I can't capture you first, I don't deserve to call myself the Alpha."

"And what happens if you don't?" I cried.

"Then you will become the winner's consort and he will challenge me to a fight to the death."

I stared at him, waiting for the punchline. It didn't come, but I was starting to feel like I was living it. "Fuck, Nicolae! You already marked me."

"My death would release you from our bond, which is minimal, since you're not a wolf or an omega." He hesitated. "You might start running out of space for the tattoos, though."

"I'm glad you think this is funny."

"I don't. This is tradition, it's as normal to us as watching a game at a sports bar on Sundays," he answered, gesturing at me with his glass. "Your reactions, however? Priceless."

"Fuck you. I don't wanna end up Mason's concubine!"

"Then I suggest you run well. Or poorly enough that I catch up with you right out of the gate."

"How the hell am I supposed to outrun a pack of werewolves?" I was fast in high school, but not *that* fast. Especially not now that I'd fucked up my knee in the mines and had asthma. Something told me I'd be needing a new inhaler.

"You're not. Not on foot. You'll have a one-day head start before the hunt begins, and you'll be given a vehicle as well as weaponry with which to defend yourself. No mode of transportation is off limits —however, due to the fact that we are at war, you cannot leave Romania."

I was listening, but none of it was sinking in. He couldn't be serious. He just... couldn't. It was bad enough when I thought it was going to be some terrifying romp in the woods, but vehicles? Weaponry? It was so intensive that I wasn't going to be allowed to leave the fucking country?

"Nicolae... you realize this is insane, right?"

"It's tradition. It's everything among our kind," he said, standing. "You will learn this."

"Did you hunt Francesca?" I asked, getting pissed at the thought. She may have been a werewolf who hardly needed the physical protection of a pathetic human after all, but she was still my wife, and the idea of him putting her at risk for any reason at all was infuriating.

"I had planned to, but she ran before I had the chance," he answered. "Before you get too judgmental, you might want to take into account that Francesca was not human. I don't care what kind of pretense she put on of being a bored, helpless housewife, but she was an Alpha and trained to kill. Damn well, I might add. Among the many privileges that come with being pack royalty, your daughter will be as well."

I'd started to come down off my high horse, but when he brought Ellie into it, I was ready to get right back on, dig in my stirrups and charge the fucker. "I don't give a damn about your traditions. No one is hunting my daughter—not now, not three years from now, not ever."

"And I never said they would. When she comes of age, Ellie will be mated to an omega who belongs to one of our allied packs. She'll be the one doing the hunting."

It took me a while to formulate a response to that. Same bullshit, different format. "We'll talk about this later," I muttered, all the more resolved in my decision to get her out of the pack as soon as I could.

"We could, but I thought you'd prefer to spend the next couple of days preparing for Ellie's return."

"Days?" He knew how to get me off a rampage, that was for sure.

"She's coming home on Monday."

"And home is where, exactly?" I demanded.

"She'll stay here. I don't trust that you won't try to run if I give you your own space."

I narrowed my eyes. "After all the bullshit I've put up with, you're really gonna go there?"

"Bullshit you put up with for her sake, not for mine," he corrected. "I did not get where I am by trusting anyone, especially not a human. You're more clever than I imagined, but still dumb enough that you fail to see that being here and taking her proper place within this pack is the best thing for her. She has no future outside of this place, and you're just prideful enough to think that you could protect her. Until you come to terms with the truth, I'm not letting either of you out of my sight." His gaze took on a dangerous glint. "And rest assured, Jack, I have eyes *everywhere*."

FOURTEEN

NICOLAE WAS true to his word about bringing Ellie home. The entire pack was aflutter with preparations for her arrival and whatever big shindig Nicolae had planned to welcome her into the fold. I'd already made him promise that it would be less intense than my own welcome. The other side of that was knowing that he was also telling the truth about keeping a close eye on us both. I'd spent weeks wandering the city out of sheer boredom, so he probably didn't think anything about my putting his threat to the test.

I went my usual route through the city center, tossing a few crackers into the fountain for the birds on my way. The square was crowded, as it usually was on the weekend, so I decided to draw out whoever was watching me another way. I ducked into the subway terminal and purchased a ticket for the museum district, then one for the busier shopping district, knowing that would show up last on the ticket booth display. I tucked the extra ticket into my pocket and pretended to be oblivious to the fact that I had any tails as I made a pitstop in the bathrooms.

No one came in. After dismissing a half-brained thought about escaping through an air vent, I ducked out through the other entrance and made a beeline for my intended stop, rushing past the dupe. There were only five people on the train when I boarded and showed my ticket to the attendant, so I sat in the back and waited. A couple of minutes passed and I was starting to relax, thinking that I was just being paranoid. If Nicolae did have anyone following me, surely they were attentive enough to stay one step ahead of a "blue-collar hick."

Just as I'd started to ease back into my seat, two burly men boarded the train, wearing the basic yet expensive dark-colored clothing that immediately identified them as *pack* to my anxiety-trained eye. I could see the confidence melt off my face in my window reflection as the strangers boarded the train and one sat in the aisle directly across from me.

The train started up and the wolf across from me folded one leg over the other, watching me with a smug look he'd actually earned the right to. "Hello again, Jack," he said in a Romanian accent even more pronounced than Nicolae's. His hair was shorter, but it was the same dark shade as the Alpha's, and he resembled Nicolae and Mason enough that I wondered if he was a close relative. Now that I was thinking of it, there had to be a lot of relation between pack members.

Of course he knew me. I might not have recognized *him* in his human form, but he was undoubtedly one of the wolves Nicolae had dangled me in front of like meat at the hunt. He knew my scent, so of course my little attempt at diversion hadn't fooled him.

At least I knew when I'd been bested, and I decided there was no point in being rude. "We've met, I assume?" I asked.

"In the woods," he answered. Before he and the others ripped another human to pieces like a stuffed dog toy.

"Didn't catch your name, but I probably wouldn't remember it if you gave it. My wolf's not much better than my Romanian."

That got him to crack a smile. Most of the pack members I'd met were as cold and driven as Nicolae, but it was hard to tell what to attribute to cultural differences and what to attribute to them being a completely different species.

"Vasil," he answered, leaning over to offer his hand. I shook it and made note of how the width from his thumb to his pinky was just perfect for strangling.

"Pleased to make your acquaintance, Vasil. Not bad at tracking, are ya?"

"Not at all," he said in a pleasant tone. "I'm better in my other form—but," he paused, looking pointedly around the train, "it's not as inconspicuous."

"You know, that's probably the nicest threat I've ever had."

A grin spread across his face. He was an oversized kid in his mid-twenties, if that. I wondered if he was one of the wolves who'd be hunting me when the time came. One of the men who'd challenge Nicolae to the death for his position if he got the chance. "When Nicolae told me I would be guarding his human, I did not think you would prove such an interesting assignment."

His human. The terminology pissed me off, so why did it make my heart skip a beat? "I'm glad I could keep you entertained."

"Are we going anywhere in particular?"

"Not really. Just figured I'd kill some time and meet the people who've been following me all month."

He chuckled. "Well, now you have. That's Lon," he said, nodding toward the other wolf on the other end of the train. Lon looked up, glaring. Or maybe that was just how his face looked. "Don't mind him. He'd rather be fighting."

"Can't say I blame him. Are you Alphas?"

"I am," he answered. "Lon is a beta."

"So... you'll be hunting me?" I asked warily.

"When the full moon comes, yes. But don't worry, I don't bite humans," he said with a wink.

I did not believe him. No one with a smile that charming was up to anything good. I liked this kid, but if I saw him anywhere near my daughter, we were gonna have a problem. "I'll keep that in mind. So, you want to be *the* Alpha?"

"Hardly," he snorted. "I prefer being a guard and a soldier, and you're not exactly my type. No offense."

"None taken," I assured him.

"Now, Nicolae's *last* mate..." he said with a low whistle.

I cleared my throat. "She was my wife, so, offense taken there."

"My apologies," he said with a laugh. His expression turned somber. "I am sorry for your loss. Francesca was a good woman. Strong. She would've made a good leader."

"Thanks. You're, uh, one of the only people I've met who seems to share that sentiment."

He shrugged. "Never said she wasn't a bitch, but most she-wolves are. The ones who get shit done, at least."

"She certainly did that."

"May I ask you a personal question?"

"You'd be the first person to ask if you could ask, so sure."

"How is it belonging to him when Francesca belonged to the both of you?"

I was surprised at his candor, but I'd lived in Europe for just long enough that I was starting to get used to it. It was a nice change of pace from the Clarksvillian habit of being cheerful to your face and stabbing you in the back as soon as you turned around. I'd grown up in a little shack in the mountains, so adjusting to town life when I'd gone to live with my aunt in high school had been a culture shock, despite its close proximity. I had learned quickly that there was a reason "city folk" didn't like "mountain folk" and it wasn't just because of our strange undertones or the elixirs granny brewed in her shed.

"About how you'd figure," I answered, deciding that was safe. "It's awkward as hell, but Nicolae promised to keep Ellie safe, and come tomorrow night, we'll find out if he kept his word."

"He always keeps his word," Vasil said in a grave tone. "That's what separates us from them."

"From humans?"

"From the Majerus pack."

"So I'm guessing that war's not gonna slow down anytime soon."

"Certainly not now," said Vasil. "Your daughter's marriage will secure our alliance with the Crow pack. Then we might actually stand a chance at finishing this thing."

I listened carefully, noting the way his demeanor shifted. He might have looked young, but his eyes told the truth about the age of his soul. He'd seen war, and he'd seen a lot of it.

"I admire anyone who's willing to put their life on the line for something they believe in, pack or country." I'd been a few months off from joining the service before Franny found me, and I chose the mines instead. I didn't regret being home to raise my daughter, but sometimes I wondered if I'd made the right choice.

"Pack is family," Vasil said in a way that made me think our conversation was not entirely unplanned. "I may not see eye to eye with Nicolae on everything, but he's a good man and he'd give his life for any of us. He proved it when he pulled me out of enemy territory half-dead and took a bullet for it. Any of us would give our lives for his in return."

"Does that mean you're gonna throw the hunt?" I asked hopefully, wishing I was remotely capable of puppy-dog eyes.

He smirked. "I respect him and our traditions too much to do that. You had better prepare yourself when the time comes."

I was sure he was right about that. The train came to a stop and I decided to buy Vasil and Lon a few drinks at the pub on Nicolae's dime to make up for dragging them around Bucharest. We weren't exactly old friends by the time evening came around, but Lon looked less like he wanted to eat me, so that was progress.

"Gonna go take a leak, unless that would be too much of a security risk," I said with a dry cough. My last sip of beer had gone down the wrong way.

Vasil flipped me off, which I was starting to realize was a gesture of goodwill in male werewolf parlance. I got up off my stool and stumbled a little. Maybe I'd lost my tolerance over the last month. I made it to the bathroom and was relieved that no one followed me in.

Taking a piss in front of a dog was one thing, but I drew the line at one who could write in cursive.

I zipped up and turned on the sink, coughing again with sudden and unexpected force. I hadn't had a fit in a few days. The air was better in Romania, if nothing else. But when I saw the black blood in the sink, I knew I was far from out of the woods, and only then did I realize I didn't have my inhaler on me. Of course I didn't. I never did anything right.

Fuck.

The coughing got worse, and I gulped down a few cupped handfuls of warm water to settle it enough to let me breathe. One night. One fucking night was all I had to get through, and then Ellie would be here.

One night.

I gripped the edge of the sink, but it did nothing to save me from collapsing, or hitting my head on the way down. I heard the bathroom door swing open while I was still trying to catch my breath and I recognized the sound of Vasil yelling, but my ears were ringing too loudly to make out his words.

A minute later, I was being dragged to my feet by both men who'd been sent to stalk me, and I was with it enough to put one foot in front of the other as they led me out of the bar. At least I probably looked like just another loser who'd had a little too much to drink to everyone else.

Vasil left us at the curb to make a phone call and I found myself leaning fully on Lon as I tried to stop coughing. Each cough had my head closer to splitting open.

"Hang on," Lon said with actual kindness in his voice as he held me up. "Don't pass out on me."

"Not —" Another cough seized me and this one sent a searing pain into my diaphragm. "Not planning on it."

"Shh," he warned, muttering something that sounded like a cross between fretting and scolding in Romanian.

A black car screeched to a halt at the curb and Vasil opened the back door. It had been all of a minute since he'd made that call, which only proved to me that Nicolae meant what he'd said about having wolves all over the city. He owned Bucharest, of that there was no question. Lon and Vasil loaded me into the car before getting in and I heard Vasil speaking rapidly in Romanian to someone on the phone. I couldn't understand more than a word here or there of what he was saying, but I knew the deep voice on the other end of the line well enough.

They were taking me back to Nicolae. Somehow, I knew I was going to be punished for this.

FIFTEEN

"WHAT THE FUCK HAPPENED TO HIM?" Nicolae bellowed as he and my professional stalkers stood aside in a mostly white room while a woman in a white coat held an oxygen mask over my face. They weren't the first words Nicolae had spoken since our hectic return to the condos, which evidently included an entire floor made up of medical facilities, but they were the first he'd spoken in English. "I told you to watch him, not get him killed!"

"He was fine," Vasil protested. "He just had too much to drink."

I wanted to interject on their behalf, but I was still coughing too hard to speak. "Just breathe," the doctor ordered. She was American, which explained the change in language.

"You sure he's not a fish?" Lon asked dryly.

"Fuck you, assh—" That was all I could make out before I started coughing again, but he got the message.

The doctor shot me a scathing look. "*Breathe*, Jack."

I tried to take a deep breath, but my lungs burned in protest. To my humiliation, once I'd finally gotten enough air to bother looking up, Nicolae was watching me. He always seemed to find me at my lowest moments. In this case, I'd been brought to his doorstep in the middle of one. I was expecting irritation in those stormy blue eyes, not the concern I found.

Somehow, that was worse. At least when he was mocking me, I could defend myself. I didn't know what to do with his pity, and I didn't want it. I'd been vehemently opposed to the idea of the hunt, but the idea that he might think twice about it because he saw me as fragile or weak made me want to have a go with the three of them right there.

I tried to tell myself I only cared about appearing strong around Nicolae because he was my romantic rival, but the oxygen deprivation was making it hard to keep lying to myself.

"Here," the doctor said, pulling the mask off my face to offer me an inhaler. "Try this now, I think you're breathing enough."

I took the small red canister and wheezed out as much air as I could without starting up another fit. Always a thin tightrope to walk. I pressed down on the aerosol pump and breathed in deep, letting the acrid vapor fill my lungs. It burned, but in a good way. I held my breath for as long as I could, which ended up being half of the recommended ten seconds. I coughed a few times and did it again. This time, the medication actually stayed in my lungs long enough that I felt the spasms subside.

I'd had my share of bad ones, but they'd never lasted quite that long or been that severe. Then again, I usually wasn't stupid enough to forget my inhaler. As soon as I could breathe again, I stopped wanting to. Nicolae, Vasil and Lon were all looking at me in varying degrees of pity and concern. "I'm fine," I coughed. "It happens."

"How long have you had asthma?" the doctor asked, frowning.

"Dunno. Five, six years?"

"Is that how long it's been since you were diagnosed, or since the symptoms started?"

I hesitated. "I don't know. Both, I guess."

"Leave," Nicolae growled to his men. Vasil and Lon tripped over each other fleeing the room. I was going to owe them more than a few beers to make up for this. So much for finally getting a couple of the pack members to like me.

Not that I planned on staying. I had to keep reminding myself of that. As soon as the chance came, Ellie and I were out, assuming I didn't get myself hospitalized before she even got home.

"What's wrong with him, Kel?" Nicolae asked.

"Hard to say without running some tests," said the doctor. She watched me closely, continuing to frown behind the thick yellow glasses that almost matched the color of her hair. "You've worked in the mines for how many years?"

I knew exactly what she was getting at, and she was probably right, but I'd been living in denial for a long time and another day wasn't going to kill me. It wasn't going to keep me from dying, either. That's what I'd always told myself so I'd have an excuse to not seek a diagnosis and hear for certain that I had an expiration date.

"My doc back home said it was just asthma."

"Your doctor whom I'm assuming is paid handsomely by the mining company you work for," she shot back.

I probably would have liked her under any other circumstances, but today, she was just another prick standing between me and my reunion with my kid. She pulled the stethoscope off her neck and popped the buds in her ears. "Take a deep breath," she said, lifting my shirt up in the back to press the cold metal against my skin.

"Do as she says," Nicolae demanded, as if he could read my mind and see the obstinacy forming.

I complied, willing my lungs not to betray me. I'd put up with enough of their shit, they owed me this.

"Again," said Kel.

I took another breath and started coughing. She pulled the stethoscope back around her neck and frowned at me again. She was going to need an ice pack if she didn't loosen her expression.

"What is it?" Nicolae asked. I could tell he wanted to make her tell him from the way his arms were folded and his foot kept tapping out his nervous energy, but he could be civil when he wanted to. Just not with me.

"I need to run an X-ray. There's a lot of rattling. It could be fluid, or it could be congestion. I won't know until I see the pictures."

"Nope," I said, standing up from the cot. "Whatever it is, it can wait until after Ellie's back."

Kel sighed and looked at Nicolae. He nodded and she left, a reminder that the answers I gave didn't matter anymore. Not when his always overrode them. That blood-laced ink on my back made sure of it.

I couldn't wait for the day I burned that sucker off and just hoped I'd live long enough to get the chance.

"You're not going anywhere until the doctor gives the go ahead and finds out what's wrong with you," he said firmly. "Mason isn't picking Ellie up from the airport until tomorrow night."

"No," I growled, my voice still raspy from the coughing. He seemed stunned into silence by my insistence, or possibly just the fact that he'd never heard the word no before, so I continued. "I don't want Mason around her. I don't trust him."

He arched an eyebrow. "That's not your call to make."

"Yes, it is. This is your pack, and she's my daughter. I've played by every rule you've thrown at me, but I'm not compromising when it comes to her."

"Mason is my son, and he's one of our best soldiers." The offense behind his words came as a relief. At least he wasn't entirely impartial toward his own flesh and blood.

"I don't care if he shits rainbows and volunteers at church on the weekend. *I. Don't. Trust. Him.* Not around her."

Nicolae's brow furrowed, and I could feel him deciding whether he was going to let my insolence slide. To my surprise, he relaxed and said, "Fine."

"Fine? Just like that?"

"I'll send Vasil. What more do you want?"

He wasn't my first choice, but compared to Mason, he was a boy scout and I wasn't going to press my luck. "Thank you."

Something told me he was only humoring me because I was sick, but I could live with that if it meant he took me seriously.

Nicolae said nothing, but I could feel the weight of the words he wanted to say pressing down on my chest, making it even harder to breathe.

"What were you doing on the other side of town?" I knew it wasn't what he wanted to ask, but I was relieved it was something I could answer honestly.

"I wanted to know who you had following me, so I tried to give them the slip at the train station and we ended up having drinks."

Nicolae snorted in amusement and shook his head. "From what Vasil told me on the phone, you gave them quite a time."

"I tried. They're better."

"They should be. They've been training since they were children."

I had to wonder what form they took then. Toddlers? Puppies? "At least now I'll be able to think, 'hey, that's my buddy Vasil' if he takes down my out-of-shape ass on the full moon."

Nicolae frowned. "We'll see."

"We'll see? Vasil said he was doing it."

"We'll see about you participating at all," he clarified.

"What? I have to. You said it yourself, the Court won't recognize us as mates unless we follow the tradition."

"If you're sick —"

"Bullshit, I'm not sick, I'm just an asthmatic who stopped working out when he got a promotion," I muttered. "I'm doing this."

Nicolae narrowed his eyes. "First, you bitch about our 'savage traditions,' and now that you're actually at risk, you're giving me a hard time about sitting out?"

"I have to bitch. I'm southern, it's what we do," I shot back. "Doesn't mean we don't follow through on shit."

"Healthy people don't just collapse and have coughs that never go away, Jack," he said in that same tone he always used when he wanted to make me feel like a child. "I thought you were just not feeling well, but it's obvious there's something more going on if you've been sick for this long."

"You don't think I fucking know that?"

He seemed surprised at my anger yet again, like he saw me as some one-dimensional idiot and occasional fucktoy who never had a thought more complex than deciding what I wanted for dinner.

"I *know* I'm sick," I said once I'd caught my breath.

"Then why haven't you gotten tested?"

"So, what, they could tell me I'm dying *and* I can't provide for my family?" I challenged. "So we could live off disability payments while Franny waited tables to make ends meet? You live in a different world. Well, so did I. In the world I was born into, nothing is free. Nothing. I grew up in a shack and never knew whether there'd be a meal on the table the next night, or whether my mother would've smoked our grocery money. When Francesca told me she was pregnant, I swore to a God I had only ever cursed up to that point that if He gave me a way to provide for them, I'd give our child the kind of life I'd only ever dreamed of. That she would never know what it was like to be cold or hungry or wonder every time her dad left for work if this would be the day he didn't come back."

I started coughing again and he was at my side the next second, grabbing my shoulders. I cursed my body and him when he held a cup of water to my lips, giving me that pitying look that made me want to kill him the way I should have wanted to the moment I'd realized who he was. I pushed him away and collected myself.

"I knew the day I set foot in those mines that I was trading my health for a better life for Francesca and Ellie," I said hoarsely. "It was a price I was willing to pay, and just because the piper's come calling don't mean I'm gonna back out now. Maybe you're right and you can give Ellie a better life than I ever could, but that's up to her. She still needs me, and I'm not gonna let my fucking lungs keep me from protecting her."

He watched me, frustration turning his blank expression to a scowl. "And letting your pride get in the way of treatment is supposed to help her? All you're doing is making sure you won't be there for her."

"I already know what those X-rays are gonna say," I gritted out. "You don't breathe coal in a goddamn tunnel for more than a decade and get good news, Nicolae."

He set his jaw and his nostrils flared as he watched me. I could see him calculating his next mode of attack, his next attempt at reasoning with the uneducated simpleton in front of him. "There are things that can be done. Money isn't an obstacle, and I can have the best doctors in the world here in a matter of hours. Maybe your pride kept you from taking care of this before, but the choice isn't yours anymore."

I wasn't sure if he was being willfully ignorant, or just arguing for the sake of arguing. He was too smart not to know that the only diagnosis that doctor was handing down was a death sentence. That left only one explanation that made any sense at all.

"You said yourself the bond between us is minimal," I said. "It shouldn't affect you when I die, as long as we're mated first and Ellie is in your custody."

He stared at me with an unreadable expression that gradually became anger. "That's what you think this is about?"

"What else?"

His growl made me jolt. The doctor came in before I could make sense of him, and I wasn't sure I wanted to. "We're ready for him," said Kel.

The habit all the wolves had of addressing Nicolae rather than me directly had always pissed me off, but I was out of energy and too tired to bother with more social interaction. "If I do this, I want you to promise me that no one looks at the results. Not until Ellie's home. I don't want this shit on my brain."

Nicolae didn't respond at first. He finally looked over at Kel and muttered, "Run the test, but hold the results until next Sunday."

Sunday. He was giving me a week to be with my daughter, untainted by the inevitability of the shadow that had been growing over my shoulder for years.

"Alright," she said, clearly bewildered by his change of heart.

"Thank you," I mumbled, at a loss for anything else to say. Usually, I'd make a snide remark and wait for his verbal devastation in response. Now all I could do was thank him.

Nicolae wouldn't meet my gaze and he didn't respond, so I left the room and followed the doctor down the hall before he could change his mind.

SIXTEEN

"SHE'S BEEN GONE for a month, not ten years," Nicolae remarked as I placed a bowl of Skittles on the counter with all the red ones picked out. Ellie had reactions to the dye, and she'd been a hyperactive gremlin for a whole summer as a child before we figured out. The Skittles were just the last offering in the buffet of all her favorites, ranging from baby carrots to spicy cheese puffs.

"You're talking to the guy who joined the scouts as a troop leader because the idea of sending his kid away on weekend trips gave him hives."

"Sounds like a perfectly healthy level of attachment."

"Hey, your kid turns into an eight-hundred pound gorilla with a dog head and he probably learned how to fire a gun before he learned how to ride a bike."

"That's beside the point, and one day, Ellie is also going to turn into a wolf," he reminded me.

I grimaced.

"That's not very open-minded of you, Jack," he taunted, reaching into the bowl of candy.

I swatted his hand with the spatula I was planning on using to take the cookies off the baking sheet once they cooled. "Those aren't for you. And I'm not open-minded at all. My mind is a small, narrow place and that's the way I like it."

"Letting your child transition isn't an entirely narrow-minded thing to do," he said, rubbing the back of his hand. I'd been getting away with murder ever since my incident, and I was not above milking it in certain regards. All I had to do was cough when he was getting testy and I'd magically get my way.

To be fair, "my way" was usually getting out of some bullshit werewolf tradition, like sitting for the traditional portrait of the pack Alpha and his new mate. No one wanted to see my hairy face staring judgmentally at them from the downstairs hallway.

"That's different."

"How?"

I shrugged. "It just is. I had my reservations at first, but after we started talking to a therapist, the stuff she was saying made sense. I realized I could either accept my daughter the way she was or end up burying her one day."

"It's hard to imagine Francesca going to a therapist," he murmured.

I chose to focus on placing the cookies on a plate. They were cool enough.

"Jack?"

"She didn't go. Not after the first time, and she walked out in the middle of the session," I finally answered.

"She didn't approve."

"To put it mildly."

Nicolae sighed. "Francesca was rather... traditional."

"Just not when it came to herself, apparently. She didn't have any problems skipping out on the good old tradition of mate marking when it came to you." I regretted the words as soon as I said them and even more when I saw the look on his face. I just didn't know why I cared. Why did it matter if I made him feel like shit when he'd done nothing but that ever since we met? He hadn't cared about my feelings when he'd tried to take back my wife, or when he'd reminded me of all my shortcomings in the forest. His words from that night still stuck with me more than I wanted to admit.

This doesn't change anything. I need you to understand that.

Those words had stuck with me, too, and I finally did understand. Two sexcapades didn't change a damn thing, regardless of how earth-shattering the sex was. I was grateful to Nicolae for everything he'd done for me and for Ellie, but there was only so much I owed him.

"No. She didn't," he said in a resigned tone that made me feel as heartless as he usually was. I still didn't know if his recent change of heart was due to pity or because he simply needed to keep me around long enough to control Ellie, but I wasn't about to trust that it was genuine. It made him all the more dangerous. I'd let my guard down around him once, and I wasn't going to take that risk again.

Walk away, Jack. Leave him burning like he left you.

"For what it's worth, you're not the only one she bailed on," I muttered. Because I just couldn't fucking help myself.

Nicolae frowned. "What do you mean?"

"I mean you're not the first guy she cheated with."

"We didn't —"

"I know. You didn't fuck while we were married," I said, dropping the last cookie onto the plate. I handed him one on a napkin. "She did, however, fuck Ellie's second grade teacher. And to be honest, her keeping that letter all these years right under my nose in the same fucking dresser I kept my socks in stung a hell of a lot more than the sex."

"You knew she was having sex with another man and you stayed with her?"

I shrugged. "We'd been married for almost eight years at that point. Seemed like a lot to throw away because of a fling she said didn't mean anything."

"Did you forgive her because you loved her, or because you wanted to stay together for Ellie?"

I looked up, surprised as his question sailed right for its target.

Sometimes, it seemed like those eyes could see through me—others, it was impossible to doubt. "I don't know," I admitted.

"You must have hated her."

"Of course I fucking hated her," I scoffed. "Especially when I walked in and found them on the living room set I'd worked overtime to get for our anniversary, but the guy left with a broken arm and she broke down sobbing and apologizing. Said she was lonely because I'd been gone so much, but I knew the truth."

"Which was?"

I leaned on the counter, trying to decide whether I wanted him to know that tidbit of my past. I decided he'd seen me in far more vulnerable states, and soon, it wasn't going to matter anyway. It was kind of nice to talk about Francesca with someone who knew who she was, anyway. Who she *really* was, beneath the PTA meetings and the smiles that never met her eyes. Someone who knew the parts of her I'd never been able to touch and she only showed to me when she wanted to hurt me.

Maybe it was because she'd hurt him, too. In the beginning, Nicolae had seemed invulnerable, and the way he'd changed whenever her name came up had made me too angry to see that it wasn't possession that changed him or even love. It was grief.

"I wasn't enough for her." It was humiliating to say those words out loud, but freeing at the same time. "She wasn't stupid. She knew I was gay, and what we had was supposed to be a one-time thing. Me figuring myself out, I guess. She said it made her insecure, that one day I'd decide she wasn't enough for me. Maybe that's why she fucked around. In her mind, she was doing it before I could."

"But you didn't."

"No," I answered. "Sixteen years, I never touched anyone but her."

"Why?"

"Because I loved her. Because I gave her my word. Maybe it wasn't the way she wanted, not at first, but I loved her with every part of me I could give and it still wasn't enough. I've gotta live with that, same as you."

"She still chose you."

"Yeah," I laughed, taking a drink. "Guess she did. Look where that got her."

"Jack... there's something you should know."

My throat tightened again. I felt the same dread when he'd first showed me his truth on the side of the road, but this time, I wasn't afraid of what he'd do to me. I was afraid of what his words would. I was afraid he was finally going to make the confession I'd expected from the beginning, that he and Francesca had been together since she'd left.

It was only then that I realized I wasn't afraid of finding out she'd broken our marriage vows again. I was afraid of finding out that she'd broken them with *him*.

I really was sick, but my lungs weren't the most broken part of me. My heart had a monopoly on fuckery.

"What is it?"

"Right now, there are three people in the downstairs hallway," he said calmly, keeping his eyes on mine. "One of them is carrying a ring of keys. The other is walking in heels."

"Okay...?"

"I know this because I can hear them," he said pointedly.

It took me a minute, but when the pieces finally fell into place, all I could do was laugh. "You're saying Francesca heard me coming that day," I said, shaking my head. "That she could've hid the guy, but she didn't. She wanted me to find them like that."

The revelation didn't really come as a surprise, but the way he reached for my hand did. My heart stopped and I stared at him in confusion. "I believe you Americans have a saying. She played us both?"

"Yeah," I croaked. "She did."

Nicolae picked up his glass and tapped it against my bottle. "To Francesca. No woman was ever more cruel, or more beautiful."

"I'll drink to that," I grunted. And I did.

There were three loud knocks at the door and I set my beer down before I realized Nicolae's hand was still on mine. He stayed behind as I went to answer the door and I found myself wondering if he was going to be on good behavior around Ellie or if she'd get a peek at his true nature as soon as she walked in the door.

As soon as she walked in, flanked by two burly wolves, one of whom had a big metal keychain dangling from his belt loop, I had to laugh. And she was wearing heels. Fuck Nicolae and his stupid wolf ears.

For the moment, none of it mattered. Not him, not the news that Francesca had done something else to hurt me. All that mattered was that my little girl was home and safe and okay enough to yell, "Dad!" when I picked her up and spun her around in my arms.

"Look at you!" I cried, setting her down. I'd expected her to come back looking as overwhelmed and out of water as I felt in the land of wolves, but instead, she looked like she'd just come back from vacation. "Are you older? You look older."

"I did turn sixteen," she said dryly.

"Oh, don't think getting kidnapped by werewolves means you're getting out of a party. I can have paper streamers here like that," I said, snapping my fingers.

Ellie rolled her eyes and groaned, so I knew she was okay. Nicolae had already warned me that the less she knew about the truth behind Francesca's death, the better. There was still a chance, if we royally fucked up and didn't appease the Court's many stipulations, that they would attempt to return to her grandparents. It would only happen over my dead body, but despite what Nicolae thought, I didn't think that would be hard.

"I'm just glad to be back," she said, wrapping her arms around me again. "I was so worried about you."

"Me?" I scoffed, stroking her hair. "I'm not the one who's been living with Claire and Damon Marjerus."

"They're not that bad," she said, pulling away to tuck her hair behind her ear. "Kind of stuffy and opinionated, but they were nice once I got there. They said they'd call you and tell you where I was." She narrowed her eyes. "They did, right?"

I could feel Nicolae watching me, the sway of him coaching me through my answer in his thoughts even though I couldn't hear them. It was weird. He'd always been able to exert control with his words, but I could feel his will even without him speaking ever since he'd marked me.

"Yeah," I said, choking down my bitter hatred toward my in-laws. "I'm just glad you're home. You're sure they were okay? They didn't hurt you?"

She frowned, like the idea was bizarre. "No, why would they?"

I took her bag and before I could put it over my shoulder, Nicolae grabbed it. I shot him a dirty look, but he pretended like he didn't notice. "Right," I muttered. "This is Nicolae Ursache. He's —"

"I know who he is," Ellie said in an icy tone, holding the man's gaze without any of the difficulty I seemed to have. "He's the guy mom ditched. The one who refused to let grandma and grandpa bring you to me."

Grandma and grandpa. I'd always felt guilty that Ellie didn't know her grandparents. Three of them were MIA and my mother was more interested in drugs, and men that had more drugs, than she was in getting clean and having a relationship with her granddaughter. I understood why she'd latch onto the idea that Claire and Damon were the happy relatives she'd always hoped was out there, but it still stung to hear those traitors' names on her lips, knowing she didn't have a damn clue what they'd taken from us. From her.

"Your grandparents have always been inventive people, and I'm afraid they've put their own spin on things," Nicolae said, proving he could be diplomatic when he wanted to. "Your father has been free to leave any time he chooses."

That wasn't *exactly* true, since he knew I wasn't going anywhere without Ellie, but for once, we were on the same side. "He's right. Nicolae is the one who helped me get you back here."

She didn't seem to know what to make of that. I could tell from the way she was looking at him that she was in the same dilemma as me. She *wanted* to hate him, because of her mother. Because of me.

Now I understood what Nicolae and Leonie had been trying to drive into my head from day once. Ellie was trapped in the no-man's land between two packs who had equally damning claims to her. Everything that pushed her away from this pack, from Nicolae, pushed her further into the clutches of Claire and Damon.

I was insane for thinking that running away would solve any of it. Who the hell even knew how much longer I had? I wanted to believe I was strong enough to hold on until she was safe, but how long would it take for two powerful wolf packs to give up on a young Alpha they both needed to secure their own futures? How many months or years I was sure I didn't have?

The Majerus pack saw her as a commodity. At least Nicolae saw her as a daughter by proxy. Hell, she probably was his by blood.

"It's a pleasure to finally meet you, Ellie," Nicolae said, offering his hand. "Your father never stops talking about you."

"That's always been a problem," she said, grudgingly shaking his hand even though she was still glaring at him. It was one of those weird fatherly pride moments, knowing I'd raised a kid who could throw shade while being polite. I could feel our ancestors smiling down on me.

"Welcome to the pack. I trust your escorts were accommodating," he said, looking up at the two men who'd remained like statues the whole time.

Ellie glanced back at them. "They don't talk much, do they?"

"I don't pay them to," Nicolae replied, waving to them. The guards left and it was just the three of us.

"So!" I said, rubbing my hands together. "You must be hungry after flying all the way from California. I made all your favorites." That was a bit of a stretch, since most of them came out of plastic bags, but it was a special occasion.

Ellie arched an eyebrow. "I can see that. But there are some things I'd like to discuss with Mr. Ursache first."

"Please, call me Nicolae."

Ellie turned back to me. "You don't mind, do you, dad?"

"Of course not," I said, unable to hide my surprise. Or my displeasure at the idea of leaving them alone and giving up the ability to moderate the conversation. Then again, from what I'd gathered, Alphas didn't really have that kind of influence over each other.

It was still so hard to think of her that way. My little girl, a wolf. Not just a wolf, but an Alpha, the kind that even made the others nervous. She'd only been gone a month, but there was something different about her. Something that had changed. I'd seen that look of determination in her eyes plenty of times, and for the first time, I saw less of myself and more of Franny.

On the one hand, I was relieved that she was far from the emotional wreck I'd expected after everything she'd been through. On the other, I was starting to realize that my hope all this werewolf stuff wouldn't change her was foolish.

"Shall we go for a walk, then?" Nicolae offered. "I can give you a tour of the building, and then show you the district."

Ellie nodded, glancing back at me as she followed him to the door. "We'll have dinner when I get back," she promised, giving me a smile that made my heart sink. I knew that smile. It was the same one I always gave her after she'd caught the tail end of an argument between me and her mother and I was trying to convince her that everything was fine.

"Sure," I said in a thick voice. "I'll be here."

Once they were gone, I picked up her bag where Nicolae had left it and carried it into the room on the other end of the condo that he'd cleared out for her.

Snooping was never something I'd been tempted to do. At least not when it came to my daughter. I'd always figured that making sure she knew she could come to me was the most important thing, and if she didn't feel like she could, I'd failed her. This time was different. I still didn't know what the Majerus pack had told her. If they'd brain-washed her, for that matter. Nonetheless, I felt a twinge of guilt as I unzipped her bag. Halfway through shaking out the contents, I caught a glimpse of a piece of paper filled with Ellie's messy and unmistakable handwriting. I was pretty sure I was the only person on earth who could decipher that chicken scratch besides her, so it might as well have been in code.

Nicolae killed mom, and I'm going to prove it. For now, we have to go along with what he says, but Claire and Damon are going to help us. I'll get us both out of here. Trust me.

I held that letter in my hands for what felt like forever. What the fuck was it with Majerus women turning my life upside-down in print? Was it too much to ask for them to give me at least some emotionally devastating news in person? At least now I knew what the Majerus pack had been feeding her.

It occurred to me halfway through crumpling the letter up and stuffing it in my bag that I wasn't even entertaining the idea that she was right. That I was the one who'd been brainwashed, not her. It was probably the more logical answer, especially considering that I had initially assumed the same, but my mind and my heart had evolved beyond recognition since then. I tried to ask myself if it could be true. If Nicolae really was the one who'd killed Francesca and was just using me to trap Ellie.

The violence with which my psyche responded to the idea prob-ably should have been proof of it, but I *knew*. I'd felt his pain as he spoke of her death like my own. I had only known him a short time, but I'd been more intimate with Nicolae than I had ever been with another person, and not just physically. If I was wrong about this, then I had already lost my sanity.

At least she was planning on biding her time. That gave me time to talk to her, to convince her of the truth. I just had to hope that it really was the truth and not my own delusion.

SEVENTEEN

NICOLAE AND ELLIE were gone for hours, and I'd already gone out in search of them when they finally came through the door. "What took you so long?" I demanded.

"Nicolae was showing me the territory," Ellie answered, slipping out of her jacket. He took it from her and hung it up by the door.

"*All* of it?" I cried.

Nicolae held up his hand before I could launch into a tirade about deserving some form of warning before they took off for that long. "Not quite, but she wanted to see the armory, and I figured that now was as good a time as any to introduce her to the troops," he said. He looked down at her, a faint smile on his lips. It was one I'd never seen before. Tender, somehow. It looked so out of place on his stern face, and yet, there was something about it that touched my heart. "After all, one day she will be leading them."

Ellie's smile was forced, and my heart sank. If she'd already started asking to see the classified shit, there was only one reason and Nicolae seemed entirely oblivious to it. Was she feeding information back to her grandparents, even now?

"At least we worked up an appetite from all the walking," she said, grabbing a handful of pretzels as she leaned on the counter, a playful glint in her eyes. "Whatever happened to the five food groups?"

"They're all here. Sugar, carbs, fats, salt, and some of the candy's green," I teased, trying not to tip either of them off to my internal meltdown before I knew how to handle this without convincing Ellie that I'd been sucked into the biggest lie of all time or alerting Nicolae to the fact that she planned on betraying him.

"I'll leave you to your feast," said Nicolae, glancing in disgust at the junk buffet. "I'm sure you'd like some time to catch up, and there are matters I must attend to for the Court."

"Thanks for the tour," Ellie said, digging around in the candy dish.

"It was my pleasure. Take a few days to settle in, and when you're feeling rested, we'll arrange your welcome party."

"I can't wait," she said, waiting until he disappeared into the elevator to turn to me. "How have you survived *that* for the last month?"

"He's not really that bad," I said, taking a sip of water since my throat was dry. "Kind of grows on you."

Ellie gave me a look of pure disgust. "Did you not find my note?"

"I did," I said slowly, knowing I had to tread carefully. "Ellie, I don't know what they told you over there, but things aren't what you think they are."

Her eyes narrowed and she just stared at me for a few moments. I couldn't tell if she was pissed at me for defending her mother's alleged killer, or just confused. When her expression finally melted into pity, I knew it was worse than that. "I should have known," she murmured, shaking her head. "He brainwashed you."

"No. Ellie —"

"Stop." The authority in her voice took me off-guard. I stared at her, bewildered as she stood up in front of me, holding unblinking eye contact. The next time she spoke, her voice held the eerily familiar tone that Nicolae's had the first time he'd compelled me. "Listen to me carefully. Nicolae *lied*. He's trying to control you."

I felt her words taking over my thoughts and the sting of betrayal was strong. I grimaced, trying to fight it. So she hadn't just been holed up in her room during her time with the Majerus pack. She'd been training, learning the truth about what she was, sprinkled in with the narrative they wanted her to believe.

"No," I gritted out.

Frustration shone in her eyes. "*Yes*. Nicolae is manipulating you, making you think what he wants you to think. He killed mom and he's trying to use you to get to me. You have to fight it."

I was. Not his influence, but hers. Under the force of her compulsion, I was actually starting to doubt it. What she was saying made sense. Too much sense, because she wasn't swaying me organically, but there was something embedded in me that was even deeper than lupine witchcraft that wouldn't let me come over to her side. Maybe the whole thing really was manipulation, but if it was, his skill far exceeded her blossoming abilities.

Now I understood why Francesca had kept the truth from her for so long. Ellie had always been strong-willed, and it had been hard enough to convince her to eat her vegetables without her having the powers of mind control.

"No," I finally managed to get out. My voice came out as a strained growl, and the look of shock on her face told me she hadn't expected me to be able to break her psychic hold. "Ellie Jessamine Mullins, if you ever even attempt to pull that trick again, you're grounded until the next time Halley's Comet passes by, do you understand me?"

Her eyes grew wide and for an instant, she seemed like herself again. "How did you —?"

"Nicolae is not the one who killed your mother," I said firmly. I knew he was going to kill me for telling her the truth, and maybe it was a mistake, but I'd made it sixteen years without lying to her and I wasn't going to start now. Not for him, not for anyone. "I know you don't want to hear this, and I am so, so sorry you have to be involved, but the people who killed her are the ones who took you."

Anger flashed in her eyes. "That's bullshit."

"It's not. Your mother didn't just turn her back on Nicolae when she ran, she turned from her pack too. Her parents were the ones who gave her to him in the first place, and she humiliated them. She came to Clarksville to get away from them, because it's protected."

"I know that," she snapped. "But she wasn't running from them, she was running from Nicolae!"

"She was running from all of them, and it's not for the reason you think," I said firmly, giving her no choice but to listen. "Those people might be blood, Ellie, but they are *not* your family. They're just using you."

"And what is Nicolae trying to do?" she demanded. "Even if what you say is true, you really think he's any different?"

"Yes. I know he is."

"Why?" she asked, folding her arms. "Why would mom have run from him if she wasn't afraid of him? Why would Nicolae give a damn what happens to either of us if it's not for his own selfish reasons?"

"Because he's your father," I blurted out, knowing the truth was the only thing that was going to make her see reason. The truth that had lingered in my mind's attic alongside the truth about my failing health, and if I unpacked it, I could keep her from turning on the one person who had the means to protect her. While she was still stunned into silence, I continued, "I believe that's why your mom ran. She knew she was pregnant, and she didn't want this life for you. She didn't want you to be a pawn for the wolves to use in their political games. She wanted better for you, and that's what happened."

"That's... that's insane," she sputtered. "*You're* my dad."

"Of course I am," I said, reaching for her hand. "I always have been, and I always will be. It doesn't matter if you're mine by blood, you are mine in every single way that matters. But I've had to come to terms with the fact that you're probably his, too. And I would rather share you with someone who can protect you than see you get used and hurt by the people who were willing to kill their own child."

I could feel her growing more livid as I spoke, and she pulled away from me. "No," she seethed. "He's lying. You're lying."

"I wish that was true, but it isn't. I think if you put aside everything you've been told and listen for what your heart says—the way I always taught you—you'll realize the same," I said gently. It killed me to know that I was hurting her, that my words were turning her world upside-down the same way Nicolae's had upturned mine, but this was the only way I could make her understand. "Nicolae may be a monster, but he's not the kind your grandparents are."

"I don't want to hear this," she growled, stalking toward the elevator. I followed her as she repeatedly stabbed the button with her finger, infuriated that her enraged exit was hampered by the slowness of machinery.

"Ellie," I pleaded. "I know you're upset —"

"Don't," she hissed, turning on me as the doors slid open. "Don't follow me." There it was again. That feral look that made her so unrecognizable, and yet so like her mother. She frowned, shaking her head as she looked me over. "I don't know what it is, but you've changed. You're not yourself."

Well, that made two of us. My heart broke as I let the doors close, sealing my baby girl away after I'd waited so long to see her. Not that I was going to let her get far. I stalked into Nicolae's bedroom and out through the fire escape. If she thought she could just run off after I'd finally gotten her back, she had another thing coming. Werewolf or not, I was *not* going to be led around by my own child.

By the time I made it to the bottom of the many, many stairs, Mason was waiting for me like he'd expected my descent all along. Hell, he'd probably heard me panting and hacking as I ran.

"Going somewhere?"

"I have to stop Ellie," I growled, pushing past him.

He grabbed me by the arm, and just as I was about to remind him that fucking his father made me his step daddy, he said, "Let her go. She's not getting far. Nicolae has people watching her."

Of course he did. "Well, I don't want her out there. It's almost dark."

Mason arched his eyebrow and scowled around his cigarette. "She's an Alpha. There's nothing worse out there."

A fair point, but it did nothing to ease the instinctive reaction of knowing my daughter was running around a strange city alone. "I don't care."

"You can go after her if you want," he said with a shrug. "I don't know what happened, but I was her age recently enough to know that whatever you're fighting over, stopping her is only going to push her further away."

I fucking hated it when an Ursache was right. Especially when it was Mason, but he had a point. "You're sure she's safe?"

"She can't hail a cab without being within ten feet of one of our soldiers, and she won't make it out of the city."

"How do you know?"

"Because Nicolae put a tracer in her phone. Come on," Mason said, putting his hand on my shoulder to lead me toward the front of the building. "You're not going to survive the stairs again."

He was probably right. "So now he's got you watching me, huh?"

"We trade off," he answered.

"You know, you really shouldn't call your father by his first name," I grumbled, needing to bitch about something so I'd feel less pathetic for being escorted back into the building like an asthmatic old man. After flying down all those stairs, I felt like one. "It's disrespectful."

"I'll keep that in mind," he said, opening the door to the condo lobby. A small brown dog was sitting on one of the couches, gnawing on a throw pillow. There was no shortage of street dogs in Bucharest, but it was the first time I'd seen one inside. It was markedly wolflike, all legs and ears and teeth.

"You guys get a pet?"

"That's Andrei," Mason answered. The pup's ears perked up at the sound of his name. He dove off the couch to run over to Mason, pawing at the young Alpha's pant leg. "He prefers this form."

"I think I do, too," I muttered. "He's not as terrifying."

The pup yapped at me and I bent down to pick him up. He squirmed and snarled like he wanted to rip my face off, but he gave up in record time when he realized I wasn't going to let him down. "Does he just run around loose all day?"

"Why wouldn't he?"

I frowned, holding Andrei to my chest at the risk of getting bitten. He was making the sounds of a possessed hamster in its death throes now that he realized he was trapped.

"He should be in school," I said.

"We tried that. He bit the teacher and ate *everyone's* homework. He's fine like this."

"He is not fine. He's as much a human as he is wolf, and he deserves to be looked after properly."

"Fine, then. You watch him. It's your condo."

I blinked. Talk about foot in mouth. I stared down at the rabid little imp who'd finally stopped squirming and snuggled into my arms, obviously forgetting how angry he was with me. *Shit.* "I'll take him until I get the chance to talk to Nicolae," I muttered.

Mason shrugged and walked to the elevator, leaving me with my new charge. I followed him, trying in vain to keep the pup from destroying the drawstrings hanging from my hoodie. I gave up on taking it away from him when he seemed to think my fingers would be a viable replacement.

The second we got back to the condo and left our giant escort behind, Andrei sprang out of my arms and stopped to sniff the air before pawing at the counter and trying to reach the snacks. At least he was too short to do much damage in this form.

"Chocolate is not for puppies," I said, clearing off the counter. "The last thing *you* need is a sugar rush."

He nipped at my heels, but I ignored him, pulling out a package of fresh steak from the refrigerator. It felt wrong to feed a sentient creature from a bowl on the floor, however much he was used to it, so I put it on the coffee table and he devoured it. At least he was slightly easier to manage when he didn't have opposable thumbs.

Nicolae was still gone and I'd managed to accept that Ellie wasn't coming back anytime soon, so I sat down on the couch to catch my breath and put on some TV to distract myself. As soon as he'd licked the bowl clean, Andrei leaped up onto the couch to join me, tongue hanging out and piercing eyes brimming with mischief. What the hell had I gotten myself into?

My nose wrinkled. "You smell like you rolled in rancid fish and washed up in rainwater."

He just stared at me. Maybe Nicolae was right about most wolves not having all their human faculties when they shifted. The lights were on, but no one was home. I scooped him up and carried him over to the kitchen sink, determined to at least make the little beast stink less. And I could use a distraction. A cute distraction in the form of a child—a wolf child, but a child nonetheless.

I lowered him into the lukewarm water and tapped my finger to his slimy nose. He had *definitely* gotten into the trash. "Stay."

"*Bek!*" he retorted, no doubt something belligerent in dog language, but despite all the splashing around, he obeyed.

I rummaged around under the cabinets in search of something to wash him with. You'd think a house full of wolves would have something, but they didn't seem to put any stock in flea shampoo. I'd heard mild dish soap was pretty much the same thing, so I poured it all over him and rubbed it into his wet fur, trying to get all the way to skin that had likely only seen water when it rained. He let me scrub him, snapping at the bubbles and grimacing at the taste whenever he succeeded in gulping one down. At least it was keeping him occupied while I rinsed him until the water swirling down the drain finally ran clear.

"Alright, now you're at least passable as a respectable house pet," I said, wrapping him up in a clean towel. "That's step one and the end game is getting them to send you back to school, so we've got a lot of ground to cover between now and then."

I doubted he understood a word I was saying, but he burrowed into the towel and seemed much less feral now that he was fed and clean. While I was busy fawning over the wild baby, the elevator doors opened and I was both disappointed and relieved to see Nicolae.

He looked about as exhausted as I was as he eyed Andrei in confusion. "Ellie has been gone all of an hour and you've already replaced her with a puppy?"

"Of course not. And he's not a puppy, he's a kid who turns into one," I corrected. "You know where she is?"

"Of course I know where she is. My guards called me the moment she left the front door."

I breathed a sigh of relief. "I guess you know what happened, then."

"Not really." He tossed his jacket over the back of the couch and came over to scratch Andrei's ears. The puppy burrowed his face into the Alpha's palm. "Care to fill me in on the details?"

"She's convinced that the people who killed her mother hung the stars and she tried to use her voice to control my thoughts. Typical teenage problems," I said dryly.

Nicolae sighed. "I warned you, this transition would not be an easy one." He paused, watching me closely. "What brought on this argument?"

"Nothing," I lied, not ready to trust him with the truth even if I didn't believe he was the monster Ellie thought he was. I knew what he'd say if he found out I'd disobeyed his order to keep the truth from her.

He kept staring and I could tell he was trying to decide whether he believed me. Finally, he nodded to Andrei. "So, how did this happen? And why do I get the feeling I'm going to need to clear out another guest room?"

"He can't just run around loose without any supervision," I said firmly. "He could get hurt."

"The betas watch him, but if you're unsatisfied with the way they're caring for him, you're welcome to take over."

I watched him through squinted eyes. "You gave in pretty easily on that."

"I never give in," he said pointedly, reaching past me for the bottle on the counter. "I just think it wouldn't be the worst thing in the world for you to have a diversion, and you're right. Andrei does need a firmer hand. Two birds, one stone."

"A diversion?" I asked. "I'm not a pet that needs to be kept occupied."

He smirked, drinking straight from the bottle. Guess it was that kind of day for him, too. "You're right. If you were my pet, I would've taken you back a long time ago."

"I'd tell you to shove you-know-what up you-know-where if *he* wasn't in the room," I muttered.

"The only words he's said in English so far are 'eat shit.' He's heard worse."

I sighed. "Guess I have my work cut out for me."

"I don't doubt you'll succeed. You're a natural mother," he replied, going into the kitchen.

I left Andrei on the couch and followed Nicolae. "We've got a problem," I said once we were out of earshot, not that the pup was likely to care about our conversation in the first place.

"We've got a lot of problems, in case you haven't noticed. You'll have to be more specific."

"Ellie pulled a mind control trick on me."

"Yes, you mentioned that."

"Well?" I pressed.

"I'm thinking."

"About what?"

He gave me a look. "You ask a lot of questions."

"You don't give enough answers," I shot back.

"I'm not surprised that Ellie tried to compel you. What's more concerning is that you were able to resist her."

"Isn't that a good thing?"

"Good, yes, at least in this case. But it shouldn't be possible."

I could certainly see why me being immune to wolf tricks would be a problem in Nicolae's book, but it came as a relief to me. Except for the fact that it was a selective ability. "I don't understand. You didn't have any trouble."

"To the contrary. You're more responsive to my control than any wolf."

"So why doesn't hers work? Is it because...?" I trailed off when I remembered that the chances Ellie was biologically mine were not high.

"I doubt it. It's more likely that the anomaly is in your response to me, but there's only one way to be sure."

"You know why it's concerning when you say things like that, right?"

He chose to send a text from his phone instead of answering me. Not a minute later, Mason came in through the hallway.

"You're using the fire escape now?" I muttered.

"I lived here before you did," he reminded me, looking toward his father. "What is it?"

"I need your help with an experiment. Try to compel Jack."

I didn't like the way his face lit up at the prospect, and I especially didn't like that he looked at me like a dog that had just been given permission to eat the cat. "To do what?"

"Something he'd object to."

"Nicolae!"

Mason set his eyes on me, smirking. "Get down on your knees."

"Go to hell," I growled. I could feel the push to obey, but after resisting compulsion so recently, it came a bit easier.

Mason shrugged. "Want me to try something else?"

"No, that will do," murmured Nicolae, studying me. "You may

go, Mason. Make sure they send me hourly reports about Ellie's whereabouts."

"I will, but the last I heard, she'd settled in a hotel across town. I think she saw the guy on her tail."

"Good," said Nicolae. "Better that she knows what she's up against."

Mason left and I was more confused than I'd been before. "What does that mean?"

"Down on your knees," Nicolae said instead of replying.

This time, there was no hesitation. No thinking, no room for resistance. I was on my knees before him and he watched me with a vaguely satisfied look in his eyes. "Only mated wolves are resistant to the compulsion of any other," he answered.

"But I'm not a wolf," I reminded him.

"You are quite human," he said with an air of affection as he reached out to pull me back onto the couch beside him. "As for what it means, I don't know. But I plan on finding out."

I leaned into him, both because I was exhausted and because for some strange reason, being close to him made me feel better even though he was the root of my stress—indirectly or not. To my surprise, he draped his arm around me and we just stayed there, pretending to sit and watch mindless TV like normal people. I knew it wouldn't last, and I wasn't even sure I wanted to, but it was the first time in at least a year I felt at home.

EIGHTEEN

WHEN ELLIE finally showed up three days later, I was at a loss for what to say despite having rehearsed what I would say when I got the chance.

"Just let me talk," she pleaded, dropping her bag by the door as Andrei took off to hide from the newcomer.

"Okay," I said, deciding I needed to sit down. The meds the doctor had given me in the interim were helping to reduce the frequency of my coughing episodes, but I still had to make an effort not to get too worked up. I just hoped she had something stronger to give me for the hunt. That was yet another fun bit of news I still had to break to Ellie.

By the way, you know that guy your mom almost married? I'm mated to him now.

"I'm sorry for leaving the way I did. What you said, it..." She frowned, and it was hard to tell if she was frustrated at herself or at me.

"I know," I said gently. "Maybe I made a mistake telling you at all. I'm not proud of the way I've handled any of this. I know I failed you, and I'm still trying to figure out how to protect you when I don't even understand this world you're apart of."

"Would you just let me apologize?" she muttered. "I *know* you're just trying to protect me." Her expression softened as she sat next to me on the couch. "You always do, but you can't. Not anymore."

She was apologizing for the words she'd spoken before, but those were the ones that broke my heart. Ever since the day I'd first held her in my arms, knowing she was mine to protect and care for was both the greatest burden I'd ever born and the greatest honor. It gave me purpose, and if I couldn't protect her, what the hell was I supposed to do with myself? It was a fear that had crossed my mind plenty of times, but hearing her voice that fear was absolute devastation.

"I'm never going to stop protecting you, Ellie. Not until the day I die."

"I know. That's what scares me," she whispered. "I know this is all a shock to you, but I think somewhere deep down, I always knew. This world... it's foreign, but in some ways, it makes more sense to me than the one I grew up in. I always thought I didn't fit in because I was trans, or maybe just because I was *me*, but now I know the truth. All those dreams I had about running in the forest—feeling the wind in my fur, becoming something more than what I was—they weren't just dreams. They were inside me the whole time. What mom kept from us both."

"She was just trying to protect you, baby girl. You have to understand that. She made mistakes, and she hurt us both, but she thought she was doing the right thing."

"So did everyone else who's ever done the wrong thing," she said bitterly. "She ran from her responsibilities, and she paid the price for it."

"Ellie!"

"It's the truth. You don't understand," she said, shaking her head. "You're not a wolf."

"You've lived your entire life as a human, too, Ellie. This isn't you."

"Yes, it is," she growled. "That's what you don't get. This *is* me. I don't know who to trust anymore, and I don't know where I belong, but I know I belong with my own kind more than I ever did with yours."

The words stung, but I could sense how hard it was for her to say them, so I made myself listen rather than argue the way I wanted to.

"You always supported me, in everything," she said shakily, taking my hand. "Even when you didn't understand, I could tell you wanted to."

"Always." Something told me I wasn't going to like where she was going with this, so I braced myself.

"I love you, daddy, but there are things you don't understand. Things you never could, and shouldn't have to. You don't know what it's like to feel like there's a monster inside of you, clawing to get out." The strain in her voice made me want to attack whatever was causing her distress, but I knew this wasn't something I could fix. The pain she was feeling came from within, and for once, I didn't know how to help her. "To know that if I'd shifted back then, I could have hurt you and who knows how many other people..."

"But you didn't," I said, squeezing her hand.

"I would have." Her eyes darkened. "And rather than telling me the truth, so I could prepare and learn to control what I was, she suppressed it. She probably would have done that forever, just so I couldn't go running back to the life she left behind. She would have let me live a lie forever so she could go on living hers."

"You don't know that," I said, compelled to defend Francesca even when her motives were a mystery to me.

"She was willing to let me be miserable because she couldn't handle the idea of me not being her precious Allen," she challenged. "Because she thought giving me the 'normal human life' I never asked for, even if it meant separating me from the only people besides you who would ever accept me for who and what I was, meant she got to decide how everything played out. To make all my choices for me. To tell me who to be."

I grimaced. I knew she was right. "She would have told you about being a wolf eventually. She would have had to."

"That's what I thought. Claire told me the truth," she said, pulling out a chain from beneath her shirt. It held Francesca's golden class ring. I still remembered Ellie receiving it on her thirteenth birthday. Francesca had always been weirdly insistent about her wearing it, but she was weird about everything when it came to her carefully guarded past. "Do you know what this is?"

"Yes. It's your mother's."

She laughed, looking down at the ring as she turned it around to catch the light in the ruby facets. "Right. Just a nice memento from her secretive past, right?" Her smile cracked. "It's cursed."

"Cursed?" I shook my head. "I don't know what you mean."

"It isn't just the hormone blockers that kept me from shifting, dad. Mom had this cursed to try to prevent it from *ever* happening."

It took some time for that to sink in, and when it did, it felt like poison in my veins. "Why would she do that?"

"Because she was fine with changing who I am, as long as it was *her* choice," she replied.

I buried my head in my hands, because it was getting hard to think. Was it ever going to end? Or was I just going to keep getting bombarded by fresh revelations that my wife, my companion who I was supposed to spend all my years with, was not the person I'd thought she was?

"I know about the affair, dad," she said somberly, breaking me out of my downward spiral. "I know about a lot of things you guys thought I didn't. I accepted who mom was a long time ago, and I'm still going to avenge her, but you have to accept it too. You don't owe her anything, and you shouldn't have to waste the rest of your life cleaning up after her mess."

"I'm not wasting anything. What are you trying to say?"

"I'm saying I want you to go home," she answered. "I want you to live the life you would have had without her and stop sacrificing everything to protect her memory. Or me, for that matter."

"I'm not sacrificing shit," I said, standing. "You *are* my life, and if you don't get that, I really haven't done my job."

She just gave me that patient smile that made her seem older and wiser even if her words were the epitome of naïveté. Maybe she didn't think she needed me, but she did. I had to believe that, even if it was only to justify my own existence. "Dad, I'm going to be okay. It's not like it was before. I have power here. Real power, and I'm going to do something with it, starting with finding out who really killed mom. Maybe then we can both let her go."

"I'm not going anywhere, and all this talk of vengeance and power stops here," I said firmly. "You might think you have everything figured out, and I'm glad that you finally feel like you belong. That's all I've ever wanted for you," I admitted. "But there's still so much you don't understand. Stuff about life that you don't have the experience to grasp. I'm not gonna let you throw it away, and I'm not letting you go back to those people. You might be wise beyond your years, but you're still a child."

"And how are you going to stop me from going back?" she challenged, standing. "If the Majerus pack is really responsible for mom's death, that's all the more reason for me to return."

"How am I going to stop you?" I laughed. "For starters, you're grounded."

She rolled her eyes. "You can't ground me, dad. We're a little far past that."

"Oh, are we now?" I raised my eyebrows. Andrei wandered over from the bone he'd been gnawing on to see what all the commotion was about. "You think becoming a wolf princess means you're too big of a deal to listen to your old man?"

"If you want to put it like that, yes," she said, folding her arms. "'I'm just doing what's best for you.' Ring any bells?"

"Sure does. But how about you try this one on for size? If you refuse to obey me as your father, you're going to obey me as the co-leader of this pack."

Her eyes narrowed in confusion. "What are you talking about?"

I turned around and pulled my collar down enough to reveal Nicolae's mark. The shock on her face would have been a bit more satisfying if I wasn't having to play power games to get my usually obedient daughter to listen to me. "You didn't..."

"I had to, in order to get you back," I muttered. "Nicolae and I had to be a united front to protect you from the Majerus family, and I did *not* give up my freedom to some Alpha douchebag who wears sunglasses indoors so you could get yourself killed running around like you're little miss thing. Consider yourself overruled."

"I can't fucking believe you," she seethed. "You whored yourself out to *Nicolae Ursache?*"

"Okay, that's it. You're grounded for a month, and if I hear another foul word out of your mouth, it's two."

"You can't do that!"

"Watch me!" I bellowed.

She stalked toward the balcony door and flung it open, glowering at me.

"Where the hell do you think you're going?"

"Out," she snapped, climbing up onto the railing. I lunged, but by the time I reached the balcony, she had already dropped down to the one below, crouched like a cat and entirely unscathed. She shot me one last glare before disappearing over the next railing.

"Son of a..."

A teenage tantrum was one thing. A superpowered teenage tantrum was not something I was prepared for. I ran to the phone and dialed Nicolae's number. To my surprise, he actually picked up.

"Jack? What's wrong?"

"We have a code red."

He paused. "What is that supposed to mean?"

"I don't know, okay? It sounded like something you'd say," I muttered. "Ellie ran off again, and I need you to have your men catch her. And lock her up."

"Lock her up? What the hell happened while I was gone?"

"A power struggle," I muttered. It wasn't one I planned on losing, either. "She knows we're mated, and there's a lot more I need to talk to you about. Just get here as soon as you can, okay?"

"I'll take care of it." I could hear other people speaking Romanian in the background and realized he was probably in the middle of some secret werewolf meeting, but he was still going to drop what he was doing to help me with my quickly unraveling domestic crisis.

When exactly had I gone from putting on a stoic face around him to seeing him as an ally?

"Thank you," I said, hanging up. I stared down at my wild puppy, who was watching me with an open-mouthed grin and wagging his tail. "I can't believe I'm saying this, but you're officially the good kid."

NINETEEN

NICOLAE MADE it home in ten minutes, and judging from how out of breath he was and how uncharacteristically rumpled his clothes were, I got the feeling he'd shifted to run the whole way. "Are you alright?" he asked, looking me over with unmistakable worry in his gaze. He gripped my arm and the touch that once infuriated me immediately released all the tension I'd been holding.

"I'm fine," I said, unconsciously stepping closer to him. "Where is Ellie?"

"Vasil found her trying to leave through a weak spot on the border. She's in custody."

"Somewhere secure?"

"If our prison is capable of holding Alphas that have transformed themselves into bloodthirsty killing machines, I think it can manage her."

"Prison?" I grimaced.

"It's only temporary, but it sounded serious on the phone, so I assumed her safety was more of a priority than her comfort."

"No, you're right. Thank you," I said, sighing. I really had to stop doing that. It always made me cough.

"Sit down," he muttered, pushing me into a chair. "Where's your inhaler?"

"I'm fine," I said, clearing my throat. "Really. Just stressed."

"That's the problem. You can't keep getting worked up like this, it's bad for your health."

I decided not to remind him that my health was probably a lost cause at this point, and decided at the same time to not let myself think about the report I'd have to hear in a couple of days. It was still a shock that he cared and I wouldn't let myself think about why.

"Tell me what happened," he said, his voice low and grave.

I chewed my bottom lip in contemplation. "You're gonna be pissed."

"I'm sure. Tell me anyway."

"First, I want you to swear to me that whatever I tell you, you're not going to take it out on Ellie."

"I have staked my entire reputation *and* my role as the leader of this pack on protecting her. She is my daughter, too, whether it's by blood or by law," he said, scowling at me. "I can't protect her if I don't know what's going on, and I can't help you if you won't talk to me."

"Okay, fair enough. I should probably start with the fact that she's convinced you're the one who killed Francesca, and she's planning on getting revenge. I talked her down, but I don't think I believe her when she admits she might be wrong. That the Majerus pack might have brainwashed her."

He stared blankly at me. "Is that all?"

"Why do you say that like you're not even slightly surprised?"

"Because I'm not." He shrugged. "It's easy enough to piece together. She is a teenager and I am, for all intents and purposes, her stepfather. God knows I tried to kill mine enough times."

"You've got some fucked up expectations of family dynamics, and we're gonna talk about that one day," I said. "But for now, aren't you the slightest bit concerned that she wants to kill you?"

"She can try if she likes. She's a young Alpha, convinced that she knows everything and drunk on her newfound power."

"Yeah. I noticed she developed the ability to scale tall buildings overnight. You didn't think you should warn me about that?"

"You were dealing with a lot. There were things I didn't want to add to your plate. The news about the ring, for example. I'm sure she told you."

"Yet another posthumous gift from Francesca," I muttered.

"Ellie is angry. At her mother, at me, at herself. You are the easiest target right now. It's not personal."

"She told me I couldn't protect her anymore, Nick. She looked me in the eye and openly defied me."

"She is a teenager. What do you expect?"

"Not that! Not from her."

Nicolae sighed. "She's a werewolf. You should expect everything. She's challenging boundaries, coming into her own as a person and as an Alpha," he said, sitting across from me. "It was bound to happen eventually. If it makes you feel any better, when Mason was her age, he went for my throat when we were on a run and tried to challenge me in front of the entire pack."

"It doesn't actually, but how the hell did you resolve that?"

"I kicked his ass and bought him a drink after."

"Yeah, well, neither of those is gonna solve this problem. I'm not kicking my daughter's ass." Not like I could've even if I wanted to.

"My point is, all adolescents try to kill their parents at some point. If it's not a literal attempt on your life, it's going for the emotional kill, saying things they don't mean in order to push you away and give them the room they need to spread their wings. The good news is, you're not dealing with this alone." He gave me a look. "Unless of course you're still planning on running?"

"How did you—?"

"I know you, Jack. Better than you think. Better than I know myself sometimes," he muttered.

I wasn't sure what to make of that, but he stood and took my hand to pull me to my feet. "Some distance will do you both good. Give you time to cool off, and her to put things in perspective. She will come around."

"What if she doesn't?"

He pulled me to him, his breath rushing over my forehead, cooling the heat under my skin. "It will work out. You need to rest."

Rest was the last thing on my mind when his hands were on me, but I nodded. "Maybe you're right. It's been a long day."

"Where is Andrei?" he asked warily, looking around the living room.

"I put him to bed in his room."

"It's *his* room now?"

"It's full of dog toys and both human and dog beds, so yeah. It's also the only containment he hasn't figured a way out of."

"I'm confused. Are you raising him as a puppy or as a human?"

"I'll tell you when I figure that out," I muttered, heading toward my room.

Nicolae took my hand and led me down the other hall. When we reached his room, he locked the door and my heart leaped. I'd been ready to collapse a minute ago, but suddenly, the idea of staying awake for a little bit longer didn't seem that bad.

"I feel like I haven't had you alone in a long time," he murmured, starting to unbutton my shirt.

I'd given up on trying to control the way my body responded to his closeness. My heart was always going to flutter and my breath was always going to be even harder to come by and my head was always going to spin. It was just the way it was, but it was a fair price for the benefit. He started unfastening my belt and I lost my English even though I didn't have another language to fall back on. Just a few scraps of Romanian, mostly words he said so beautifully that they got stuck in my memory. "I didn't think you wanted me alone."

He looked down at me, his eyes ablaze as he pushed me gently up against the door. "I want many things that surprise me these days. All of them revolving around you."

I swallowed hard. "What am I supposed to say to that?"

"Nothing," he said against my lips. They were the only soft part of him and when they brushed mine, my knees gave. Good thing his knee was there between my legs. The only things separating us were my boxers and his slacks, but that was easy enough to resolve. "Say nothing. Let me distract you."

He took my face in his hand, sweeping his thumb across my lips. They parted in a gasp as he dipped his thumb into my mouth and slid it down over my tongue. My lips closed around it instinctively and I closed my eyes, imagining something other than his digit. When I finally opened my eyes, his were nearly black with desire.

"It's wrong," he breathed, lowering his hand to my throat. My head fell back against the door as his grip tightened, not enough to actually inhibit my breath, but enough to send a thrill that went straight to my half-erect cock.

"What is?" I asked, afraid to lift my voice above a whisper. I assumed he meant the fact that I was half-naked and we were quite obviously about to fuck.

"What you do to me," he answered.

I wet my lips and tried to collect myself rather than begging him to choke me harder. What was it he'd said? *I want many things that surprise me.* Well, I wanted things that terrified me.

"Tell me something," he demanded, brushing his lips over my jaw with tenderness that felt cruel. "Why do I want to open you up and pour myself into you until there is no part of you that isn't tainted by me?"

A rush of breath escaped me and I found myself incapable of taking another, but this time, I couldn't blame my traitorous lungs. This malady was all him, and only he held the cure. "Couldn't tell you," I rasped. "Sounds like something only a psychotic wingnut would say."

The toothy smile on those devil's lips was obscene. "And what does that make the man who begs for my touch?"

"I ain't begging for shit, fleabag," I grunted. "That was a one-time deal. Your words, remember?"

"I seem to remember making you come twice," he said, reversing our positions to push me onto the bed. "Or was it three times?"

"I don't remember. Must've been forgettable."

"Is that so?" He lowered himself onto me, only putting pressure on my crotch as he pressed his thigh against it. He'd been treating me like I was broken ever since they'd dragged me home from that bar, but I was too bewildered by the way he was stroking my hair to call him on it. "Then I'll have to give you something to remember."

He reached past my waistband and squeezed my dick just hard enough to hurt, easing up as soon as it did. I smothered a moan in his neck, my arms wrapped tight around his neck. He wasn't even stroking me, all he was doing was running his fingers around the tip to make me even more sensitive. He tugged my boxers down and brought his fingers to his lips, sucking off the precum like it was a drug and he wanted to savor the essence until it was gone.

"On the bed," he said with the casual air of a man who knew he wouldn't be questioned.

I needed to sit down anyway, before I passed out. He took his time undressing before he sat down at the head of the bed. He wasn't even fully hard, but I had plans to change that. Before I could touch him, he pulled me onto his lap, maneuvering me to face him while I straddled his powerful thighs.

"You're going to ride me," he said, as if he was just filling me in on his plans. Lucky for him, I'd thought of little else since he'd started touching me, but I had to remind him that I wasn't just going to roll over and do whatever he said. Not without being a hell of a lot closer to orgasm, anyway.

I raised myself, pressing my shaft against his muscular chest, and gripped a fistful of his hair. His eyes widened in surprise, but he could have pulled my hand away or scolded me and he didn't. I kept my eyes on him as I reached down and stroked his shaft with my free hand. Three times and he was stiff as a board. He was also slick enough for me to consider taking him without bothering with lube, but he had other ideas. He pulled the bottle out and I snatched it from him in frustration.

"Eager tonight, are we?" he asked, clearly amused.

I knew he was only having me ride him because it was "safer" for me, but I wasn't going to pass up the chance to be in control, even if I was still getting fucked. I ignored his remark and slicked up his cock before positioning it at my entrance. I tossed the half-empty bottle aside and wiped my hand off on the sheets we were going to ruin anyway before gripping his shoulders for balance. I had a harder time getting him in than he had, and he was well aware.

"If you need help..." he offered in a smug tone.

"I can do it myself," I growled. "The angle's just hard, that's all."

"Mmh. It's nice from where I'm at," he mused, running his hands down my chest. The touch made me shiver and his lubed up member slipped out of position.

"Would you stop groping me until I'm on your cock?"

"I'm fairly certain *those* words have never been uttered outside of a whorehouse."

"That's where you're gonna have to go if you don't hold still," I grunted, readjusting. He reached underneath me and grabbed his own dick, slipping it in along with a finger to pry me open. I dropped down a little in response to the breach and he slipped in even further.

The new position made me all the more aware of how thick he was and with his assistance, I moved my hands back to his shoulders. "It's like trying to sit on a fucking tree trunk," I muttered.

"Now that I would pay to see."

"Oh, shut up." I grimaced as I lowered myself a little more and decided it was a good thing I'd let him talk me into lube. Taking him without it was not only impractical, it was impossible.

Nicolae's hands closed around my sides, his fingers tickling my back. It was one of those zones he'd spoken of, and my body responded powerfully. I shivered and arched myself into him instinctively, relaxing enough to impale myself fully. He let out a lustful snarl and his grip tightened as my cock slapped against my torso from the sudden drop. Nicolae pushed his hand up against the underside of it like he was trying to knead the orgasm from me.

"Fuck," I gasped, surging up against him once more. His nostrils flared as he swallowed a moan from the way I tightened up around him. Two could play the cock torture game.

"*Tu diavol,*" he growled, nipping at my neck. Not hard enough to make me bleed and spread his venom, just hard enough to make me fear it. If he had any idea how much I craved that lethal bite...

Hell, if I was gonna die anyway, maybe that was how I wanted to go.

I didn't understand his words, but the intonation made it clear he was accusing me of something. Whatever it was, I decided to prove him right and ground my hips forward even though the pain was almost unbearable. He hadn't prepped me like last time, and I wouldn't have tolerated it. I was tired, but I needed release more than I needed sleep. I needed him. Pain was part of it. It wasn't a kink so much as another way to feel him.

Nicolae's breathing grew shallower the harder I rode him, and in my attempt to brace myself, I realized my nails had drawn bloody crescents on his shoulders. He didn't seem to notice, or mind if he did. His hands were much gentler as they ran up and down my thighs, teasing my cock with their close proximity. I wanted him to touch it, but I didn't want him to stop what he was doing. It felt equally erotic. Anywhere he touched me instantly shivered with lust. His right hand finally wandered back to my throbbing shaft and he gave it a tug.

My hips bucked, driving him deeper into me. His fingers glided over my sensitive tip and gathered precum on their tips. My cock was weeping with arousal, and the pleasure of him guiding himself into my spot with every rock of my hips had finally exceeded the ache.

"Let me adjust," he said suddenly, pressing his hand to my chest. "I need to pull out a little or I'll knot you."

"Give it to me," I whispered greedily, guiding his hand back between my legs.

"Jack, you're not well."

"Would you stop reminding me?" I grunted, clenching around him to hasten the process. I knew it was going to hurt, but I was more than willing to suffer for the thrill of it. "I need you. All of you."

He stared at me like my words made no sense at all. "You *enjoyed* that?"

All I could do was nod, dragging my nails down his chest to trace the path the beads of sweat dripping down from his neck were leaving. My teeth sank into the flesh of my bottom lip until it was swollen and sore, the same kind of addictive ache that made me want to keep bucking my hips and sinking down onto him.

He whispered something else my heart understood perfectly, even though it was in Romanian. His gentle, adoring intonation spoke to my soul. His hips lifted slightly and I felt his knot swell once more, inflating to compress my prostate and deliver a surge of pleasure and pain that short-circuited my brain. Nicolae's hand covered my mouth to muffle my scream and my teeth clamped down on his flesh out of instinct. I tasted blood and he groaned, but he didn't pull away. Instead, his other hand rested behind my head and he covered my mouth tighter since I was still making the sounds of the damned as I rode his knot and came onto his chest without even needing to touch myself. He finally wrenched his bleeding hand from my teeth and pulled me down for a crushing kiss.

The taste of his blood on my lips seemed to have some intensely erotic effect on him, and his cum exploded into me in violent spurts, hot and filling. I returned the kiss, burying my hands in his hair and rocking against him as he filled me with one load after another. My climax subsided long before his, and when we were both finally spent, he wrapped his arms around me and I collapsed against him.

I could still feel his pulse inside of me and took comfort in knowing he'd stay there for a while. "How was that for memorable?" he whispered.

I answered him with another kiss and smiled against his lips. "Next time, you ride me."

He cupped my cheek and rubbed his against the other side of my face to mark me with his scent, a surprisingly catlike gesture. Like it wasn't already coming out of my pores. "Never going to happen," he said in a breathless voice that was even more heavily accented than usual.

"Never hurts to ask."

It did, however, hurt to have a wolfman pull his knot out of your ass, even when it had mostly gone down. The pain was just a price I was willing to pay.

TWENTY

TIME FLIES by when you're waiting to find out how soon you were going to die. Nicolae was avoiding me, and I couldn't tell if it was because we'd fucked and that was just what he did, or because he didn't know what to say. Comforting wasn't his schtick, and being consoled wasn't mine.

Nicolae was like the tide. Every time he drew closer, I knew it was only a matter of time before he drifted even further away. He couldn't help it. It was just who he was. I wasn't going to be the one who changed him, and I didn't want to.

Whatever this was, I'd already promised myself that I wouldn't ruin it by wishing it was something it wasn't. That didn't mean I always succeeded. Every night since that one, we'd slept in our separate rooms, but I'd still roll over expecting him to be there. It was strange how someone who'd been your constant companion for sixteen years could become a distant memory in one, and how someone you barely knew could imprint themselves so deep in you that their presence became a pillar in a matter of weeks.

Sunday morning, I got up and got dressed. I didn't hear Nicolae, but he was always gone by that time of day, so I didn't bother to look for him. I went down the hall and got Andrei ready instead. I'd realized that bribing him with food was the only way to get him to hold human form for more than a few minutes, and he would only tolerate his damn pajamas, but at least we had progressed to the point where he was dressed and sitting at a table and holding a fork. He was holding it grudgingly and grasping it like a knife he planned to stab someone with, but he was holding it nonetheless. I felt an absurd sense of accomplishment as I watched him jab his waffles with it, snarling before he took a bite.

It occurred to me as we went about our breakfast routine that it was cruel to let him get attached to me when I might not be there for the little scamp much longer. I'd already made arrangements for him to stay in the pack daycare while I went to my doctor's appointment. The teacher wasn't happy about it, but I assured her that we'd worked past devouring markers and toys and hoped it wouldn't turn out to be a lie. It would be good for him to form other connections.

Once we were done eating, I took Andrei downstairs and he was perfectly happy until we reached the daycare room and he heard the other kids laughing and playing. He put on the brakes and clung tighter to my hand.

"It's okay," I reassured him. "You're just going to be here for a little while until I get back from the doctor."

He shook his head violently, blond curls spilling out everywhere. With a vocalization that sounded an awful lot like a "no," he buried his face in my sweater.

I knelt down to be at eye level with him. "I know you don't like all the noise, but you're going to make friends. You'd like that, wouldn't ya?"

He scowled at me as the teacher came over. "Hello, Andrei," she said pleasantly. "Are you coming to join us?"

He bared his teeth at her.

"Sorry. Just give us a second," I pleaded. Once she'd gone back to the other children, I faced Andrei and looked him in the eye. "Listen, kid. I know you understand more than everyone thinks. Now, I'm gonna tell you what I told Ellie on her first day of school. Everything worth doing starts out scary. You're gonna make friends and play games and do crafts and eat snacks, and you're gonna have so much fun you won't even wanna leave, but you've gotta take that first step. And I'm going to be right down the hall."

Maybe it was wishful thinking, but he seemed to be listening and thinking about what I'd said. "Come back?" he finally whispered in his soft, raspy voice.

My heart ached. "Yeah," I choked out, knowing there was probably going to come a day soon when the answer would be different. "Of course I'm coming back. And soon."

He grunted in acknowledgment and hesitated at the door a second before carefully putting his foot over the threshold. I couldn't help but smile as I watched him inch into the room. A little girl came over immediately and whacked him on the arm with a cry of, "Tag, you're it!"

Andrei blinked at her in shock before he took off after her with a roar. The other kids shrieked and laughed, and I watched just to make sure he wasn't going to go completely feral when he caught one. When I was satisfied that he was going to be alright, I closed the door and turned only to find Nicolae watching me from the hall. "How long have you been there?"

"A while," he answered, slipping his hand into his pocket. "I've never heard him talk before."

"Neither have I," I admitted.

"You're good with people," he murmured, walking toward me. "Even Mason is starting to hate you less."

"That's not much of an endorsement."

"Oh, it is. Mason still hates *me*," he snorted. "It's rare for the pack to accept an outsider. Rarer still for them to accept a human."

"Guess it's just that southern charm," I teased. "I was starting to think you'd moved out."

Guilt flickered over his expression. "I'm sorry I haven't been around. I needed time to think."

"You don't need to apologize. You don't owe me anything."

He seemed to want to say something, but I decided to spare us both. "I should get going, I'm due across the hall in five minutes."

"Jack, wait," he said, taking my wrist. It wasn't the first time, but as firm as his grasp was, it was gentle. When I met his eyes, they were full of desperation. "I want to be with you."

I stared at him, afraid of how my heart shaped itself around those words even though my brain knew I'd heard them the wrong way. "I guess you can come if you want."

"No. I mean, yes," he said, frowning like he was as confused as I was by his momentary lapse in composure. "But that's not what I was trying to say."

"What *are* you trying to say?" I asked, as afraid of his answer as I was to my reaction to it.

"I want to be *with* you. Not just now, but always. Not just as my mate in name only, or the man I fuck because I can't convince myself to stay away." His voice was so raw and full of passion that it might have sounded like anger, if I didn't know the subtle shades of him so well. "Whatever those X-rays show, I want to care for you and call you mine for as long as we have. As long as you'll allow me."

Call you mine... Those words were too good to be true. He was speaking too plainly for me to doubt that he'd said them, which meant I had to be dreaming. The constant pain in my chest said otherwise. "Nicolae... I don't know what to say to that."

He pulled something out of his jacket and I began to reconsider the possibility that I was dreaming, or hallucinating, when he got down on one knee. A few wolves who were walking across the corridor gave us some strange glances, but they didn't say a word. "Say 'yes.' And remember, I can make you." He said it in a wry tone, but the look in his eyes made me doubt he was entirely joking.

"You're fucking serious," I muttered in disbelief, my face burning with a combination of humiliation and infatuation. "Have you lost your damn mind?"

"Absolutely. I've had three days to trace back my steps and I've come to the conclusion that there's no reclaiming it, so I may as well dedicate myself to insanity." He grabbed my hand and pulled the ring out of the box. I was torn between a racing heart and a dead one as he put the ring on my finger alongside the band I still wore from my union with Francesca. When he looked up at me, I just quit. I quit trying to pretend like my entire world didn't revolve around this man, I quit trying to pretend like I hadn't fallen in love with him, I quit trying to pretend like there was any part of me left that was strong or decent enough to resist that this thing we'd both been trying to fight was going to drag us to hell.

"It is ironic, is it not?" he asked, brushing his thumb over the stacked rings on my left hand. "When we met, the sight of you wearing this band enraged me. I couldn't stand the thought of sharing her with you. Now I cannot stand that you were hers. I'm every bit the savage monster you saw me for that day on the side of the road, and I must possess every part of you, past and present."

I couldn't breathe. Not in an "I'm dying" kind of way, but in an "I think I'm experiencing two-decades-delayed alcohol-induced brain damage because this can't actually be happening" way.

"Jack?" His tone was impatient, because even down on one knee, he was still an entitled, egotistical fuck who thought he shouldn't have to wait for anyone. And goddammit, he didn't.

"Just to clarify. You're asking me to *marry* you?"

He frowned. "What else would I be doing, you backwoods brat?"

"Would you just stand up?" I muttered, looking around. We were still being watched. Now there was a fucking crowd.

"Say 'yes.'"

Now he was using humiliation rather than compulsion to force my hand. Prick. "Yes," I growled through my teeth.

He gave me a victorious smirk as he rose to tower over me once more. "There, that wasn't so hard, was it?"

"I can't believe you."

"You said yes, didn't you?"

"That doesn't mean anything!"

"You're already my mate, what's the problem with making it official by human standards?"

"It's just... it's weird, okay? And unexpected, and," I lowered my voice, "there's a chance I'm not even gonna be around for the honeymoon."

A shadow came over him, like something had blocked out the sun. "I'm not letting you go that easily. You may have already given up, and I know you're afraid to face this, but I'm not leaving you a choice. You're mine. Whether it's for a month or a lifetime, you're mine and I will not let you do this alone."

I tried to swallow, but the knot in my throat wouldn't let me. "So," I said, realizing if I didn't say something, the tears in my eyes were going to give him fodder for weeks to come. And I knew him well enough to know that, yes, he would absolutely mock me minutes after he proposed to me, and then I would have to tell him to fuck off in front of his pack. It was kind of our thing. "How long've you been carrying around that ring, or did you just get it out of a vending machine this morning?"

I realized he'd never let go of my hand when he pushed his fingers through the spaces in mine and pressed his forehead against my bangs. "You'll find out if your finger turns green, won't you?"

Smiling was just about the last thing I imagined I'd have reason to do today, but it was so hard to fight it when he was this close. "I hope you realize, you made me late for my appointment."

"It doesn't matter," he said, kissing my cheek. "I know the management."

"Oh, yeah. I heard he's a real prick."

His husky laugh made me wish we weren't in the middle of a public floor, surrounded by wolves trying to pretend like they were just going about their business. "So I've heard."

KEL'S OFFICE was the kind of place that made you feel like you had the flu even if you didn't. As I sat on a lumpy exam table staring at the blank gray slate that would soon be lit up with images of my insides, I felt like time had slowed down on purpose. The day I'd been putting off for years was finally here, and it was punishing me for running from it for so long.

Nicolae was across the room, looking absurd in the clinical surroundings with his black duster and black boots and black clothes and the aura to match. He'd taken an interest in the cotton balls sitting in a canister by the sink.

"You know, you don't have to be here for this. I'm sure you've got other shit to do," I said.

He gave me a look that said it wasn't even worth bothering with a verbal response and turned back to the cotton that was infinitely more interesting than my latest attempt to boot him out of the room.

A knock at the door announced the end of my stay in purgatory and possibly the beginning of the afterlife. The look on the doctor's face as she came in with a thick folder packed with white-edged X-rays didn't bode well. Neither did the fact that she needed so many of them. If there was nothing to see, there'd only be a few, I figured.

She seemed surprised to see Nicolae there, but she adjusted and gave me a nod. "Good to see you again, Jack."

"I'd say the same, but I get the feeling you're not gonna tell me anything I wanna hear."

She gave me a sympathetic smile. That was never a good sign, especially from someone who looked like she lived for watching political documentaries and giving out expired raisins on Halloween.

I watched her arrange a few of the X-rays on the lighted screens, and before she said a word, I knew the cloudy white splotches on the screen blocking out full view of my ribs weren't just cotton candy.

"As you can see here, your X-rays show some considerable abnormalities," Kel began, using her pen to gesture to the largest lesion. "I believe without a doubt that we're looking at advanced coal workers' pneumoconiosis," she said slowly, giving me time to process every word.

"Black lung disease?" Nicolae demanded, already prepared to fight.

I didn't know how he even knew what that was if I didn't, but then again, I'd been keeping my fingers in my ears all along. I'd been so prepared to hear it was cancer that my mind went AWOL for a minute, but I quickly composed myself. "Sorry, what is that? And can you put it into layman's terms?"

She sighed. "You can go without symptoms for years before it progresses to a point where your lungs are necrotic and your other organs are impaired. It comes from inhaling coal dust."

Nicolae gave me the filthiest look yet and turned back to Kel. "How do you fix this?"

"It's incurable."

"Bullshit," Nicolae snarled, flinging everything off the counter with one swipe.

"Nick!" I snapped. Kel didn't seem phased.

"What about a lung transplant?" he demanded.

"He wouldn't receive approval, not at this stage. The chances of success, even if he *was* approved —"

"Fuck the chances, and fuck the list. I'll find some fucker with good lungs and cut them out myself."

Kel paused to let him recover. She had more practice dealing with Alphas in raging denial than I did, and my head was still full of... everything. Memories. Realizations of all the things I'd always said I would do and didn't. Francesca's voice.

"This job is going to kill you, Jack."

"What the fuck am I supposed to do, Franny, go into Clarksville's thriving banking sector?"

It was the only argument I ever won, because she knew as well as I did that we needed the money. Braces didn't come cheap. Neither did a mortgage, cars, cable packages or any of the other staples of suburban life.

Nicolae was still arguing with Kel when I finally came back to earth. I checked in on the tail end of, "—wouldn't survive the surgery, sir."

"How long?" I asked suddenly. They both looked at me like what I'd asked didn't make any sense, so I clarified, "How long do I have?"

"Maybe a year, maybe less. It's a wonder he's made it this long without coming in," Kel answered somberly, looking at Nicolae like she expected him to lash out again. He said nothing. He was stone and I was ice, melting fast.

The silence didn't last long. "There's a doctor in Warsaw who specializes in diseases of the lungs. We'll fly him in," Nicolae said firmly. "We'll do whatever it takes."

I stared at Nicolae in disbelief as he rattled off his research and Kel listened patiently. And here I thought he'd just been avoiding me. Knowing he'd taken the time or even cared enough to chase any threads that might keep me with him longer meant more than anything he'd said down on one knee. It meant more than anything anyone had ever said or done for me, and all I could do was wonder how the hell we'd gotten here.

Not *here*, in this sterile office at this appointment that had been inevitable for so long, but *here* with him actually wanting me to live and me not wanting him dead.

"We'll do everything we can," Kel said finally. I felt a camaraderie with her, because we'd both already accepted the thing that Nicolae was fighting like *his* life depended on it. He knew it, too, but he was nothing if he wasn't pride incarnate, and he would still probably be clinging to false hope while I was rotting. "For now, there are drugs I can start him on."

"Nothing with side-effects," I said suddenly.

"Jack," Nicolae scolded, looking at me with the same exhaustion I'd felt during the countless hours I'd spent trying to convince Andrei that vegetables were not going to kill him.

"I'm not saying I won't try anything," I assured him. There was no point long-term, but hell, if it gave me a few more months with my very small circle of loved ones, I'd deal with the sickness. I'd just be trading one type for another. "But it has to wait until after the hunt."

"I told you, it's not happening."

"So we're just going to let the Court give Ellie back to her grandparents, then?" I challenged. "I'm going to immediately start taking drugs that turn me into a walking corpse, and I'm going to suffer through the last few months I have knowing that they're going to take Ellie away from you as soon as I'm gone?"

He was livid. I could see it in his eyes and feel his rage pulsing in the suffocating energy that filled the room. He hated me right now, because if he didn't let the rage out that way, it would turn into fear, and he was not a man who could give in to it. I knew, because it was the same thing that had kept me out of his arms for so long even if it hadn't kept me out of his bed.

"You can't handle it. The stress alone could kill you."

"There's gotta be something I can take that won't make me sick, right?" I asked, looking at the doctor. "Breathing treatments, maybe? Let me have something experimental so I can give these fools the slip for a few weeks, and I'll comply."

Kel hesitated and looked between us, like she was trying to decide if agreeing with me was worth incurring Nicolae's wrath. "There are some things I can give you for pain, and we do have that serum."

"What serum?" I asked.

"We've been working on a drug that utilizes the venom injected by a werewolf bite," she explained. "The experimental concentration only possesses as much venom as our saliva naturally contains when we're not biting. It has healing properties. It's worth a try."

I gulped. Yeah, I knew all about that. Intimately. "Great. I assume it has to be injected painfully?"

"Sorry," she said with an apologetic smile.

"I'm good," I said, rolling up my sleeve. "Just get it over with."

Kel hesitated, looking up at Nicolae for permission. Because I belonged to him and if anyone in this damn building went two seconds without reminding me, they'd explode.

He nodded reluctantly, but I knew the arguing was far from over. One broom-sized needle in the arm later and I was actually starting to feel like I wasn't dying. I'd forgotten how nice that was.

"I'll give you a moment," Kel said, giving me another pitying smile before she left the room.

As soon as the door shut, Nicolae opened his mouth to argue and I knew I had to shut him up somehow. "I'll marry you."

His jaw hung open for a second and he gave me that perplexed frown I knew so well. "What? You already agreed to that."

"Yeah," I said, reaching out to hook my finger around his belt loop and pull him closer. "Except this time I'm not saying it so you'll stop embarrassing me. I mean it."

I could see the irritation in his gaze, but it faded fast and he snorted in amusement. "What changed your mind?"

"You," I admitted, smoothing down the collar of his shirt. "My whole life, I've been taking care of other people. My mother, my family, my employees. I'm not saying I *need* you to take care of me or that it's going to do any good in the long run—"

He rolled his eyes.

"—*but,* it means a lot that you want to."

"Not enough for you to let me do my job and keep you home."

"You know we can't get out of this, Nicolae."

He closed his eyes and sighed, wrapping his arms around me. It was unexpected, but I relaxed into him like I belonged there. Maybe I did. "I know," he answered. "And I think I prefer it when you call me Nick. Except in the bedroom. In that case, I like listening to you trying to say it."

I smiled into his shoulder, squeezing him. "I'll keep that in mind."

TWENTY-ONE

IT HAD BEEN a week of brutal honesty, but when the time came to tell Ellie the truth, I still felt unprepared. She'd been moved to more comfortable yet no less secure facilities in the main building the pack resided in, but I was sure she was still pissed off at me for keeping her under lock and key, even if it was for her own protection. I expected an ambush when I walked through the door, but I was surprised to find her reading on the couch. When she looked up, she actually didn't look like she wanted to kill me, which was a start.

"Hey," I said, closing the door behind me. I'd convinced Nicolae to let me do this alone, but he still insisted on guards right outside the door. Like she was going to shift and try to make a run for it.

"Hey." She closed her book and bit her bottom lip as she watched me like she didn't know what to say any more than I did.

"I'm sorry," we both started at the same time.

"You are?" I asked, surprised.

She looked away, scowling at the floor. "I was upset when you told me about Nicolae. I took it out on you, and I know you're just trying to deal with all this the same as I am."

"That's a pretty mature outlook," I said, wandering over to her.

She rolled her eyes. "I still hate him."

"That's fine. I hated him too, at first. You don't need to like him, but you do need to respect him," I replied. "If not as my partner, then as the leader of this pack."

"I know," she muttered. I'd expected her to fight me on it, and there was still a chance she was just telling me what I wanted to hear. "I'm going to be stuck here forever, aren't I?"

"Not forever. Just until the hunt is over and there's no chance of the Majerus pack getting you."

Ellie watched me, searching my face intently. "You really trust him, don't you?"

"I do," I answered, no hesitation.

"With your life?" she challenged.

"With something a hell of a lot more important than that."

Her indignation turned to sadness. "You're not a wolf. You don't have to go through this ridiculous tradition just to protect me."

"Have to? No. But I'm going to."

"I guess you've already made up your mind."

"Yep. You didn't get all of your stubbornness from your mother."

She smiled, and I could tell she didn't want to. The concern came back into her gaze as she looked me over. "You really are different. Your scent is, too. Now that I can shift, I notice things more."

I swallowed hard. I'd heard plenty of stories about dogs being able to smell when someone was sick, so it was probably a matter of time before she figured it out anyway. "There's something I need to tell you."

She looked nervous, which was understandable considering the last bombshell I'd dropped on her, but she didn't say anything.

"I'm sick, Ellie. I don't really know how else to say it, and you know I've never been good at this kind of thing," I sighed, raking my fingers through my hair. I couldn't bring myself to look at her, and when I finally got the spine to do so, her eyes were full of confusion.

"What do you mean sick? You mean, like...?"

"Black lung disease," I answered. "It's... not good."

"Oh, God," she breathed, covering her mouth.

"I know this is out of left field, but I need you to know where I'm at. You've always been the greatest source of joy in my life, and protecting you is what gives me purpose," I said, reaching to brush a strand of hair behind her ear. "I'm not going to be here forever, Ellie, and I need to know you're safe. I need to know you're with people who will protect you the way I would, and I know you don't trust Nicolae to do that. But I do, and I need you to trust *me*. Promise you'll let him keep you safe. Can you do that for me?"

She pursed her lips and the tears welling in her beautiful eyes cut me to my core. For a second, I thought she wasn't going to answer.

"Yes," she croaked. "But I don't want you to leave. You can't."

"I'm not planning on it anytime soon. You know me, I'll do whatever it takes to stick around and nag you for as long as possible," I teased.

She cracked a pained smile, but it crumpled and the tears started spilling down her cheeks. She fell into my arms and I held her like I always had, no matter what the pain was from. The kids at school, her latest fight with her mother... I'd always taken pride in knowing that no matter how shitty the world was, I was a safe place for her, and knowing that I wasn't going to be able to keep being that was the worst part of all of it. It was too much to think about, and I felt myself shutting down. I had to. How was I supposed to comfort her if I was falling apart?

We talked for what felt like an hour or so, but by the time I realized she needed to be alone to process this, the night was far from young. She stopped me at the door before she left and placed her hand on my arm. "Do you have to do this?"

I knew she meant the hunt. She'd been as opposed as Nicolae was to the idea from the moment I'd told her. I nodded solemnly. "It's the only way I'm going to be able to focus on getting better, sweetheart."

Well, fuck. Guess I couldn't pat myself on the back for not lying to her anymore. There was no *better*, not in any permanent sense.

There was only prolonging and managing. I'd done the same research Nicolae had, even if my lack of denial had led us to different conclusions.

"I'll be back before you know it," I promised. "Then, assuming you don't try to make anymore great escapes, we'll have that welcoming bash Leonie's been prattling about since before you got here."

Ellie rolled her eyes. "It wasn't that great if I didn't even make it out of the city."

"True." I grinned. "Stick around and I'm sure Nicolae will be happy to teach you all the tools of the trade."

"Trade?" She arched an eyebrow.

"Yeah. Being a furry pain in the ass."

TWENTY-TWO

MY FIRST FORAY into Nicolae's world had involved watching the whole pack turn into monsters, then hearing them kill a human one. I was the prey this time, and as I stood outside the car that would be my initial ticket out of Bucharest, saying goodbye to Nicolae and the life I'd just begun to settle into, I felt like a scared rabbit.

"You're sure you brought enough ammo?" Nicolae asked, frowning as he stood in front of me like a fretting parent sending a kid off to a sleepover for the first time. I would know.

"If I brought more, I'd be packing more than the national army."

"That's not necessarily a bad thing."

"I told you how I feel about shooting your packmates," I muttered, fully aware that Vasil and the others I'd grown attached to would be along for the hunt and not cutting me a break either.

"And I told you, hesitation will mean capture for you and death for me."

It was a sobering reminder that the games the wolves played were winner-takes-all. "I'll be fine. I grew up in the sticks, you think I don't know my way around a gun?"

He grunted. "You have your cards, your cash, your medication—"

"And some snacks for the road, ma. I'll be just fine," I said, leaning up to kiss him. It still felt kind of weird, being so openly affectionate with my one-time enemy, but I'd never really stood a chance against Nicolae in any capacity. Working with him, on the other hand, held its pleasures.

He returned the kiss and grabbed me by the arms. At first, I just thought he was being his usual possessive and aggressively affectionate self, but he leaned in to whisper to me instead. "Varna. It's a city not far into Bulgaria. Vasil will meet you there and keep you safe until the full moon has passed."

I froze. "What happened to the importance of tradition and honor? Playing by the rules?"

"Fuck the rules," he growled in my ear. "This is war, and all that brings you home to me is fair."

Those words crushed any doubt I had that Nicolae loved me, even if he wasn't the kind of man who could bring himself to say the words easily. Hell, neither was I. Not after Francesca. The doing meant more than the saying, anyway.

"When I get back," I whispered, resting my hand on his chest, "there's something I want."

"Anything."

I smirked. "Fine. I want to fuck you."

He said nothing and when I looked up, his expression was blank. "Jack."

"Well, you said anything."

His lip curled and I fully expected him to tell me to fuck off. "One time. Once. And I'm on top."

"You're serious?"

"You're not? Fine, then I take it back."

"That's just poor sportsmanship."

He rolled his eyes. "Get out of here before I decide *not* to come looking."

I grinned, opening the car door. I started the vehicle up, and as I planned to get lost before the full moon, I realized that Bucharest—

and more specifically, the pack protected within its borders—had become my home. Even more specifically, Nicolae had.

TURNED OUT, road trips weren't as much fun when you weren't seventeen.

I wasn't sure how the hell I was supposed to get out of Romania when there were allegedly wolves watching to make sure I followed the rules, but I figured Nicolae would have thought ahead to every possible contingency.

Hoped, anyway.

The moon wouldn't be full until the following night, and I was already starting to feel the effects of being on the road. The serum helped, and I didn't feel weak like I had the past few weeks. In fact, I hadn't so much as coughed in the last couple of hours. I told myself it was probably the fresh air. Nonetheless, I couldn't help but feel like something was... off.

No matter how hard I blasted the AC, I still felt like my skin was made of hot coals. I pulled onto the first exit that popped up to get some gas and another bottle of water since I'd drained the last three I had with me. I knew it would be wiser to just check into a hotel for the night, but I'd already decided that my safest bet was to drive to an eastern train station and hop one that ran to my actual destination at the last minute. I knew Nicolae and the others would be tracking me, even though I was using cash everywhere I went and the hunt hadn't officially started yet.

For all I knew, he'd gotten the others to play along. Of course, that was contingent upon them not double-crossing him just to get a shot at taking the throne. That was a lot of trust to put in people I barely knew.

My five-minute pit stop sapped all of my reserves, and I decided that stopping for the night was going to be a necessity after all. If I got up early, I could still make it to the station in time to get into Bulgaria by moonrise safe and sound.

The phone I'd bought halfway according to Nicolae's recommendation burned in my pocket, but I knew calling him would be game over. It had only been a day. Was I really that needy?

I set the fuel nozzle back into the machine and wiped my brow only to realize I wasn't actually sweating. So I just felt like a melted candle on the inside. Fun. Must have been some side effect the doctor hadn't warned me about.

The next few hours on the road made it clear that I wasn't going to make it to my intended destination by nightfall. My vision was blurry and no matter how many times I rubbed my eyes, I still couldn't see the road right. I'd unbuttoned as much of my shirt as I could without looking like I was auditioning for a rodeo, and I was horny to boot. If I didn't pull over, the sex flu was going to land me in a ditch.

I took the first exit that promised a rock-hard bed and a shower that hadn't been cleaned in weeks and checked myself into a room. The clerk didn't seem to give a single fuck, which was good, because that meant she wouldn't remember me. The room was as lackluster as I'd imagined, but as soon as I got in, I went to the sink and splashed cold water on my face. It helped some, just not enough.

The bathtub wasn't actually as bad as I'd expected and didn't look like it had been used to dissolve dead bodies, so I turned on the water and stripped down. The cold water surging over my body was a relief, but it wasn't a cure for whatever it was that ailed me. It wasn't doing as much to ice my libido as I'd hoped, either. I kept thinking of Nicolae and of what he was doing right now in the interest of hunting me down.

It should have been an unsettling thought, and it was, just in a different way. I felt like a junkie in withdrawal. I *craved* him. His breath on my neck, his heat against my back, his hand crawling up my belly and his long fingers teasing my nipples until I was ready to explode before he'd even gotten to my cock.

Jerking off in a dirty hotel bathroom was hardly my idea of a romantic evening, but the thought of him was going to drive me insane if I didn't find release, and he wasn't even here. Wasn't commitment supposed to put a lid on the flames? All it had done was ignite them. I shuddered, one hand propped against the wall as I came. My teeth cut into my bottom lip to keep his name out of my mouth.

God, I missed him. How had I ever thought running was an option when I couldn't be away from him for a day without turning into a needy mess?

I toweled off and slipped under the covers, determined to at least get a decent night's rest before the fun began. Fully trusting Nicolae didn't mean I had to fully trust any of the others. Not even the man who was supposed to keep me out of harm's way until this backwards ritual was over.

Sleep was easier said than done. I found myself watching the clock for hours, still restless, even though jerking off had made one aspect of my discomfort tolerable. I ended up kicking off the blankets, then the sheet, because it still felt like my boiling blood was heating me up from within.

Nicolae had sent me with a first aid kit, just in case I suffered some injury less severe than a wolf bite to the jugular, and I opened it up to take out the drugstore thermometer tucked in with the rest of the supplies. I propped it under my tongue and rooted around in the cabinets for a plastic cup to fill with water so I could pop the aspirin within the kit. When the thermometer finally chirped, I took it out only to realize the thing was busted.

One-hundred and five degrees.

Sure, I felt like crap, but I didn't feel *that* bad. I tried again and the reading was a little higher, so I chucked the defective thermometer in the trash, popped the aspirin and turned out the lights.

Eventually, I fell asleep, but the pornographic nature of my

TWENTY-THREE

I WAS late to get back on the road because, by some miracle, I'd managed to get some real rest. It just happened to come when the sun was peeking through my curtains, so it still sucked, but it was something. I'd grabbed something to eat, but it wasn't sitting well, and I had to keep the AC on with the windows rolled down to deal with the nausea and feverishness. It wasn't as bad as it had been that night, but I was still miserable. Of course the ritual had to happen right after I came down with a mysterious case of wolf flu. I was starting to hate the full moon and all the tradition and superstition that revolved around it.

The train station was crowded with the afternoon rush by the time I reached it, and I could only hope that if any of the wolves had chosen to check the station instead of the airport I'd bought a decoy ticket for, they wouldn't notice me going to the booth. Just in case, I got six others to wildly different destinations in hopes that might at least slow them down.

As I settled into my car and found a row of seats that were unoccupied, I marveled at the convenience of the European transit system. Growing up, it had taken upwards of an hour to the nearest department store. Here, that could get you to a whole different country.

The exhaustion I would have appreciated the night before hit me all at once and I fell asleep leaning against the wall of the train. It was probably just as well. In addition to feeling like shit all-around, I was not in a talking mood. Hell, I probably would've shot whoever came after me without a guilty thought if I hadn't ditched my weapons with my car.

The shriek of wheels grinding to a halt as the train came to a stop at the station woke me and I checked my phone to find that all three hours of the journey had passed. I'd lost signal at some point during the journey. Wonderful. But the sign outside said I'd made it to Bulgaria, and it was almost dark, so I had other things to worry about for now.

Finally. It was over. Nicolae really must have rigged it, because that had been a hell of a lot easier than I'd thought. Not that I was about to complain.

I got off the train with the rest of the passengers and realized that I actually felt out of place in a sea of humans. Maybe I would never be one of the wolves, but I'd changed enough in my time with them that I felt more at home in the pack than I ever had outside of it.

In time, I hoped that Ellie would come to feel the same way.

As I made my way through the murmuring crowd waiting to board the evening train or reconnect with their loved ones, I resisted the urge to stop at one of the station's kiosks. I was starving, but I still had to find Vasil. I'd assumed he would be at the station, but there was no sign of the towering man through the shuffling travelers.

Maybe I did have time to grab a bite after all. I started to head toward a promising hot dog stand when I noticed a payphone and realized there was a greater temptation than a greasy stick of meat. I told myself I wasn't actually going to make the call. They'd been monitoring Nicolae, and I was sure they still were. Any attempt at contact could jeopardize everything, but I could at least call Ellie. She wasn't part of this, and he wouldn't have contact with her.

I picked up the receiver and checked my pockets. Of course, the one thing Nicolae hadn't armed me with was pocket change.

"Here. Let me help you."

A man's deep, accented voice filled my ears like incense smoke, smooth, rich and seductive. The accent was subtler than Nicolae's, softer but still of that steady Eastern European drawl. I turned around to find myself face-to-face with a blond man who looked Vasil's age, if not a bit younger, even though he was a good deal more muscular and had the appearance of a soldier. He would have been decent competition with Nicolae in a fight, all else equal, but his light gray eyes were full of amusement.

"Do I look that much of a tourist?"

"Americans have a certain... energy," he said with a pleasant smile as he offered me a quarter in his palm.

"Thanks," I said, reluctantly taking it. The moment my hand touched his, it felt like I'd been struck by lightning. I cried out in alarm and dropped the quarter. A few people stared as the coin rolled down a groove in the station tile.

"Sorry," I muttered, dropping to my knees to retrieve it. When I looked up, the stranger was on his knees in front of me.

"Relax, I have more," he said, reaching out like he was going for the quarter only to brush his fingertips along the inside of my wrist. I shuddered in an all too familiar way, only rather than lust, his touch stirred only dread.

I leaped to my feet and slammed the phone back in its place. "I just realized I don't need to make that call after all, so... thanks anyway."

I kept walking and when I glanced over my shoulder, the weirdo was still just standing there, watching me. I would've been less alarmed if he'd tried to stop me.

He was a wolf. An Alpha. Had to be. The only question was, why the fuck did I respond to him the same way I did to Nicolae when none of it was supposed to be possible?

Fuck Vasil. I was done waiting around in a foreign territory that was obviously just as full of wolves as Romania was. Only in this country, Nicolae's word wasn't law and that symbol inked on my back meant nothing.

I followed the English signs to the concourse where all the car rental places were and prayed they had something fast. When I caught sight of another unnaturally large guy at the other end of the concourse, I had a change of plans and ignored my racing heart as I fast-walked up the moving sidewalk the wrong way.

I had to get out of here. Whatever was drawing these freaks to me seemed to be more like a flashing beacon than a magnet. Maybe I was just being paranoid, or maybe they were part of the hunt. Had they figured out Nicolae's plan to cheat the game and come after me despite the hard-and-fast territory laws?

Deciding that poaching a cab was my safest way out, I left the train station and headed to the curb. Just as I'd caught sight of a banana-yellow taxi up ahead, a black car screeched to a halt in front of me. The door swung open and nearly took me out. Before I had time to recover my balance, a man stepped out from the other side and one came from behind me.

I caught a glimpse of the face of the creep at the telephone kiosk as the other stuck a needle through my shirt and into my arm. He glanced both ways and clamped a hand over my mouth to muffle my indignant yell. I elbowed him hard and chomped down until his blood filled my mouth, but whatever he'd drugged me with worked a hell of a lot faster than Kel's.

I pitched forward and they both caught me by the arms before shoving me into the back of the cab face first. I blacked out the second the car started moving forward.

So much for being safe at base.

———

WHEN I CAME TO, I heard the fucker who'd given me a quarter talking with some other douchebag I assumed was an Alpha. I was in a hotel room, judging from the tacky painting on the wall that looked nailed in. I was on a bed and I couldn't feel half my body, but I didn't think they even had me bound. Not a good sign if they weren't even afraid I'd try to escape.

"You fuckin' kidding me?" Quarter Douche demanded. "I'm not handing over a human omega to the fucking Majerus cunts."

"I'm tellin' you, his picture was posted with the girl's. They were offering six million for her."

"Yeah, and a guy like this would fetch a hell of a lot more than that on the black market. That shit isn't even real. We've got a fucking unicorn on our hands."

Now that was a new one. I'd been called a fairy, a flamer and all kinds of other unpleasant monikers, but never a unicorn.

My head was killing me. I could barely remember how I'd gotten there. It was like someone had taken all my memories from the past few hours and shaken them up in a box, leaving me to sort through them one by one.

"I say we just wait for the next auction, and have a little fun with him in the meantime," Quarter Douche suggested.

"Not until I call Majerus and figure out what they're offering," the other growled. "Stay put."

I decided there was no point in pretending like I was asleep, since someone foul enough to assault me wasn't going to hesitate to do it while I was out, so I opened my eyes and glared at my guard. "You have no idea what you're doing." I was slurring like I'd spent the night drinking.

He smirked, walking over to the bed. "That so?"

"I'm not an omega. I'm not even a fucking wolf," I informed him. "But I do belong to a man who'd make a little bitch like you piss his pants, so if you think you're getting away with this, think again."

"Belong?" He laughed. "You're not claimed. There's no mark on you."

"Guess again."

He narrowed his eyes like he was trying to call my bluff. "Where?"

"Back of my shoulders."

He grabbed me and tore my shirt open in the back. I knew the second he saw Nicolae's mark, because he stumbled back. "Boris!"

The other scumbag came back into the room with a cordless phone to his ear. "What?"

"He's marked. He's got the Ursache family crest inked on him."

Boris' eyes widened as they landed on me. "Shit," he breathed. "Yeah!" he exclaimed suddenly, nearly dropping the phone. "Yeah, you'd better put me through. I got something they're definitely going to want to pay top dollar for."

Fuck.

"Whatever they pay you, Nicolae will triple it," I said, looking intently at the other wolf. I knew if Francesca's parents got ahold of me, they'd just use me to get to Ellie.

"We're counting on it," he said with a wicked smile. "I expect there to be a bidding war. You know, you're not the first omega I've poached, but I get the feeling you're gonna fetch the highest price I've ever gotten."

I gulped. "What makes you think I'm an omega?"

"Your scent," he answered, like it should be obvious. "I could smell you before the train even came to a stop. You're in heat."

My heart palpitated. "What? Bullshit."

"How do you think I found you?" he challenged.

I decided not to tell him there were others after me, and I was still reeling from that humiliating little revelation. *Heat?* I knew Nicolae thought I responded to his touch like an omega, and my bizarre experience at the train station made it seem more likely than not, but *heat?*

I wished I'd paid more attention to what Leonie had told me about omegas. I knew they went into heat on a full moon, but in all my years of living, I had yet to become a walking flytrap for hungry wolves. Living in Clarksville aside, I'd passed a full moon under

Nicolae's watch without anything weird happening. If this sickness was part of heat, I'd certainly never dealt with it before.

Fuck, I couldn't even believe I was entertaining the idea. I didn't want it to be true.

Boris was off the phone and I tried to tune back in, realizing that they might well be talking about the end of my life.

"They'll be here tonight," Boris announced. "They said if everything checks out, we'll be getting ten million at the very least."

"*Ten?*" the other wolf snarled, giving his partner a shove. "Are you crazy? I could get more than that pimping him out!"

Man, I wanted these bastards dead in the worst way. The murderous fire rising up from my core surprised me, but I chalked it up to being part of the heat.

I was already trying to formulate a rational explanation for how I'd become something that wasn't supposed to be possible. I certainly wasn't a werewolf or I wouldn't be dying from inhaling coal dust, but maybe Nicolae's mark had infused enough of him within me that I was taking on some of the traits. Or maybe my captors were just as out of their minds as they were incompetent. That was definitely a possibility. So was Kel's goddamn burning serum. Maybe I had that dreaded werewolf rabies after all.

Whatever the case, all the talk of negotiations and payment seemed to distract them from their even more twisted plans. When the one I heard Boris call Milan slipped out of the room for some smokes, I finally relaxed.

"You know of Nicolae, don't you?" I asked, propping myself up against the wall. My legs were still numb and so were my hands.

Boris looked up from his phone and grunted. "Who doesn't?"

"Then you know what he'll do to you when he finds me."

"If he wants you back, he'll pay. Otherwise, you'll go to the Majerus family."

"You're in the middle of a war here, Boris. I don't think you wanna be on the losing side."

He snorted. "So you smell like a wolf and now you talk like one.

Tell me, do you writhe like a whore for your Alpha's knot like a typical omega?"

"Fuck you."

He laughed and went back to his stupid fucking game. At least Milan didn't come back. When the door finally opened, a tall man and a woman who was nearly his height in black stilettos came into the room, followed by an entourage of guards who were most certainly wolves. Humans didn't come that stacked.

I didn't recognize the man from Adam, but I'd know the woman's shrewd golden-brown eyes anywhere. She looked younger with her face all done up and her dark hair was cut into a short, spirited bob, but as impossible as it was, just like everything else about this night, I recognized her immediately.

She was, after all, my wife.

TWENTY-FOUR

"FRANCESCA?" I breathed, convinced that she was a hallucination my drugged mind had failed to separate from reality. Or a ghost, here to taunt me, to remind me that I'd failed her and our daughter yet again.

She didn't answer me, only stared in that passive disapproval I knew so well. I watched as the others entering the room moved around her, trying to determine whether any of them could see her.

"Hello again, Jack," Franny said calmly, her hands folded as she stood in the middle of the room the men who came in behind her were searching. Boris and Milan looked half as bewildered as I was as their little trade quickly got out of hand.

"How the fuck—?"

"You two know each other?" Boris asked, suddenly all business.

"He's my husband," Francesca said, casting the man beside her an apologetic glance she'd used on me plenty of times. "Or rather he was before I had a death certificate."

"And who the hell are you?" I asked the man, more confused than angry even though I got the feeling I had reason to be plenty of both.

"This is Ansel Crow," Franny answered for him. "He's my destined mate. The man who helped me escape from you."

"*Escaped* from me?" I cried in disbelief. This was all too much. Too fucking much of everything. I'd grieved this woman. I'd buried her body in the earth and held our daughter while she sobbed as the casket was lowered. I'd picked up the pieces of the life her murder had shattered.

Now she was here, very much alive, and claiming to belong to some pasty-faced dick in a poorly fitted suit.

"Come on, Jack." She said it in that casual way she'd delivered so many soul-crushing blows as she sat on the mini bar and kicked it open with her heel. She rummaged around and pulled out a small bottle of vodka. "You didn't really think I'd be happy slumming it in a shitty town with a shitty man like you if I had a choice, did you?"

I stared at her in disbelief. Not because the words came as a shock or seemed even the slightest bit out of character. I'd always suspected that was how she felt, but she'd at least had the decency to mask it in wispy little lies like, "Of course I'm happy, dear," and, "I know you try your best."

"You're dead," I choked. "I buried you."

"You buried a crackwhore," she said flatly, taking another chug of vodka with her legs crossed over the fridge. "Not a very good one, I might add. I compelled you and the necessary bumpkins that it was my body at the morgue, and that you should have a closed-casket funeral to avoid upsetting Allen." She paused. "Oh, I'm sorry. Is *she* still going by Ellie?"

"You're sick," I breathed. It wasn't an accusation, just acceptance of what I should have known all along. This woman—this Alpha, who'd deceived me about her identity at every level, up to and including letting our daughter think she was dead—wasn't just cruel, she was twisted. I hated her, but I pitied her more.

"I'm not the one who reeks of mating pheromones and death, love." Her gaze swept over me with a shake of her head. "Marked by two wolves and loved by none. Then again, that is less than you deserve for breaking your promise."

"My promise?" I asked through clenched teeth.

"To stay in Clarksville." Her tone turned icy as she cast aside the empty bottle. "I didn't run to that little hick town and fake my own death to get away from Nicolae and my parents just to have you drive our son back into their clutches."

"We don't have a son," I seethed. "And you don't deserve to call her your daughter, you frigid, psychotic bit—"

Ansel had been silent the entire time like a good little lap dog, but he backhanded my face hard enough with his ring that I tasted blood. My right ear was still ringing from impact by the time I saw Francesca give him that "we're talking about this in the car" look she'd given me so many times.

"Patience, Ansel. After all, he is an omega." Her melodic words were meant to humiliate me. It had always been her favorite sport. Why should now be any different?"

"You knew," I muttered.

"Of course I knew. Only an omega would be pitiful enough to roll over for a woman he isn't even attracted to who treats him like shit and raise another man's child without ever questioning it," she laughed, propping her knee up on the bed to straddle my lap. She wrapped her bright red claws around my neck and pushed my head up against the wall. "Tell me, Jack, didn't you ever once ask yourself if it was all a *bit* too good to be true?"

My windpipe felt like it was ready to collapse, and she'd drawn blood with all five talons, but I wouldn't give her the satisfaction of blinking. "Baby, there were a hell of a lot of things that crossed my mind about you, but that was never one of them."

Her eyes narrowed and the look in them had me convinced she was gonna kill me then and there. Why not? She'd killed everything else. My spirit, my pride, my hope in the family I'd been trying to hold together for years.

"She's not yours. You know that, don't you?" Her sweet tone was dripping with vindication.

"I figured when I realized she wasn't dumb enough to put up with your bullshit."

Boris cleared his throat. "About the money," he interjected, probably saving my goddamn life.

"Ah, yes. Forgive me," she said, climbing off my lap to face him. "What was it we agreed upon?"

"Ten million," Milan answered stiffly. "But that was before we knew there was a connection between you two. You know, a human omega's exotic as hell. We could get that much easy at an auction."

"Of course," she said in a sweet tone. Only Ansel and I seemed to know that voice meant a hurricane was coming. "Ansel, love, hand me my pocketbook, would you?"

The blond wolf smirked, offering the sequined black clutch to her. She opened it and fished around for a second before pulling out a small handgun and firing directly into Boris' heart. "That's one," she said, turning to do the same to Milan before he could pull his own. "And two. They're solid silver, boys, but I'll have to owe you the rest."

Francesca's heavily armed entourage was already dragging the bodies into the bathroom. I didn't even want to know what they were going to do with them, since a similar fate was probably going to befall me soon.

When I'd made the mistake of sending up a prayer that I wouldn't die of cancer, I really should've been more specific.

"Ansel Crow," I muttered, eyeing the other poor bastard Franny had sucked in. "I assume you're of the Crow pack Nicolae considers his closest ally?"

Ansel smirked. "My father has other ideas about the direction of our pack's future. You'll go a long way toward helping with that."

"So you're going to use me to blackmail Nicolae?" I laughed. "I'm dying. He's not gonna pay you shit for another few months with a man he only marked to protect our daughter from *your* parents," I said, looking back at Franny. "Just out of curiosity, do they think Nicolae killed you, too?"

"Of course," she said without remorse. "Don't look at me like that. I've been used all my life, first by them and then by Nicolae. I'm not the villain just because I got sick of it and decided to take my life into my own hands."

"And what about mine?" I growled. "What about Ellie? Were you just going to let her think you were dead forever?"

"Of course not. When Ansel gained control of his pack, I was going to bring her home. Until you got the brilliant idea to leave."

"Good to see your ability to twist literally every scenario until it's somehow my fault hasn't changed in death," I taunted.

Dead or alive, the woman got on my last fucking nerve.

Before she could respond, one of her guards chimed in with, "We've got a situation on the ground floor."

"What is it now?" Francesca snapped. "If it's security, just kill them."

"It's not that. There are wolves."

"Of course there are. He's an omega in heat, he's like a lighthouse. Kill them too."

The humiliation still stung worse than the betrayal, especially in front of her. At least now I knew why she'd always seen me as a second-class citizen. In her mind, I was below human. The way Nicolae talked about omegas made it sound like some sacred thing, but on her lips, the truth was clear. To her, being an omega made me disposable.

The entourage had been gone all of one minute before I heard snarling through the window. Given the fact that I was in heat, I doubted any wolves who'd pursued me there had any noble intentions. At least the humiliation and shock were keeping my mind off of the fact that Francesca was here.

Franny. Alive. Here. Being the sociopathic asshole she usually only revealed herself to be in my dreams.

The window shattered behind me and a shard of glass sliced into my eyebrow, turning everything black with blood and blinding me as a soul-shaking bellow filled the room. I could see just enough with the right to watch Francesca and Ansel transforming in tandem. It was the first time I'd seen her as a wolf, and under any context, I might've found her ethereal even as a snarling beast. Now she was the stuff of nightmares, all teeth and fury. It took me a moment to make out the object of their rage, but when I did, my heart leaped. *Nicolae.* He towered over the other Alphas, the black fur on his chest soaked in the gore that hung from his bared fangs in ribbons. The sight should've terrified me, but it didn't, not even when he effortlessly tore off the head of the guard who'd just entered the room.

I stayed hunkered between the bed and end table as Nicolae turned on Ansel next, knowing that if I dared to move, I'd be wolf chow. They wrestled fearsomely, tearing and slashing, but Ansel was no match for the larger beast until Francesca threw herself into the fray with a vicious roar. He went down under their combined weight, but they didn't have the upper hand for long before he rose up with Ansel's head between his massive hands. With a sharp turn and a deadly snap, Ansel's life was extinguished.

As the Alpha's body sank to the ground, Francesca let out a cry of pain and regret I was sure she'd never felt a fraction of on anyone else's account, but her grief was short-lived. It morphed into horrifying rage as swiftly and violently as she'd physically transformed. She lunged and her claws drove into Nicolae's broad shoulders like knives. He roared and slammed her against the wall, trying to throw her off, but she held on with everything she had left and plunged her fangs into his throat.

I lunged for the fallen Alpha's discarded gun and managed to curl my finger around the trigger without firing prematurely. I had to wait for an open shot and the blood running down my face had rendered me half-blind, but time was running out. I could see Nicolae's life draining before my eyes as the she-wolf tore at his flesh, her face buried in his bloodied mane as every bite brought her closer to his jugular. I was terrified of hitting Nicolae instead, but if I didn't take a shot, she was going to finish him off regardless. I trained the gun on the she-wolf, willing myself to fire, but seventeen years of history held me back. Everything she'd done to me, all the ways she'd used me... none of it was enough to convince me to pull the trigger.

Ellie was. Nicolae was. I could forgive her for what she'd done to me, even though I knew she would never ask for it if she lived for all of eternity, but knowing that she would bleed them both dry for her own happiness was what I needed to see the she-wolf for the monster she was and not the woman I'd devoted my life to.

The shot rang in my ears and the fighting ceased all at once. The she-wolf fell from Nicolae's back and landed on the floor beside Ansel. The bullet hole in her back was still smoking as she stared life-lessly at the only other person she'd ever come close to loving. Not her daughter, not her parents, not me.

Nicolae's shaggy head turned and he fixed his smoldering eyes on me, and for a moment, I wondered if he was going to turn on me even though I was the one who'd rescued him. I'd saved him from *her*. The woman *he* loved. The woman whose death he'd been trying to avenge all this time. The woman who'd held his heart long before I ever had.

He reached for me, and when I didn't flinch away, he pulled me into his arms with a gentle, saddened growl. I let him hold me against his massive chest, enveloped me in black fur and blood. I didn't care. In that moment, I didn't even care about Francesca, or Ansel, or the fact that I was somehow inexplicably an omega. I only cared that Nicolae was with me. That he was alive, and this goddamn hunt was over, and he didn't hate me for killing the woman we'd shared and grieved and suffered for.

I realized only then that the heat and the fever and the pain were gone.

TWENTY-FIVE

"HOW ARE we going to tell Ellie?"

It was the first I'd spoken since Nicolae had taken me to a house on the border of Romania. I didn't know if he owned the place or if it belonged to one of his many "friends," but I was still too shaken up to care.

I'd killed Francesca. Francesca was *alive* as of a few hours ago, and now she wasn't because *I* had shot her. How was I supposed to reckon with that? How was I supposed to make sense of any of it at all?

And Ellie...

Nicolae considered my question in silent contemplation for a few seconds. "We'll tell her it was me," he finally said.

"What?"

"There's no reason she needs to know you're the one who did it. After all, you were only saving my life."

Every damn time. Every time I thought it was impossible for my heart to open any more to him, the bastard had to go and prove me wrong. "We're not doing that. She's already been lied to all her life," I muttered. "For another thing, she already hates you. If she thinks you killed Francesca, she's never going to stop trying to get revenge."

"A fair point. I suppose that means you're going to tell her the truth about her paternity."

I thought about it. It had slipped my mind in all the shock, but it was a good question. "She already knows it's likely..."

"But knowing beyond doubt is different, isn't it?" he said in an understanding tone, sitting next to me on the couch to rub my shoulders. Relief washed over me like healing waters. I was far more prone to the effect of his touch in this state, and I could only guess whether it was from heat or exhaustion. "You don't have to tell her. Certainly not on my account. Perhaps I could, if you really want her to know."

I shook my head. "No. I have to. She deserves that."

Nicolae leaned in and pressed his lips to my cheek. God, he was so cool to the touch. He healed every part of me his hands and lips swept over, even if it was only temporarily. I wished I could put my soul in his hands, because that was the only way it ever felt like it would be whole again.

"I can't believe this is happening," I said quietly. "Any of it."

He wrapped his arms around me from behind and pulled me close, tucking my head beneath his chin. "Let's face it, Jack. We both knew she was twisted, but she still played us both. She played me against the Majerus pack, and us against each other."

"For what?" My voice cracked but I couldn't make myself sound strong when I felt like I was crumbling. "I still don't understand what made her do this."

"I do. It's the same reason I fought so hard to get her back. She recognized early on that if she wasn't out for herself, no one else would be, and she lived every day of her life by that principle. She did not care who she hurt, only what others could do for her. I know because I was the same way, before you. And before Ellie."

I swallowed hard, leaning back against him. "You're nothing like Francesca," I murmured.

He kissed me. "And you deserve better than us both, but I'm

afraid I haven't evolved quite enough to let you go now that I have you."

"I'm not complaining," I said with a small smile. It faded as soon as the grief set in again. "You know what's fucked up?"

"Hmm?" he asked, stroking my thigh as he held me in his arms.

"I always felt like the worst person in the world when she died. I didn't feel anything I was supposed to feel. I felt the anger and the loss, sure, but not the grief, no matter how I tried. I thought I was just in denial and that it was going to be a process, but now... I don't know."

"She marked you," Nicolae said thoughtfully. "The link between you was faint because you're human and you weren't destined mates, but it was enough that you subconsciously felt the truth. That she was out there still."

"Fuck," I breathed. "Is that why it hurts this much now? After everything she did, is that why I finally feel the pain I should have felt then?"

He wrapped his arms tighter around me. "It will end," he whispered. "Every day, it will get a little easier, and I will help you through it."

I nodded, touching his hand. "I'm sorry, Nicolae."

"For what?" He sounded genuinely confused.

"For killing her. I know why it happened, but I know you still loved her."

He said nothing for a long time. If he pulled away from me, I would understand. It would kill me, it would hurt worse than the pain and guilt I felt now over Francesca's death, but I would deserve it and bear it with dignity. Instead, Nicolae turned me to face him, pressing his palm to my neck as he so often did when he wanted my attention. I wasn't sure if it was simply a wolf gesture or just his need to claim the most vulnerable part of me with his touch, but either way, it made me shiver.

"I love *you*." It was the first time he'd said it, but his words were so deliberate and his gaze so full of the echo of them that I couldn't doubt it. "And she nearly took you from me. I would have killed her myself if you hadn't, even if she took me down with her. You are my mate, Jack. My destined one. Nothing short of death itself can stand between us, and I'd fight that, too."

"Destined?" I asked in disbelief.

His gaze softened. "I didn't think it was possible. In the beginning, I hated you so much that I was able to explain away the intensity with which I was drawn to you. I don't know how you are an omega, or how you are mine, but the reasons don't matter."

"Nicolae—" I began to protest, until he kissed me and I found myself capable of accepting things my stubborn and insecure heart was too fragile to hold on its own. I returned the kiss, fingers brushing over his aquiline features to remind myself of them so I wouldn't need to open my eyes and break off the kiss. Alone, the intensity of the changes that had come over me were overwhelming and unpleasant, but in his arms, they were new and thrilling and intriguing.

As my heat reignited, I wanted more. I wanted to fully awaken to this state I was so ill-prepared for because I knew he'd keep me safe. Body, soul and mind. The fire of our bond drove out my guilt, my grief and the shame until all that was left was the all-encompassing beast I had fallen for.

He pushed me onto my back and brought his weight down on top of me. I ground against him, no longer caring how needy and desperate I seemed. There was no point hiding the truth, and at least now I knew why I craved him so fiercely. I was his omega, and he was the answer to every question inside me, the cure to every ache and the weakness I'd grown tired of resisting. Even so, his passion energized me and I felt damn near immortal in his arms.

Once more, his teeth scraped my neck and I wanted the bite more than I ever had, even knowing it would kill me. Every caress and nip and growl drove away every last shred of logic. When he kissed me instead, I must have groaned in defeat, because he laughed huskily in my ear.

"I don't know how I ever doubted what you were," he remarked, removing our clothes casually like he was plucking the petals on a rose while I kept trying to pull him back for more. I was too feverishly hungry for him to realize that delaying him was only prolonging relief.

"Hold still," he scolded gently as I guided his hand down to my cock. I needed his touch, even though the brush of his fingertips pushed me dangerously close to an unsatisfying climax. He seemed to notice I was too wound up for direct contact and worked a finger into me instead. That just proved to be another kind of torture, so I grabbed his wrist and made him withdraw. He looked down at me in confusion as I rose up and maneuvered his body back into the same position he'd had me in.

I knew if he was the one taking the lead, he'd insist on preparation I didn't need, teasing and torturing in his attempt to be gentle. Awareness touched the lust on his face as I straddled him and he propped himself up on his elbows, allowing me to come down onto his cock on my own terms. It hurt so fucking much more than it had before, but the relief of having him inside of me was worth it.

I snapped the tie that bound his hair and watched it unravel against the wine-colored sofa as he gasped from pleasure. Once I finally managed to work his entire shaft into my ass, his nails bit into my sides until they drew blood and as he moaned my name, I kissed him hard to swallow down the sweet sound of it. For once, I was the one who'd taken his breath away and I was never going to get sick of it. I rode him as aggressively as I would fuck anyone else and I realized what it meant to be Alpha and omega in an instinctive understanding that surpassed the language our tongues didn't have time to form, all tangled with each other.

Nicolae ravished me with his hands and his tongue, and when he flipped our positions to fuck me on my back, I was more than happy to trade the lead. He'd always been somewhat careful with me, and he still was, but there was something different this time. As he thrust into me, his fist tangled in my hair as he bent over my writhing body to kiss my bare neck, it was like he'd finally given himself permission to take what he wanted without worrying he'd break me. To take what I needed so desperately to give him.

His knot inflated against my prostate and my cock shot hot streams of white cum onto his chest. I hoped the neighbors weren't the shy types because the cries of climax that came out of my mouth were absolutely filthy. Nicolae growled and clutched me to keep me in position as his hips jackhammered into me, his balls striking my quivering ass with each trust. His orgasm infused me with his energy and his scent, and for the first time, I could feel it permeating every-thing. Claiming me, for him. For my Alpha, my twin flame, my world.

Nicolae shook with release and trapped my body against his as I wrapped myself around him and breathed him in greedily. If it was possible to come again that soon, I would have just from the way he whispered my name, like it held all the meaning of a sonnet.

"That was..." I couldn't think of the word. It was always amazing, but there was something else this time. Something more that I couldn't put into words and wasn't sure I wanted to.

"Yes," he whispered in agreement, nuzzling my neck. Every time he moved, his knot pressed into the right place and made me tremble.

"Why?"

I knew he understood my question. He kissed me again and touched his lips to my ear. "Because it's the full moon and, to put it in scientific terms, omegas always get incredibly horny."

I snorted. "Why didn't I last time?"

"I don't know," he admitted. "It's just part of what we're going to have to figure out."

His answer satisfied me enough and I relaxed in his arms to enjoy the fulfilling sensation of him inside of me while we were tied. My bliss possessed me and I decided I could live with not knowing the answers right away. Especially if the investigation involved more experiments like this.

TWENTY-SIX

RETURNING to the pack was a bittersweet moment. On the one hand, there had been part of me that was convinced I'd never see it again, and as Nicolae led me back into the building that stood out like a blue gem against the gray sky, it felt like home. On the other, I had the unenviable task of telling my daughter the truth about her mother's deaths, real and staged.

Nicolae insisted on me seeing the doctor first, no matter how many times I assured him that I wasn't injured, and I knew he was at least partly trying to give me an excuse to put off the conversation. Soon enough, we would have to deal not only with coming clean about Francesca but informing the Crow pack that their late son had died a traitor. Something told me that wasn't going to go over well.

Kel stared at us both like we'd gone off the deep end as Nicolae explained everything that had happened. Not that I could blame her. It all sounded absurd to me, and I had lived it.

"A human omega?" she muttered, shaking her head like she just couldn't convince herself it was a possibility. "I don't know, Nicolae."

"He's my mate," said Nicolae. "And not just because I marked him."

"That's subjective, with all due respect." She was probably the only person who had the balls to say that to him, but all he did was scowl. "I'll have to run more tests."

"There are tests for this kind of thing?" I asked skeptically.

"Not exactly, but I'm still going to run every last one I can think of before I'm willing to accept this as a possibility."

At least she was honest. "How many of those are going to hurt?"

Kel smiled. "How are you feeling after the hunt?"

"Dead," I admitted. Her refusal to answer was pretty telling of what I was in for.

"I'll give you more serum," she said. "That should help you while I'm working on a theory."

"You have one?" Nicolae demanded.

"It's rough as sandpaper, but if Jack was marked by two Alphas, I suppose it's possible that he's manifested some latent werewolf qualities," she mused. "The change became pronounced after your mark, didn't it?"

"That's right," Nicolae answered.

"Are you saying I'm part wolf?" I asked, bewildered.

Kel shrugged. "Hybridization is possible, but it's rare. I suppose you might have had a distant wolf ancestor somewhere back in the family tree."

"Clarksville," muttered Nicolae. "Maybe someone who abandoned his pack to be with a human."

"Who says it was a 'he'?" said Kel.

Nicolae sighed. "Just do whatever you can. I want this to take top priority."

"I have an entire pack to care for, you know," she replied flatly.

"Not anymore. I'm bringing another doctor in to take over for the day-to-day."

She grunted her disapproval and left the room.

"You know," I said, staring at him, "you could try not to make everyone in the pack hate me."

"They'll live," said Nicolae.

"What does it mean if I have wolf blood?" I asked warily, not sure if I should be nervous or relieved. I did know I was getting tired of receiving startling news.

"I don't know. But it would explain a lot."

"Yeah," I muttered, unable to believe I actually meant it. At one point, this would've just raised more questions than it answered. It did raise the question of if I was doomed to die from lung disease after all, but that wasn't a conversation I had the emotional energy for. Not yet. Not when there was another to be had. "Come on. We should go tell Ellie we're back."

Nicolae studied me with concern. "Are you sure? You're exhausted. If you want, I can go alone."

"This is something we need to do together," I said, taking his hand. I didn't know how long 'together' would be an option, so I was going to make the most of it while it lasted.

ELLIE'S RELIEF TO see me was short-lived when she picked up on the apprehension Nicolae and I were both feeling. He wasn't kidding about being destined mates, and the bond between us now was proof enough. It was like the full moon had opened up another dimension I had once been oblivious to, and it was both daunting and incredible.

Now, it was time to face the music.

I explained for the most part, and Nicolae let me, only cutting in to put up a defense on my behalf when he thought I was being too harsh in my retelling. Ellie listened and I couldn't tell if she was just in shock, or silent because she was too angry to speak and put her feelings into words. Like her mother, she had always been prone to shutting down and closing me out when she was upset, and by the time I finished, all I could do was hope she wouldn't hate me forever.

If she did, I'd understand.

The tears filled her eyes finally and overflowed along with the guilt welling in my heart. "I'm so sorry, Ellie," I whispered, too ashamed to speak at full volume. "I know it doesn't mean much, but I—"

She rose and Nicolae flinched, like he was ready to stop her if she tried to attack. Instead, she threw her arms around me and started sobbing. So did I. Through everything, I'd managed to keep from breaking down in front of her no matter what was going on in our lives, but I couldn't do it anymore. I held her and we both cried like it was the funeral all over again, and I guess it was.

It was a death, it was a betrayal, and it was a new beginning for her. I knew that as much as she loved her mother, there was a part of Ellie that was relieved. I'd seen the terror in her eyes when I got to the part of the story where Francesca came back, and I'd realized then that she was just as afraid of the woman as everyone else. Francesca could be sunlight on a spring day when she wanted, but she could also be the wildfire that left your heart in smoking rubble. She took and she gave on her whim, and in the end, she left those in her wake with nothing.

Once we'd finally collected ourselves, Ellie was the first to speak intelligibly. "I don't blame you," she said shakily. "I blame her."

"Ellie, I —"

"*No.*" Her gaze turned sorrowful as she took my hand. "I know you only defend her because you're trying to protect me, but I learned today that one of my parents wasn't truly mine, and it isn't you. What she did to you, what she did to both of us, is just proof of that. I'm not angry that you killed her, I'm angry that she wasn't dead to begin with," she seethed. I knew her anger and the pain that caused it. I was finished making excuses for a woman who'd never deserved them. Who'd never deserved the life she had so happily thrown away. "Losing her the first time was hard, but the worst part was feeling..." She broke off, like what she wanted to say shamed her deeply.

"Relief," I offered.

Ellie's eyes widened in shock.

"I know how it sounds, and maybe that's why we both went so

long without saying it," I murmured. "Francesca was cruel. Even before we knew the truth, she left scars in us that are going to be there for a long time. Losing her hurt. So did loving her."

Ellie covered her mouth and I could tell she was trying not to start crying again. I hoped she succeeded, because if she started, I was going to.

"It's okay. To feel whatever it is you're feeling," I told her. "We'll figure it out together."

She nodded, looking up at Nicolae. He'd given us space, but he'd been a solid pillar of support throughout the hardest conversation I'd ever had. "So," she said, regaining her voice. "I guess you're where I get my temper from."

He gave her a faint smile, looking calm on the outside even though I could tell he was at least as nervous about her reaction as I had been. "I wish I could offer you some words of comfort about how it gets easier to manage with age."

"Thank you," she muttered. I could tell she had a hard time getting those words out.

Nicolae's face was blank with confusion. "For what?"

"For bringing him home," she said, nodding to me. "And for taking care of him when I was... you know."

His gaze softened with understanding. He was so different when he spoke to her. Maybe they had sixteen years of catching up to do, but I had no doubt that they would. I finally let myself breathe, knowing that when I was gone, whenever that was, he would protect her and they would be there for each other.

"We have at least one other thing in common," Nicolae said. "I love your father very much. I don't expect that being your biological father gives me any right to special treatment or your trust, but I do hope that we can begin to build a relationship based on that."

She smiled a little. "Yeah."

"Since the hunt is over, you're free now," he mused. "Or at least you're as free as an Alpha can be."

"Not free enough to get out of this 'welcome home' bash, I assume?" she asked hopefully.

He chuckled. "I'm afraid not. If so, I'd have played that card a long time ago."

She groaned. "Guess we'd better get it over with, then. Can we do it sooner rather than later?"

"I thought you might say that," he replied. "Leonie has been planning this thing since you arrived, so I'm sure the short notice won't be an issue."

"This isn't a black tie thing, is it?" I asked hopefully.

Nicolae rolled his eyes. "You'll find a way to manage if you have to wear a tie for one night."

"A tie, fine. A bowtie is where I draw the line."

Ellie snickered. "You're fighting an uphill battle."

"You're probably right," Nicolae agreed.

"Don't you two start ganging up on me now," I huffed. Inwardly, I'd never been more relieved. They were getting along.

Nicolae grinned at Ellie. "We should probably start getting your stuff moved in, since you're no longer...well, grounded."

"About that," said Ellie. "I was kind of hoping I could stay here. I mean, without the guards."

"Here?" I echoed. "Why?"

"No offense, but I'm not really interested in sharing an apartment with you guys and a biting gremlin doesn't exactly sweeten the deal."

I sighed. Hopefully Andrei wasn't giving Leonie *too* hard of a time. She was the only person I'd trusted to watch him, but she'd made it clear she had no plans of being a regular babysitter. "I don't know how I feel about you moving out. You're sixteen. You're a baby."

Ellie stared blankly at me. "I'm going to be taking a mate in the next few years. If I don't enjoy my freedom now, I never will."

"She has a point," said Nicolae. The moment I whipped my head around to glare at him, he held his hands up in immediate deference. "But that's up to you two to work out."

"I guess you could, on a trial basis," I muttered. "But that's contingent on you getting back into school, getting good grades, and staying out of trouble."

"Deal," she said immediately.

Nicolae and Ellie started talking about the local high school, and my weary mind tuned out. It probably *was* a good thing for her to get used to a little independence. I couldn't hold onto her forever. Chances were I couldn't even hold onto her for another year.

TWENTY-SEVEN

THE PARTY WASN'T QUITE as formal as I'd feared, but I got the feeling that was more for Ellie's sake than because Leonie wanted it that way. She'd informed me that it was my duty as the Alpha's mate to stand at the door and greet every guest as they came in, and by the time the party was in full swing, I was more than ready to leave.

At least Ellie seemed to be fitting in. Most of the pack had readily accepted her, and the ones who hadn't were smart enough to keep their mouths shut about it. Even Andrei seemed to be enjoying himself. He'd tolerated the tiny tux just to make me happy, but the little imp couldn't help tearing off his bowtie and stealing all the deviled eggs.

Nicolae was busy charming the wife of the neighboring pack Alpha. He'd invited more than a few new allies to make up for the one we'd lost in the Crow pack. Ansel's betrayal had already been reported to the Courts, so his parents couldn't take revenge without starting up another pack war, but that didn't mean we were on friendly terms. Another development—one that was both unpleasant and ultimately positive—was that the Majerus pack had sent a representative as a gesture of good will. Damon and Claire still refused to show up, even though Nicolae had extended an invitation on Ellie's behalf, but it was a start.

"You look like you're being tortured," Ellie remarked, finding her way over to me.

I stared at the drink in her hand and narrowed my eyes.

"It's just sparkling apple juice, dad," she said. "Relax."

I snorted. "Good. Just because you're an Alpha doesn't mean you can get away with everything."

She gave me a patient smile. "I know, I know. At least I —" She stopped talking and her face went blank as she fixed on a spot across the room. I followed her gaze to where Leonie was standing, laughing and teasing one of the other Alphas' sons. "Who's that?"

"That's Mario Padovano, I think."

"Not him. Her."

"Oh. That's Leonie. I haven't had a chance to introduce you yet," I said, waving her over since she seemed to have grown weary of her conversation partner.

Ellie turned white as a ghost and clutched her glass in both hands like she was trying to hide behind it. Leonie wandered over, smiling pleasantly at us both. "You're looking well, love," she said, touching my arm before she turned her attention to Ellie. "And here's the guest of honor. Hope you're enjoying the party."

"The party's great," Ellie said stiffly, staring at the beta like she was looking at an actual wolf that was about to bite. "Thanks for doing it. Planning, I mean. I—I like your dress."

Leonie gave an awkward laugh and I almost laughed too. I'd never seen Ellie so tongue-tied and I was at a loss for words myself. "No trouble, I live for this kind of thing. And thanks," she said, smoothing her hands down the soft fabric. "I made it myself."

"Leonie is the best damn werewolf designer in Europe," I said when it became clear Ellie really had forgotten how to speak. *What the hell?*

If Leonie noticed, she didn't let on. "You should come by my studio sometime," she said to Ellie. "I'd love to design something for you."

"Okay," Ellie squeaked.

"Well... I should go make sure the other guests are doing alright. It was nice seeing you, Jack, and nice to meet you, Ellie," Leonie said, giving us both a warm smile before she left us.

"What was that about?" I asked, turning to face my daughter.

"Nothing. Um, I need to go," Ellie said suddenly, setting her glass on the refreshment table before she took off toward the side door.

"Ellie, wait!" I called.

"I wouldn't." Kel's voice gave me a start, especially since she was so short I had to look down to see her when I turned around.

"Geez, are you trying to give me a heart attack before my lungs rot out?"

She gave me an unapologetic smirk. "Sorry. But I've treated enough Alphas over the years to know what that's about."

"Well, in that case, do you mind telling me? Because I don't have a damn clue."

"It's a mate bond," Kel said, shrugging.

"A mate bond?" I frowned, doing a double take. "With *Leonie?* Ellie's only sixteen!"

"The fact that she's an Alpha is more of an issue," she mused. "A mate bond doesn't mean acting on it, it just means there's a connection that will one day lead to romance."

It took a while for her words to settle in. "But she's supposed to be betrothed to some omega in another pack."

"Yes. I can see how that would present a problem. Glad I'm not her," said Kel. "Anyway, that's not what I came to tell you."

I was still reeling from her bombshell about Ellie, but whatever was important enough for Kel to feel the need to find me at a party couldn't be good. "What is it? I'm not dying *tonight*, am I?"

"No," she laughed. This woman's idea of humor was a bit off. Then again, she was a werewolf. "But I did find something interesting in the secondary analysis of your blood."

"Okay..."

"The first time, I was just looking for flags of disease. This time, I found a marker that's only present in werewolf blood."

"So I am part wolf?"

"Well, just a little. It's distant. I'm afraid one of your ancestors has some explaining to do."

"Yeah, well, one was a conman and another ran off to join the circus, so it wouldn't be the first," I said. "What does that mean for treatment? Or is that a conversation we shouldn't have right now?"

"It means that there is an experimental and incredibly risky option we could try if all else fails."

"You mean like we know it's going to?"

She didn't answer, but I knew she agreed. Nicolae was the one who couldn't accept it. "If you are wolf enough to have manifested the traits of an omega after being marked by two Alphas, then I believe there's a chance, albeit a small one, that you could survive a transformative bite. I'd estimate your odds of survival to be about twenty percent."

"That's a hell of a lot better than my odds right now," I said as the news sunk in. My nonexistent odds, to be exact.

She nodded. "I'm telling you because I'm certain that once Nicolae knows it's an option, he'll run with it. I thought you deserved the chance to consider it on your own."

"Yeah," I said, feeling out of my body again. "I appreciate it. And I'll definitely think about it. Thank you."

Kel nodded. "Enjoy the rest of your evening."

"Enjoy" was a strong word, especially when I quickly went back to watching my daughter like a hawk to make sure she stayed away from the less innocuous drinks, but I certainly had a lot to think about.

TWENTY-EIGHT

IT TOOK me a few weeks to work up the courage to tell Nicolae about Kel's theory. I wasn't sure why I'd put it off for so long. There was no particular reason, the right time just never seemed to come up. I wasn't sure if I was scared he'd say no, or scared he'd get up hope only for the plan to be called off because it turned out the odds of success were just as bleak.

Dying was a pretty open-ended thing. I'd known my body would fail on me eventually, and I'd figured it wouldn't be pretty, but if I allowed Nicolae to bite me and it failed, it meant a rapid descent into madness followed by certain death. And I wouldn't even be myself. I couldn't help that I was afraid, and I liked to think I'd taken the news of my inevitable demise in stride, all things considered. But I was more afraid that Nicolae would just flat-out refuse. It was dangerous, and he was fixated on half-baked therapies that carried no risks.

When Nicolae came home with another stack of papers, I knew it was time. He was pissed that I'd put off other forms of treatment that were definitely destined to just prolong my suffering by a few terrible months, and that was if I got lucky. I knew I was breaking my promise to try everything, but if I only had a little bit of time with him, I wanted to enjoy it. I didn't want to spend it exhausted and wasting away. Just running after Andrei took enough energy those days. I didn't want the people I loved to remember me like that.

It was one point in favor of Kel's option. It would allow me to maintain my dignity, at least until I turned into a ravenous monster.

"Nicolae," I began in hopes of preempting his spiel on the latest drug studies he'd printed off the Internet.

"Don't," he growled, dropping the papers on the counter. "You've been putting this off ever since we got back, and I'm done. We are going to talk about this *tonight*, whether you want to or not."

"Fine, we'll talk about it. But can I tell you something first?"

He stared at me skeptically, like he thought this was another diversion tactic. "Okay," he said, grudgingly sitting down. "What is it?"

"Kel told me about a new experimental treatment. There's only a slim chance of success, but it's better than what we're working with. The only problem is, if it *doesn't* work, it'll definitely kill me."

His eyes went wide as he listened. "When was this? You didn't tell me you had an appointment today."

"I didn't." Now the guilt was setting in. "She told me at the party."

"The party?" he cried, standing. "Last month?"

"I'm sorry I didn't tell you sooner. I just needed time to process."

"What's there to process?" he growled. "How could you keep this from me if it was so important she'd seek you out over it? And what is it, this 'experimental' treatment you felt the need to hide?"

"I'm part wolf, Nick." He seemed to shut down at that revelation. We'd both talked about the possibility, but actually knowing was another thing. "It's not much, but Kel thinks that there's a chance I could survive your bite and it would heal me."

For a few minutes, his face showed absolutely nothing. Then it became a screen that projected only anger. "That's insane. Even if you do have some distant wolf ancestor, that means nothing! You're human. I'm not going to be the one who murders you based on some theory."

"I'm dying, Nicolae," I said slowly, hoping that this was finally the time the words would sink in. For a long while, I'd tried humoring his denial, hoping he just needed time to ease into it, but Ellie had accepted it better than he had. Out of the two of them, he was the one I worried for most when I was gone. Ellie was fearless and strong, a pillar even more solid than Francesca. Nicolae hid his weaknesses well, but they were there, waiting to undermine him. "Whatever drugs I take and whatever surgeries they try, it's only going to make me suffer longer."

"You don't know that," he snarled, pacing the room. "You've given up, but that doesn't mean it's true. There are new therapies coming out every day."

"Nicolae, I'm *dying*," I repeated, walking over to him since I knew he wouldn't come to me when he was like this. I reached to touch his face, but he turned away from me. I took his hand instead, squeezing it, and his eyes finally met mine.

The anger in them was a poor cover for the fear. The pain. The doubt. "It's over if we don't try this," I said softly, closing the gap between our bodies and our lips. "You know that."

"No," he gritted out. His eyes were red even as his voice softened. "I just found you."

"I know," I whispered, touching his cheek. "And I would give anything to stay with you, but it's not going to be enough."

I realized only then what I'd been afraid of. It wasn't him saying no or saying yes. It was the fact that no matter what he said, I already knew what my choice would be. Either this worked, or I was going to lose him. Ellie. Andrei. There was no magic bullet, no waking up from a bad dream. His bite would either save me or kill me, and the time for weighing the decision was drawing to a close.

Nicolae grimaced, touching my hand to hold it close to his cheek. "You don't know what it's like to be as powerful as I am and utterly powerless to do the one thing that matters."

"Even you can't stop this, Nicolae," I told him, pleading with him to look at me. I knew it hurt, but I needed him to understand. "If I only have a little time left, I want it to be on my terms. You understand that, don't you?"

"I understand," he said bitterly. "I hate it, but I understand."

I smiled. "I can deal with that."

He looked away, frowning off into the distance like he was considering another argument, but he released a burdened sigh instead. "When?"

"I'd like to hold out as long as I can," I admitted.

"When you are ready, then." He sounded so broken. Defeated.

"There's something else I should have told you earlier," I said.

His eyes narrowed. "What else?"

"I think Leonie is Ellie's destined mate."

He stared at me like he was waiting for me to announce it was a joke. "She's a teenager."

"Preaching to the choir," I muttered. "But if you'd seen her at that party, you'd understand."

"She's a teenager," he said again, stuck on that just as much as I was. "And Leonie is a beta! It's against everything we've planned for."

"I know, but it's not like we're on speaking terms with the Crow pack anymore," I reminded him. "And we don't have a whole lot of room to talk when it comes to what's conventional. What are we going to do, tell her she's grounded from falling for the wrong person?"

He grunted in irritation, but I could tell he was coming to the same conclusion I had. Whatever became of that bond in the future, being set against it would only make things worse for everyone involved.

"Has Ellie said anything to her?" he grumbled.

"Not as far as I know. She hasn't talked to me about it, either."

"Well, that needs to change."

I gave him a look. "I know you've been a parent longer than I have, but when it comes to a teenage girl, you're playing by *very* different rules. When Ellie wants to talk, she'll come to us. That's the way it's gotta be."

I was sure he was going to keep arguing, and he'd probably have ended up echoing my own concerns, but instead, he pulled me into his arms and breathed in my scent. I leaned on him, relieved that we weren't going to spend the night fighting. "What am I going to do without you, Jack?" he murmured.

The question broke my heart, and I didn't have an answer that wouldn't break his. I just held him and prayed for a miracle.

TWENTY-NINE

WEEKS BECAME months and I sucked the marrow out of every last moment of it, but around the seven-month mark, I felt my body slipping even if my spirit remained strong. I'd always imagined that dying would be something sudden that happened without you realizing it, but it felt more like it creeping up on me. Death was the approaching shadow of a storm overtaking a summer field. Every minute, it was just a little bit darker. A little harder to see the sun.

The fear of fading out was the only thing that outweighed the fear of letting go. I knew it was time. So did Nicolae. And so did Ellie. Even Andrei had lingered that morning on his way to class, which wasn't like him now that he loved school and had friends to see. Leonie had given me a hug that morning for no reason at all when I'd passed her in the hall.

A hundred years wouldn't be enough to spend with the people I loved, but the only chance I'd ever have that I'd get to experience half of them was going to pass me by if I waited any longer. I just had to find a way to say the words. To say I was ready.

That morning, rather than going out to deal with the pack's latest problems like he usually did, Nicolae was still there when I came back from dropping Andrei off at school. He was sitting at the kitchen table with an untouched cup of coffee in his hand and a cigarette hanging out of his mouth.

He'd banned smoking in the building altogether when I was diagnosed, and the fact that he was doing it himself meant something was different. Today was either an end or a beginning and the rules no longer applied. Not in this liminal space between life and death, hoping and fearing, relief and regret.

"We're taking a trip," Nicolae announced, putting his cigarette out in his coffee before he stood. "Get ready."

I nodded and went into the bedroom to grab a jacket. What else were you supposed to bring to your death? Sensible shoes seemed like a given. I decided I didn't need my wallet, or my phone. Whatever happened, Nicolae would tell the people who needed to know in the event that I wasn't there to, and it wouldn't come as any surprise.

We'd kept the others from the truth about our plan, both because it felt unfair to give them false hope and because I'd had so many hard conversations with Ellie that I hadn't wanted to sour the last time I might see her. Instead, we'd talked for hours just like we used to, and I wanted that moment to remain if I didn't.

I followed Nicolae out of the condo and downstairs to the parking garage. He was silent on the drive and made no attempt to tell me where we were going. I didn't ask.

The sky was clear blue, which was a rare thing in the land of stony castles and endless rain. It almost looked like the Tennessee sky I'd grown up under. I stuck my hand out the open window and let the air drift through my fingers just like I'd always done as a kid, when my grandmother would take me with her on the long drive down the mountain to the only market in town.

I realized we were heading toward the mountains on the horizon outside the city skyline. My heart ached the same way it always did whenever that old country song that had always put Ellie to sleep as a baby came on the radio. The mountains were full of memories both good and bad. For better or for worse, those razor-sharp ridges were the element of my soul, and if I had to die anywhere, I couldn't imagine a better place. And I couldn't imagine anyone else I'd rather have holding my hand.

I looked over at Nicolae when he finally pulled the car to a stop on the side of a slender dirt road once we'd driven as far into the mountains as we could. He didn't say a word. He just got out of the car and opened my door before I had time to do it myself. He was fast, and I was a lot slower these days. I winced as he helped me out of the car. My body had been aching lately on top of everything else, and there weren't many parts of me that weren't in pain. At least the crisp mountain air filling my lungs made it a little easier to breathe.

I held Nicolae's hand as we walked up the mountain path and the forest grew thicker and darker around us. Nicolae seemed to anticipate when I needed a moment to rest before I did and he'd stop, giving me time to catch my breath. The weakness that had come over me recently, overtaking my body confirmed that I'd made the right decision, whether he thought so or not. Maybe he was okay with narrowing the focus of his life to caring for me, but I wasn't. I was a human, an omega. I was already weak in every way that he was strong, and I wanted to be able to walk beside him until the end, even if it killed me.

"Just a little further," Nicolae promised, as if he knew I was close to shutting down. He was already doing most of the work keeping me on my feet, but I'd refused to let him carry me and warned him that I'd be biting *him* if he tried again. I knew it was selfish to refuse to let him help as much as he wanted to, but if I was about to lose everything, I at least wanted to hold onto my pride.

The sunlight that had almost vanished in the most densely forested part of the trail suddenly broke through the leaves in shining splendor. I stared in awe at the mountaintop clearing and the view that stretched on as far as the eye could see. Glorious mountains, green and blue and white, cutting a breathtaking silhouette against the sunset. Just like the ones I remembered, not the depleted, flattened peaks I'd left behind.

The moon was full, her light already illuminating the trees against the shadow steadily creeping over us. For once, it didn't feel ominous. It was more like a blanket gathering softly over me.

Nicolae stood beside me, his face impassive and immune to the beauty before us. I took his hand and his eyes met mine. I didn't have to speak, and neither did he. I just needed him to know that if this was it, if this was the last thing I ever saw, it was enough.

He sat down in the grass, pulling me with him and into his lap. I sat between his legs, my back against his warm chest, and realized that for once, even in heat, my body temperature was lower than his. He wrapped his arms around me and I felt his steady heartbeat against my back as we watched the sun sinking into the horizon. The sky was cloaked in royal blue and the full moon stood out like a giant pearl broach above the mountain's peak. We were so far from the city that the stars all clustered together in streams of hazy white light rather than the pin pricks I was used to seeing from my window.

Maybe the wolf in me was no more than a sliver, but when the moon was full, I felt her lunar pull so strongly. I felt the shards of her light embedded deep in my soul, soothing the scars left by the loss of Francesca and my family and my dead-end town. All the painful things that had worked their way into me, leaving my heart tender and bleeding from the inside.

One way or another, this night would put an end to me—to my humanity, or to my life itself—and all the wounds left on my soul. Either way, I'd be free. I closed my eyes, but it wasn't enough to keep the tears back.

God, I wished the mark on my back was enough to bind me here forever. In his arms, as his mate, as his pet. Anything.

Nicolae must have smelled the salt of my tears because he turned me just enough to kiss them away. He touched my neck and my flushed skin tingled, because even though the fire in me was quickly burning itself out, he was still capable of rekindling it. A spark, a flare, a moment stolen with a kiss that tasted like heaven and felt like hell. I'd already lost my breath, but he didn't let me go and I made no attempt to escape. He kissed me harder, like he planned on suffocating me himself. I wouldn't have complained, but when he finally pulled away, I caught just a glimpse of the grief in his eyes before he pressed his lips to my throat.

I smoothed my fingers through his midnight hair. "It's okay," I whispered.

He let out a choked sob that he muffled in my neck as his fangs sank into my flesh. He held me tightly, and I was glad, because my reaction to the blinding pain of his bite—nothing compared to his venom—was to writhe and try to escape. He crushed me against his chest, barely allowing me room to breathe, let alone move.

My heart raced, spreading his toxin through my veins like wild-fire, and God, it burned. My body lost strength and gave up the fight, and I stared up at the moon watching over us as he bled me until my consciousness was fading.

When Nicolae's fangs finally left my neck, he pulled away. His lips were painted with my blood and his pupils were wide, sucking in the light, and he looked like an animal as he watched me. My heart felt like it had been doused in kerosene and lit with a match, but I was too weak to show my agony.

Maybe it was better to let him think I'd slipped away peacefully. He didn't need to live with the truth. He held me, stroking my hair as he came back to himself.

"Jack," he whispered pleadingly, holding me and rocking me, every movement endless torture. "Please, baby... stay with me."

I felt my body shutting down organ by organ, my spirit slipping with each hoarse breath. I was fading, not because of his venom but because that last struggle had sapped me of the few drops of energy I had left in my veins.

Then something else began to stir. A new fire. A new pain. My lungs filled suddenly, a shot of adrenaline that sent me surging upright and out of his arms. I caught myself face-down on the grass before him. I saw him watching me fearfully. Saw him reaching for his gun. I'd made him promise to put me down if I went feral so I would never suffer that kind of indignity.

As I coughed up blood and felt the venom bubbling under my skin, rage wiping out every other subtle shade of emotion I'd once been capable of, I realized it was too much to ask him. I had to take the gun and do it myself before my mate let me tear him apart, but I was in too much pain and my body was no longer mine to control.

There was another spirit in me, and it seemed to rise up from within, going from a voice so faint I'd never consciously heard it to a howl so loud it felt like war drums shaking the mountains. Did he hear it, too? I clutched my head to drown the sound out and my own screams almost did the trick.

The pain was beyond comprehension. The light of the moon was no longer soothing but glaring, mocking, maddening. I wanted to tear it out of the sky myself and rip it open until the gooey white substance of its light slid down my throat like blood.

Nicolae touched me and I struck him away automatically, sending him flying. I was still just myself enough to turn and run, ignoring his pleas for me to stop. I felt him close behind me and the sound of his footsteps doubled. He let out a roar of warning and my foot slid on the side of the mountain. I went tumbling, ribs cracking as I hit the rocks over and over again, but it was nothing compared to the sensation of my bones shifting beneath my skin. When I finally rolled to a stop, caught in place by a small tree stuck in the mountain, my flesh seemed to melt as I groped to claw my way up the earth.

Claws. Big ones. Sharp and white, just like Nicolae's fangs. I pulled myself up with a body I didn't recognize, staring down at fur as reddish brown as the earth that sifted beneath four paws that wouldn't work the way I wanted them to.

The beast I knew so well appeared before me, eclipsing the moon, and pulled me up with hands far more human than my clumsy paws. He kept me in his arms and only collapsed once we reached a plateau, his chest heaving as laboriously as mine. He was far stronger, but he was exhausted. The past months had taken their toll on him, too.

We stared at each other as his clawed hands explored the foreign slope of my head, thick finger pads sweeping over my fur and taking in every strange new angle. He was so far from human, but I could still read the look in his eyes. Relief. Shock. Love. He held me so close it felt like he'd crush me and his growl instinctively made my wolven self shudder, but I was still myself enough to know that he would never harm me.

My ability to think like a human was beginning to fade, but as it did, other instincts and modes of being came in to take its place. Touch and scent suddenly meant so much more than they ever had. As he shifted back, clutching me to his bare chest, his rushing words of gratitude wouldn't have made any sense to me even if they were in English. But his hands in my fur... that, I understood fully.

I had survived. I was a wolf now, *his* wolf, and I was going to live.

THIRTY

IT HAD BEEN a month since my human life had ended, and life as a wolf was more than I had ever imagined. More sensory experience, more anger, more hunger, more thirst, more oxygen in my lungs and more time to take it all in.

Even when I was human, I felt like I didn't quite belong in my own skin. Nicolae and Ellie both assured me that it would pass. The first few months were always the hardest. The more time I spent as a wolf, the easier it would be.

Running with them was unlike anything I had experienced. It was pure exhilaration, and the only thing that slowed us down was when we brought Andrei out with us and we had to make sure the little guy could keep up. Sometimes, it was just me and Nicolae, and I'd come to realize I was closer to him than I'd ever been when I was a human. Not because he put any barrier between us, but because there was only so much a human could feel.

What I lacked in articulation in my wolf form, I made up for in depth. I knew and felt and sensed in ways that had once been unfathomable to me, and I felt the same echo that united the rest of the pack reverberating deep inside of me.

This was going to be our first full moon together as full-fledged wolves, and Nicolae had promised it would be special. He'd taken me up to a mountain cabin to ride out the full moon. The first few transformations under her light would be the most difficult to manage around humans. I had always relied on Nicolae to keep me safe from his kin. Now I relied on him to keep everyone else safe from me.

We'd been running all night, and it was helping my bloodlust stay under control, but it was doing nothing to quench my desire for him. When we finally circled back to the cabin and shed our fur in exchange for skin, I pushed Nicolae up against the outside wall and kissed him hard.

He laughed at my desperation and I nipped at his bottom lip, tasting blood. He tangled his fist in my hair and jerked my head back with a scolding look. "Behave yourself."

"Fuck me and I will," I muttered.

"Oh?" He arched an eyebrow. "And here I thought I was going to reward you by trying something different."

"Different?"

He ignored me, walking inside the cabin. I caught the door before it shut, following him. The one-room cabin was not quite as luxurious as the rest of his haunts, which suited me fine. Nicolae said it was because I was liable to tear the place apart in my current state and I didn't doubt him.

"Nicolae, what did you—?" He silenced me with a kiss and pushed me down on the sofa by the hearth. The fire was already crackling, casting a soft glow on the room, but I didn't need the ambiance to be all over him.

"Stay," he ordered like I was already an unruly dog, disappearing into the bathroom for a moment before he came back with something clutched in his hand. I looked down, trying to figure out what it was, but he grabbed my chin with his other hand and made me look at him. "If we're going to do this, it's on my terms."

My eyes widened as I realized what he had in mind. I'd forgotten all about the hopeful bargain I'd made with him nearly a year ago. "You're actually going to let me fuck you?"

"A promise is a promise," he muttered, shoving the bottle of lube into my hand. "Finger me."

He was quite possibly the only person in the world who'd said those words in that commanding tone, but I'd be damned if I was going to pass up the opportunity. I wet my fingers generously in the silky liquid and slid my hand underneath him as he straddled my lap. His expression was as stern as I'd expected as I slicked his hole, wincing only slightly as I slipped a digit into him. He was as tight as I'd imagined, too, and as I pushed my finger further in, my cock went hard at the thought of being buried in his ass.

Nicolae's hands rested on the back of the couch behind me and his dark hair fell over his shoulders as he readjusted himself. His breathing ceased as I worked another finger into him. "Hurry up," he growled.

Fuck, he was hot when he was obstinate.

He clenched around my fingers as I started pushing in and out to get him ready for my iron-hard dick. His eyes were heavy-lidded and his lips moved slightly, as if he was murmuring something without being conscious of it. I felt his prostate under my fingers and took my time stroking it, pressing until he bit down on the lip that was already swollen from my bite.

"Feels good?" I asked knowingly.

"Fuck," he groaned.

I could tell he'd never done this with anyone but me. He was too hard, too responsive, too breathless. I wanted to be inside him, but I wanted him to enjoy this first. To make him feel something he never had before, and know I was the only one who'd ever see him like this. Vulnerable, yet still in control. Just willing to give enough of it over to me to share something new.

I placed my left hand on the outside of his thigh and he jolted, tightening around my fingers. When I ran my hand up over his taut abdomen, teasing and stroking down to the very base of his cock, he shuddered. "Bastard."

"You're beautiful like this, you know?" I murmured, taking the chance to look at him. Usually when we fucked, I was on my back and his face was buried in my neck. He never missed a chance to sink his teeth in now that he knew it wouldn't kill me, and I found myself wondering just how much superhuman restraint he'd needed before. Otherwise, I was on my hands and knees, robbed of the opportunity to see his perfect face cast in pleasure as he rammed into me from behind.

"Shut up."

"I'm serious," I said, trailing my fingers down the underside of his cock. It jerked for me and I dipped my finger in the well of his arousal pooling at the tip. "You're too perfect. It could give a guy a complex, you know?"

He looked down at me, his eyes blazing as he rode my fingers and brought his hands down to my shoulders. His nails dug in like claws. He was rougher with me now, and I liked it. I liked knowing I could give him all of me and he could take it without restraint or fear, and tonight, I was going to show him how it felt.

"Are you going to keep whining or are you gonna fuck me?"

I grinned, pulling my fingers out so I could wrap my hand around my cock and hold it steady for him to mount. The tightness around my fingers was nothing compared to the resistance his ass gave the head of my cock, but I let him go at his pace. He gave way for me and moaned, freezing in place to accommodate my tip.

"Nicolae," I moaned, skimming my hands up his sides as I bent forward to take the hard pebble of his nipple into my mouth. He shuddered and sank down a little more, his hips surging forward as he angled me and I fell back to enjoy the show.

"Fuck," he growled, his lip still dripping blood as he came down hard on me, like he was growing impatient with his own body's resistance.

I could tell he regretted that decision from the way he tightened up until I felt like he was going to snap my dick. I pulled him in for a kiss to soothe him. "Easy," I warned him, stroking his cock to help distract him from the pain.

"You make it look like nothing," he grumbled.

I laughed, and he glared at me. "I'm a little more used to it. Besides, after taking your knot that first time, the rest of it didn't seem that bad."

His eyes lit up with desire, like the reminder of me stuck on his knot was more consolation than what I was doing to his throbbing shaft. Silky fluid spilled out from the slit as I stroked him hard and slow.

"Like that," he moaned, grinding against me. I pushed up into him and he grunted in pleasure as I ran my finger back and forth across his sensitive head. "Just like that."

He grabbed a handful of my hair again and leaned down to kiss me, as demanding with his mouth as he was riding my cock. I groped him with my left hand, satisfying my fingers with his loose hair and his brawny shoulders as I worked his cock with the other.

He repositioned himself suddenly and came down hard, driving me into his prostate. His hips bucked as his torso ground against mine, using me for his pleasure and heightening mine in doing so. "I'm starting to see why you make all those sounds," he moaned.

I squeezed his shaft and he cried out with a new sound of his own. With my other hand, I stroked his long hair back and kissed him, turned on by the fact that for once, he was letting me take the lead. I didn't know if it was a one-time thing and it didn't matter. I just wanted to make this as good for him as possible. I'd never seen him like this, and I was closer to climax every time he breathed my name to beg for more.

And then, he stopped begging and started demanding. He lifted his ass and slammed back down on my cock, his breath rushing against my neck as he tongued my jugular and whispered, "You'd better still be stretched from this morning, because I'm not going to have the patience to prep you after."

His words made my cock quiver and I started stroking him harder. He snarled and ground back into me in response, his ecstatic profanity making it clear that there was at least one thing I was better at doing than him. Knowing that I could touch him better than he could himself was a hell of an ego stroke. I had him where I wanted him, his cock ready to explode in my hand and mine ready to bust inside of him.

I wasn't sure when I started kissing his shoulder or when his hand had started cradling the back of my head to encourage me. Biting him seemed natural, even though it once would have been a completely bizarre act, and as I tasted his blood, his cock pulsed hot cum through my fingers that sprayed my chest. I bit deeper and he came harder as I lost control and my cock spasmed and released. He tightened with his climax and his grip on my shaft became semi-painful, but that was good, too. It was all so fucking good. The taste of him, the way he felt, the way my body still ached for his to claim it.

He didn't climb off me right away, but when he did, he kept kissing me right where we'd left off. He pushed me onto my back and switched our positions to take the lead he was so damned good at. As promised, he had no time for preparation, and I had no patience for it, either. I'd been the fragile human for so long, and only now did I understand just how close I'd been to shattering every time he touched me. Now I was strong enough to stand beside him, to lie beneath him, to take my fill of him in every permutation.

I'd always belonged to Nicolae. Before we'd met, before he'd marked me, he was the thing my heart had waited for, the empty space I'd imagined would always be there. Now he belonged to me. My bite wouldn't mark him the way his had marked me, bringing me back from the clutches of death, and it was already healing as I swept my fingers over it and stared up at him. By morning, it would look like nothing had ever been there. But I'd know, and he would know, and that was enough.

He was mine, too.

Nicolae fucked me until I forgot who I was and reminded me

with a kiss before he collapsed on top of me. He slid down between my legs and dipped his fingers in his own blood to paint some letters I couldn't read on my chest.

"The hell are you doing?" I asked, still trying to catch my breath. My lungs worked just fine, but Nicolae had a way of bringing even a healthy body to its limits.

"Writing something," he answered, looking up at me. Fire lit his mischievous eyes, dancing within them like the devil he was. "You can't read it."

I huffed. The written word was still something of a sore subject where he was concerned, but I was too exhausted and well-fucked to care. I'd already started to fall asleep by the time he finished and pulled me into his arms.

Halfway through the night, I woke up thirsty and stepped over Nicolae's slumbering body on my way to the bathroom. I cupped a few handfuls of water into my mouth before I caught sight of the dried blood on my skin and stepped back to read it. My backwards Romanian was as shit as my forwards Romanian, but it looked like *sufletul pereche.*

"What the hell did you fingerpaint on me, you fuckin' psycho?" I yelled, laughing, when I heard him moving around outside the door.

He leaned over so I could see his head through the door, his hair brushing the rug. "It means soulmate," he answered, stretching out lazily. Sometimes I'd swear he was a cat rather than a wolf.

Nicolae's words always took me off guard. His words had gone from cutting me on so many occasions before our hatred had transformed into love, and now his words made me feel loved and accepted and safe in all the ways I needed. This time, it was something else entirely. Something I didn't have a name for. Maybe there wasn't one.

I turned on the shower and he appeared at the door like some ghost summoned by chanting its name in a mirror three times. With his pale white skin and that almost-black hair down his shoulders, he looked like one. "A shower in the middle of the night?" he chuckled.

"I'm going to wash the blood off," I said, taking my hand to pull him in with me. "Wanna join me? I'm in heat, after all."

His eyes darkened as he pulled me to him and kissed me. It was rare for him to follow anyone's orders, let alone mine, but tonight was full of firsts. As we made love again and the water washed my skin clean, the words he'd painted remained carved in places the water could never touch.

The End.

ABOUT THE AUTHOR

Joel Abernathy, also writing as L.C. Davis, is a trans author of MM romance. He enjoys writing dark and emotional romance about men loving men in all genres.

CPSIA information can be obtained
at www.ICGtesting.com
Printed in the USA
LVHW050910161022
730814LV00005B/197